TIM O'LEARY

The Woman in the Road

Dr. O'Neil Callahan —
A great doctor, woman and an even better friend. — Thanks for keeping this love of my life healthy. All the best,
Tim O'Leary

Copyright © 2023 by Tim O'Leary

All rights reserved. No part of this publication may be reproduced, stored or transmitted in any form or by any means, electronic, mechanical, photocopying, recording, scanning, or otherwise without written permission from the publisher. It is illegal to copy this book, post it to a website, or distribute it by any other means without permission.

First edition

ISBN: 979-8-218-20596-6

*This book was professionally typeset on Reedsy.
Find out more at reedsy.com*

For Pat

*For me, the most important part of PATIMIKERRY
and the larger family we've become.*

Acknowledgement

This book was a cooperative effort with my friend Joe McDonough. Most of our collaborations took place over coffee and tea at a Dunkin' in Rowley, Massachusetts.

Joe has lived in Massachusetts, California, Bahrain, Qatar, the United Arab Emirates, and Oman. He has been a political nomad and crisscrossed the United States organizing and speaking with and for every Democratic Nominee for US President since Jimmy Carter. Joe has more political stories than CNN and FOX, and tells them better than both.

Joe has a bit of the Forrest Gump. He has met some great people and had adventures with luck and good timing. A life with more bizarre twists than a reality TV show. Some, I gave to the principal character in this book. Others are:

- At a college party he had a good-natured wrestling match with Tommy Lee Jones.
- He once gave Ed Asner the finger for stealing his parking space. Mr. Asner responded by inviting Joe to a Hollywood party and introducing him as his Buddy.
- Joe met and spent an hour with Bobby Kennedy the day he announced for President because they got snowed in together at an airport. Kennedy's to Joe on why he was running made the *New York Times*.
- Joe once made the Technology/science section of Time

magazine for showing the Dukakis Campaign how to use satellites for local TV interviews instead of flying to them.
- Joe became a member of the "Grand Clong" Club during the Carter Campaign. You have to be a member to know what it means.
- Each St. Patrick's Day, Joe dons his "classy but cheap, $100 tux and attends the Anniversary Celebration of the founding of the Charitable Irish Society.
- When he was a young boy, Joe broke his hip and had to leave an altar boy class run by Reverend Paul Shanley. Later, he learned the priest had molested, among others, three of the five other boys in that class. One of his few regrets in life was not being to help the other boys, who were not as lucky as him. He remembers them and his broken hip on cold, rainy days.

The principal character in this book is loosely based on Joe, although except as a law student and brief stint as an Assistant District Attorney at the Woburn Court in Massachusetts, he has never been a "serious" prosecutor. And he has never been a member of the CIA.

Of the former, I am quite certain. The latter? Maybe, not so much.

Tim O'Leary

May, 2023

I

Part One

Chapter 1

At eleven-thirty, the morning of January 11, 2022, Alice Ruth Fox, Ph.D. climbed the steps to the Penobscot Judicial Center on Exchange Street in Bangor, Maine. To Fox, who had made this trip on several occasions, the bland, brick rectangular three-story building reminded her of the Pennsylvania grammar school she had attended, more than it did a courthouse. The day and sky had a cold, midwinter pre-storm look, a brooding somberness. The sun as pale as an old dime. Alice tightened the woolen coat over her forest green business suit, hugged her brown leather briefcase, and entered through the thick wooden doors.

"Over here, Ma'am," a tall, lumpy man with thinning hair and tired pink skin, walked toward her and extended a guiding hand toward a metal detector and a conveyor belt for her briefcase.

"It's *Doctor* Fox," she said. She brushed aside his arm, and dropped her briefcase on the belt. At this time of day, the morning rush of lawyers, defendants, jurors and witnesses was over, and she passed through security in less than a minute.

Fox went up the staircase to the second floor and sat on a long oak bench against a drab beige wall running between courtrooms 2 and 3. She placed her briefcase beside her and dropped each arm to the bench to provide a measure of balance. At five feet two inches, her sensible brown shoes barely touched the floor of the corridor, and only if she sat erect at the front edge of the bench. It was a precarious position for Fox as the polished bench was slick and inattentiveness could lead to a fall to the tiled floor.

Fox was there to testify as a defense witness for Robert Palfrey, who was being tried on thirteen charges of sexual assault of minors and one charge of statutory rape. The allegations all stemmed from his nine years as a volunteer volleyball coach at a small private high school in Bangor. The prosecution's case relied on the testimony of five former players, and a gymnast, who met Palfrey through a friend on the volleyball team. All the victims were now in their mid-twenties. According to the testimony of psychologists, provided by the prosecution, the memories of the victims had been repressed. They had come to light at varying times as each graduated from different colleges and began careers in business, teaching, and, in one case, as a Catholic nun working in an orphanage in Troy, New York.

Their testimony was admitted over the strenuous objections of the defense, who was now forced to rely on Alice Fox to refute the reliability and science of repressed memory and create the reasonable doubt Palfrey needed to escape spending the next thirty or forty years of his life in a cell.

Fox glanced around the empty, dark corridor. There was little light coming from the large windows at either end of the hallway. The other benches were empty and the three sets of double doors, with frosted glass panels, that led to the courtrooms were closed. Silence hung in the air like the smell of wet paint. *The halls of justice are gloomy, quiet, and are housed in what should be an elementary school*, she thought.

She swung her small feet front to back, a habit she picked up as an adolescent and struggled to stop her entire life. Now fifty-six, Fox was unattractive, and had been since birth. Even as a baby and a young child, her appearance drew stares and little praise. Her closely-cropped reddish hair sat on a thin longish face, bookended by small pointed ears and centered by dark brown, almost black, eyes and a narrow nose. Alice Fox had the perfect name, or perhaps an unfortunate one, for her appearance.

Fox was a highly intelligent, aggressively confrontational, tenured faculty member of the Psychology Department at the University of Southern Maine in Portland. Her students feared and loathed her. Most gave her low evaluation grades upon completion of her course, calling her stubborn, and accusing her of narrow-mindedness and using outdated materials and terminology.

None of that mattered to Fox, or to USM, which prided itself on having a faculty diverse in opinion, as well as race and social-economic status. She used her doctorate degree in psychology to question the efficacy and accuracy of many of its practitioners, as well as the tenets of the profession. She published a book, Liars for Hire, calling most of psychiatry "Junk Science" and referring to the so-called expert psychologists scurrying through court houses offering testimony in exchange for checks, as "articulate hucksters spewing psychobabble with the scientific foundations of a palm reader or Ouija board."

As a result, Fox was controversial and acquired a national reputation. She came to Academia later than most, but living in a shroud of controversary and acclaim me, she was a star on the talk radio circuit and actively recruited by some colleges. She was now in her tenth year as a tenured professor of psychology. While passed over several times for Chair of the Department, she was firmly ensconced in a place where most of her colleagues, and virtually all of the University's Administration, expended considerable energy to avoid her.

"They're ready for you, Ms. Fox," a tall, burly, African-American court officer in thick black shoes, dark blue trousers, and white shirt and badge, called to her from an open door ten feet away. Fox looked and saw he was not carrying a gun.

"It's *Doctor* Fox," she snapped in a sharp voice. She slid off the bench and draped her coat over her shoulders like a cape. She walked to the door, the footfalls of her low heels echoing behind her as if she was being followed. The court officer stepped aside, and Alice stopped briefly at the open door. The courtroom was filled with spectators, including a row of reporters and a TV camera. Fox spied what appeared to be a woman in a nun's habit sitting with five other young women. *Ah, the victims*, she thought.

Fox took a deep breath and entered the courtroom. She felt the eyes of the room and enjoyed the twelve second walk to the witness chair.

Show time!

Chapter 2

Robert Palfrey sat at the defense table in an ill-fitting brown suit, pale green shirt and yellow tie. He was just over six feet, with a beaked nose, close-set green eyes, and a black – too black - widow's peak. He tilted his head back, the better to peer down his nose, and watched the woman, hired to save his ass, walk to the witness stand. *Christ,* Palfrey thought, *I wouldn't fuck her with a stick.*

Gretchen Harris, a sixtyish, heavy-set woman with an elaborate hairdo, stepped over to the witness chair. "Ms. Fox, please raise your right hand."

She stood. "It's *Doctor* Fox. Try to remember that." She raised her right hand and took the oath.

Bitch, Gretchen thought. She administered oath, and took her seat at the table below the Judge's elevated perch.

A tall man in an immaculate dark blue pin-stripe suit, pink shirt and a dark blue tie with thin pink stripes stood. "Doctor Fox, I'm Trevor Chandler." He drifted behind the chair of Robert Palfrey and placed his hands on Palfrey's shoulders. "I represent Mr. Palfrey, the gentleman seated here." Chandler removed his hands and walked in front of the table, blocking Fox's view of Palfrey. "Doctor Fox, I'm going to ask you a series of questions to establish your background and areas of expertise." Chandler was a handsome square jawed ex-jock with bleached teeth and a smile he'd perfected in his bathroom mirror. He stepped closer to Fox and exposed the great smile. "Before we begin, would you like a glass of water?"

Fox smiled and revealed a mouth of small coffee-stained teeth. "No thank you, I'd prefer to get started. I'd like to be out of here before the one o'clock lunch break."

Judge Rebecca Farmington, a tall African-American with the looks, demeanor and style of a homecoming queen, generally preferred to let attorneys try their cases without interruptions or comments from her, leaned forward. A shadow of annoyance crossed her face. "Ms. Fox, I decide when it's time to recess for lunch, and it's not always at one o'clock. I expect your testimony and cross-examination will take most of the day. We will recess for lunch, of course, but you might want to have some water handy."

Fox turned towards the Judge. "I don't understand why it is so difficult for you folks to address me as doctor, as I have requested. It's who I am. Ms. is a pronoun manufactured to soothe the feelings of insecure women ashamed or embarrassed by their marital status. Imagine how annoyed you'd be if I addressed you as Ms. or Rebecca and not Your Honor."

A silent pall descended. Gretchen Harris, the clerk who had administered the oath, began to sort papers and rearranged the pencils in a small plastic tray on her desk.

Judge Farmington nodded. "Please get Doctor Fox a glass of water," she said to no one in particular.

CHAPTER 2

***

Forty-five minutes later, after questioning from Trevor Chandler and the prosecutor, Elaine Blass, a pretty brunette in her forties, with a tight, willful mouth, and tough blue eyes, Judge Farmington qualified Doctor Fox as an expert witness and ruled she would be allowed to express her opinions on repressed memory and related issues. "However, before you do so," Farmington said. "The Court will stand in recess for ninety minutes. Enjoy lunch, everyone."

Fox made a show of checking her watch, and turned to Judge Farmington. "One o'clock. Imagine that."

"That's strike two, Dr. Fox," Judge Farmington whispered. She rose and left the bench so fast that her robe flowed behind her like the black gown of the grim reaper.

***

At two-thirty, court reconvened. Trevor Chandler slowly rose from his chair, made a show of buttoning his suit jacket and approached Fox. "Doctor Fox," he began, "would you please explain to the jury the theory of repressed memory?"

Fox shifted in her seat to face the jury.

"First of all, it is theory, not fact. A repressed memory, according to the theory, is one our brain hides (Fox flashed the universal quotation sign with her fingers around the word hides) from us to help avoid stress or trauma from the event that created the memory."

"And do you have an opinion on this theory, Doctor Fox?"

Fox turned to the jury and smiled. "I do not agree with it. Common sense and experience tell us the problem following most unpleasant experiences is an inability to forget the event, rather than some form of amnesia to help us forget it. The theory is most often raised in connection with sexual assault or molestation." Her voice was clear, not halting and expressed in a conversational tone. The answer was delivered exactly as rehearsed by Fox. She smiled as several jurors nodded, while others scribbled furiously in their note pads. Fox turned away from the jury and faced Chandler.

Chandler nodded thoughtfully, as if he heard the answer for the first time, and actually learned something. Two weeks earlier, Fox told him she would make a specific reference to sexual assault to establish her credibility with the jury. If they saw she was not afraid to make a specific reference to the charges his client faced, her ultimate opinion that repressed memories could not be accurately recovered would be more believable.

"So, Doctor Fox, you disagree with what the psychologists the prosecutor marched before the jury last week said about repressed memories?" Chandler asked.

Fox turned again to the jury. "I wasn't here to hear their testimony. I was simply doing what you asked me to do: offering the jury an explanation as to what the theory of repressed memory is." Fox took a small sip of water, creating the pause to set up her next comment. "And, I was not offering an opinion as to whether or not memory can be recovered or whether or not a memory alleged to have been recovered can be believed." The hum of several murmurs rolled from the back to the front of the court room. The jury sat a bit straighter.

"She's an experienced witness," Elaine Blass, the prosecutor, whispered to her assistant. "Full of shit, but the jury's eating it up."

Chandler feigned surprise at the answer he had heard more than a dozen times. "Well, thank you for that clarification, Dr. Fox." He walked to the defense table and flipped some pages of the yellow legal pad, pretending to look for an important note. He looked back to Dr. Fox. "Tell us, Doctor Fox, do you have an opinion as to whether or not a memory that has been allegedly repressed can be recovered?"

"I do," Fox said.

"Please tell it to the jury," Chandler said.

Elaine Blass rose to her feet. "Objection, Your Honor. Preserving it for the record."

"Overruled," Judge Farmington said. She looked to the jury. "I have already ruled the witness has the requisite expertise to offer her opinion. Please remember my having ruled the witness has the requisite knowledge to qualify as an expert, does not mean her opinion must be accepted by you, the jury." Farmington nodded to Fox. "The witness may answer the question."

Gretchen Harris smiled and thought. *"The witness. Good one, Judge. Don't call her doctor."*

Chapter 3

Trevor Chandler walked over to the jury box and turned to Fox. "Tell us Doctor Fox, in your opinion can a repressed memory, assuming it exists, be recovered?" He rested his elbows against the top of the ornate wooden structure in which the jury sat, becoming one of them.

"Please move, Mr. Chandler," Judge Farmington said. "You're obstructing the view of several jurors."

Chandler turned and gave an elaborate bow to the jurors in question. "My apologies, Your Honor." He strutted to the defense table and sat down. "Would you like me to repeat the question Dr. Fox? I'm sorry for the distraction."

"I remember the question," Fox said. She shifted again to face the jury, like a teacher with adoring students. "The brain processes information and stores it in different ways. Most of us have had unpleasant experiences, and we remember them in great detail. However, some memories become so vague you wonder if it's real. It feels like a dream you've forgotten over time. These memories are not, in my opinion, repressed.

CHAPTER 3

They've simply been forgotten."

"Can an event be misremembered?' Chandler said.

"Yes, there is a limit as to what the brain can process, so even with an important event -like a wedding - the bride will remember many of the specifics, but forget or not remember whether or not a particular person attended the event."

"So, if something unpleasant occurred, say a guest accidently pushed over the wedding cake, you'd expect her to remember that occurred," Chandler said. "Not likely she'd forget that happened, correct?"

"Objection," Blass said.

"Overruled, He can have it. Save it for cross-examination, Ms. Blass." Farmington smiled, "Is it okay to refer to you as Ms. Blass?" There was the smallest ripple of laughter, and several of the jurors smiled. "The witness may answer."

"Highly unlikely any bride would forget that," Fox said. "But over time, her memory could fade to the extent she might not remember the specific guest's name, or what he or she was wearing."

"Assuming she forgot the guest's name or whatever he or she was wearing, could she someday suddenly remember it?" Chandler said.

"Of course, the name might suddenly occur to her, less likely whatever he or she was wearing, but it's possible. It's natural to forget things and then remember, but to label a forgotten memory as repressed and to suggest it can be recovered in therapy is ..." Fox paused as if searching for the word. She shrugged her shoulders as if giving in. "Well, it's not surprising clinicians who get paid to recover these so-called memories believe this theory in far greater numbers than researchers."

Chandler decided to let Fox's words hang over the jury for several seconds. He went back to flipping the pages of his legal pad as if some greater truth would appear. He looked up at Fox. "A number of the prosecution's witnesses have testified, under oath, they were sexually abused by my client a number of years ago, and each has said her memory of the event was suppressed and suddenly recovered in therapy. Are you suggesting each is lying?"

"I am not suggesting anything," Fox said. "I am saying there is no scientific evidence to support repressed memories, or that we can believe the accuracy of any so-called suppressed memory that has been recovered."

"Could these women inaccurately, but honestly, believe their testimony is the truth?" Chandler said.

Blass rose. "Objection. Speculative."

Judge Farmington's face twisted in thought. "Overruled," she said. "Mr. Chandler, let's not dwell too long on hypotheticals or conjecture." She turned to the prosecutor and smiled. "Ms. Blass, I will give you broad leeway on cross-examination."

"Thank you, Your Honor," Chandler and Blass said simultaneously. Each wanted the jury to believe the other had lost the brief skirmish.

"You remember the question, Doctor Fox?" Chandler said.

"I do. Let me answer this way. "There are people who sincerely believe they were abducted by aliens. They describe in vivid detail, the aliens, the ship they were carried away on, and the experiments these so-called aliens performed on them. Is this credible evidence of aliens kidnapping people?"

Chandler chucked softly and nodded his head, as if he'd never heard the example Fox used. He assumed a thoughtful and serious pose. "But why does this happen?"

"Objection, Blass said in a pleading I-told-you-so-tone."

As a general strategy, Blass avoided objections. She thought they drew the jurors' attention to the testimony about to be offered. She was confident of her skills on cross-examination, and didn't want the jury to think she was afraid or even concerned about anything Fox had to say. She silently cursed herself for violating her own rule.

Judge Farmington sighed. "Overruled. Mr. Chandler let's get away from aliens and spaceships and simply ask your witness how so-called false memories come about?"

"Thank you, Your Honor," Chandler said to signal another triumph. "Doctor Fox could you please explain how an honestly believed but false memory can come about?"

Fox turned again to the jury. "There are numerous ways this can occur. Our brains and emotions are not infallible. There is one famous study where false memories were created in a laboratory experiment, involving children. The study found after repeated questioning by those conducting the experiment, a significant number of the children believed they had once been lost in a mall, when in fact, no such incident had ever occurred."

"How did this happen, if you know?' Chandler asked.

"Therapists can implant memories."

"Objection," Blass said, rising to her feet. "Unless, Mr. Chandler is prepared to offer evidence of implanted memories in this case, the witness is offering conjecture based on her own bias."

Chandler turned to Blass and smiled. "Madam Prosecutor, the witness cited a study involving youngsters. She is an expert and can offer her opinion."

"Overruled," Judge Farmington said. "Ms. Blass, you have cross-examination to address your concerns"

"Please continue Doctor Fox," Chandler said. "How can memories be implanted?"

"We know our brains can be influenced by questioning, and it can impact our memories of an event. Most false confessions result from interrogation tactics used by the police. So too, the memories a witness may have of an event can be influenced by questions he or she is subjected to by the police, or others. This is particularly true when the questions are being asked by a trusted source such as a therapist."

"Objection, move to strike the answer," Blass said in her well-practiced voice of indignation.

"Overruled," Farmington said. "Let's move it along Mr. Chandler."

"Thank you, Your Honor. I'm almost done." He picked up his yellow pad and flipped a page. "Doctor Fox, are there other explanations as to why an honestly held memory can be incorrect?"

"There are many," Fox said. "As I said our brains are not perfect and neither are our memories. A dozen people can see the same event and each might remember it differently, or remember different parts of the event. Over time, as memories fade, which is normal, the disparity will become greater. Yet, each will believe his or her memory is more accurate than the others." Fox took a well-timed sip of water. "Also, we all have an internal drive to manufacture excuses to explain failure, weak or faulty behavior." Fox made a show of turning to the jurors, as though announcing her next words mut be remembered.

"I call it the I-was-abused-as-a-child-so I can't-be-expected- to perform-like-others excuse. It gets developed early, and as the person recites the false claim, and adds details, she or he becomes convinced t actually occurred."

"You fucking bitch," Samantha Cronin, the gymnast and one of the victims, stood and screamed. Samantha was petite and barely visible in the crowded courtroom. But she had a loud, sharp voice that quickly drew the attention of those around her. She began to sob. The nun beside her pulled her back to her seat and placed an arm around her.

"I move for a mistrial, Your Honor," Chandler said. "This is outrageous, and prejudicial. A blatant attempt to influence the jury."

"What's outrageous is the nonsense coming out of your witness," Blass shouted over Chandler. She pointed a finger at him. "You and your quack precipitated this outburst."

Farmington slammed her gavel on the wooden block. It sounded like a shot. Silence descended, broken only by the smothered sobs of the woman. Farmington pointed the gavel at Samantha, her head buried in the fabric of the nun's habit. I want her escorted from the courtroom." The court officer stepped from the back and marched down the courtroom aisle.

Farmington turned to the jury. "You are to disregard that outburst and what was said. Erase it from your memory as if it never happened." She paused and took a breath. "If any of you believe you cannot do that, if you believe you can no longer deliberate and honor the oath you took at the beginning of this trial, raise your hand, and I'll appoint one of the alternate jurors in your place." She paused again. No hand was raised. "Very well, Mr. Chandler, your motion for a mistrial is denied. Please continue your direct examination."

"Your Honor, I'd like to be heard on my motion for a

mistrial," Chandler blurted. His face was red as was his bulging neck tight against the stiff collar of his pink shirt, as if his head was about to erupt.

"The motion was denied," Farmington said. "Your objection is noted for the record. Please proceed with your direct examination."

"Very well, Your Honor," Chandler said. He made a show of consulting his legal pad and nodded affirmatively as if all he had wanted to ask had been asked. He smiled triumphantly and said, "I have no further questions."

"The court will be in recess for fifteen minutes," Farmington said. She slammed her gavel to end discussion on the issue.

Chapter 4

Trevor Chandler sat across the table from Alice Fox in the room provided for the defense during trial breaks. "Well done, Doctor Fox," he said. "I think we have jurors three, six and eight."

Fox sat on the edge of her chair, her feet swinging front to back. "I think maybe juror nine as well," she said. "The outburst from the so-called victim didn't help her cause. You think it was spontaneous or part of some calculated maneuver?"

Chandler shrugged. "Don't know, but it didn't work, and, it proved you were effective." Chandler clapped his hands. "Even better, it showed Samantha Cronin was not Miss Purity." He laughed. "Using the F-bomb in court while sitting beside a fucking nun." Chandler shook his head and grinned. "Alice you are absolutely the best."

"It's Doctor Fox."

* * *

Elaine Blass sat in her darkened office taking slow deep breaths in through her nostrils and out her mouth, a technique to delay the onset of a migraine. Sitting quietly in one of her client chairs was Samantha Cronin, the woman who hurled the F-Bomb, while sitting next to a fucking nun.

"Please tell me Sister Alicia didn't know of your plan," Elaine muttered softly between breaths.

"Don't worry, she didn't, Samantha said. "You realize, of course, this is the first time she's worn the full religious habit in years. Usually, she's in pale brown dresses with long stockings and sensible shoes." She laughed. "As for me, it wasn't planned. It was an emotional outburst triggered by the insulting innuendos of that cunt Fox."

Blass tightened her closed eyes. "It's Doctor Fox," she said.

* * *

Judge Farmington stood in front of the desk in her chambers making circles with her outstretched arms, an exercise to relieve neck spasms. "Christ, that woman gets under my skin," she said to Gretchen, her clerk.

"You mean Ms.-Call-Me-Doctor-Fox?' Gretchen said. "Me too, but I'm afraid the jury likes her."

Farmington dropped her arms and stared. "You're shitting me. Right?"

"I wish I was," Gretchen said. "She's tough to look at, but

she has a nice way of explaining things to the jury." Gretchen shrugged. "She might be pulling them her way."

"I can't believe the jury will buy her shit," Farmington said. "My God, we have seven women on the panel." She shook her head. "No, no, they're not buying her bullshit. I know it."

"I hope you're right, Gretchen said. "But unless Blass cuts her down in cross-examination, we may be headed towards a hung jury."

"Blass will destroy that fuckin' bitch," Farmington said. "You wait and see."

"It's Doctor Fuckin' Bitch," Gretchen said. "Why is it so hard for *you folks* to remember that?"

* * *

Robert Palfrey sat on a small bunk in the six by nine foot holding cell in the basement. Two weeks ago, he was out on bail, enjoying life. Unfortunately for Palfrey, he was arrested for operating under the influence and driving after a license revocation. More unfortunate for Robert, was the fourteen-year-old girl in the car. While she supported his claim of simply driving her home, and the matter was still under investigation, it was enough for Farmington to revoke bail. *Miserable cunt*, Palfrey thought.

Palfrey's anger at Judge Farmington, dissolved and a smile emerged on his pale face. He was delighted with Doctor Fox's testimony, and now believed an acquittal was in sight. "Samantha Sammy Cronin," he muttered to the empty cell. "Still shooting your mouth off." He laughed at the memory of

Fox's face when the words, "fucking bitch" flew at her from Sammy's mouth. Then, he thought about the nun. *Hmmm, what is Donna Fletcher doing in a nun's habit? Never would have figured that. Man, I'd love to take a peek under that costume. Yum.* Palfrey laughed. *Nah, she's too old.* He laughed again and leaned back, lifting his feet off the floor. He slammed them to the floor and clapped his hands. "I'm going home, soon!" He shouted to the guards he was certain were somewhere close. "I'm going home!" He repeated, the words echoing in the dark, basement corridor.

* * *

Court reconvened at ten minutes past three. Judge Farmington looked over to Blass, who was standing. "Ms. Blass, any questions for the witness?"

Doctor Fox looked up to Farmington. "Would it be too much to ask that you refer to me as Doctor Fox and not the generic term, witness? It's who I am."

Judge Farmington looked at Fox. "You're a witness. That's who you are in my courtroom." The Judge turned to Blass. "Please proceed."

Chapter 5

Blass walked towards Fox. "Doctor Fox, she said. "Are you married?"

"None of your business," Fox snapped.

"Objection," shouted Chandler, struggling out of his chair.

"Sustained," said Farmington.

Blass smiled and nodded her head. She turned toward the jury. "I agree it's none of my business," she said. "That's why I prefer Ms. I could use doctor, since I have a JD Degree, but I prefer Ms." She paused and turned back toward Fox. "I suppose you think that means I'm an insecure woman ashamed or embarrassed by my marital status. Isn't that, right, Doctor Fox?"

"I have no opinion on you or your psychological profile," Fox said.

Blass drifted closer to the jury, careful not to obstruct their view of the witness. "But, Doctor Fox, didn't you say earlier that Ms. was a pronoun manufactured to soothe the feelings of insecure women ashamed or embarrassed by their marital status? You remember saying that?" Blass glanced at a forty-something female juror and caught her quick smirk.

"Objection," Chandler shouted. "This has nothing to do with the issues at hand. The prosecutor is harassing Doctor Fox."

"Overruled," Farmington said. "This is cross-examination. The witness will answer the question." *Strike three*, Farmington mouthed to Fox.

"I've forgotten the question," Fox said.

Blass stepped closer to Fox. "I can help you. I asked if you remembered testifying earlier that Ms. was a pronoun manufactured to soothe the feelings of insecure women ashamed or embarrassed by their marital status?" Blass turned to the jury with its seven females.

"I was not expressing my professional opinion," Fox said. "I was being sarcastic. You clearly misunderstood me."

"Really," Blass said. "Did I also misunderstand you when you said the young women who have testified in this case, one of whom is in a religious order serving in an orphanage in New York, may have made this all up to explain their own failures or inadequacies? The 'abuse excuse' you called it."

"That's not what I said," Fox said.

Blass walked over to the stenographer, sitting before a tripod, head down fingers pushing black, soundless keys. "Would you like your testimony read back to you?"

"I was commenting on one of the ways a mistaken memory can become one that is firmly believed, as if it really happened." Fox's shook her body, like a bird ruffling its feathers. "I don't know the young women in question"

Blass turned to the jury and asked her next question while looking at them. "Did you make any effort to learn anything

CHAPTER 5

about the young women in question"

"I'm not sure what you mean," Fox said.

"Did you hear the testimony of the six young women in this case?"

"No, I was not here."

"Did you view a video or other recording of their testimony?"

"No."

"Did you read a transcript of their testimony?"

"No."

"Have you ever spoken to, or even met any of the six women?"

"No," Fox said. "It wasn't necessary for my testimony."

Blass turned to Fox. "Really," she said, infusing the word with two extra syllables. "Would it surprise you to learn each woman testified to events or actions that she said happened to her personally?"

"No, I wouldn't be surprised. I'm well aware of what is being alleged here," Fox said. The first hint of anger and exasperation seeped from her mouth.

You think the experience of being raped or molested is equivalent to seeing someone tip over a wedding cake," Blass said, incredulity infused into every word. Two of the women jurors began writing in their notebooks.

"Objection!" Chandler shouted, trying to slow down the assault. The prosecutor is mischaracterizing Doctor Fox's testimony."

"Overruled," Farmington said. "You have redirect." She looked at Fox, who was staring up at her. "The witness will answer."

"I'm not sure I remember the question," Fox said.

"Funny how that never happened on the questions asked

by Mr. Chandler," Blass said. Two of the jurors smiled and nodded their heads. A male juror gave out a muffled laugh.

"Objection," Chandler shouted. "Move for mistrial on the grounds of prosecutorial misconduct."

"That's absurd," Blass said.

"Let me make the rulings, Ms. Blass," Judge Farmington said. "Motion for mistrial is denied. She turned towards the jury. "You should disregard the comment by Ms. Blass and any innuendo it might carry." She smiled to soften the tension of the moment.

Blass faced the jury. She gave them a quick eye-roll. "I understand, Your Honor." She turned her attention back to Fox. "I asked you if you thought being raped or molested is equivalent to seeing someone knock over your wedding cake?"

"I was simply responding to a hypothetical posed by Mr. Chandler concerning what would be an unpleasant experience."

"Is that how you view rape or child molestation? As an unpleasant experience?" Blass said. She turned to face the jury.

"Well, no, I mean yes," Fox said. She took a quick sip of water, "I mean any nonconsensual sex or inappropriate intimate touching would, at a minimum, be unpleasant."

"Would you concede rape or molestation would be, for most, a traumatic experience and not just an unpleasant one?"

"No, not all of these horrible incidents will produce trauma." Several of the female jurors flashed quizzical looks, one shook her head in apparent disbelief.

"Do you acknowledge that PTSD Post-Traumatic Stress Syndrome is real? Blass moved a step closer to Fox and crossed her arms.

"I think it's over-diagnosed," Fox said.

"That's not what I asked you. Do you acknowledge it exists?"

"Yes."

"You remember your testimony about false memories being honestly believed?"

"I do," Fox said.

"The examples you gave all involved situations where several witnesses to an event may recall it differently while each believed his or her memory is more accurate that the others. Isn't that right."

Fox paused and fidgeted.

"Objection," Chandler said in his practiced voice of indignation."

"Overruled. The witness will answer."

"I'm sorry, I don't remember the question," Fox said.

Several jurors groaned audibly. Others shook their heads. One smiled and wrote in her notebook.

"Perhaps it's been suppressed," Farmington said. Some laugher came from the jurors.

"I'll repeat the question," Blass said. "The question was with respect to your testimony about mistaken memories that are honestly held. I asked wasn't it true that the examples you gave all involved situations where several witnesses to an event recalled it differently while each believed his or her memory is more accurate that the others."

"I suppose you're right," Fox said.

Blass said, "Suppose?" She let the skepticism ride on her voice. She turned back to the jurors, to measure their interest, or boredom. "Would you like the stenographer to read back your testimony?"

"No, that's an accurate statement on my testimony on

mistaken beliefs, honestly held."

"And, you've already acknowledged the emotional impact on a person experiencing a rape or molestation is not the same as the emotional impact on a person witnessing an event, isn't that true?"

"Yes, that's true, but I believe both can have mistaken memories that are honestly held," Fox said.

"Did you know each of the six women who testified in this case used a different therapist?"

Fox shrugged. "I think I knew that. Must have read it somewhere."

"Is it your opinion each of these women and each of the clinicians conspired together against the defendant and made-up stories of abuse?"

"Objection," Chandler shouted while rising to his feet. "Move for mistrial."

"You seem anxious not to let this jury make a decision," Blass sneered while turning toward them.

"The objection is sustained," Judge Farmington said. "The motion for mistrial is denied." She leaned in the direction of Blass. "Ms. Blass, another gratuitous comment like that, and your cross-examination is over."

Blass gave the jury another quick eye-roll. "I apologize, your Honor." She turned to Fox. "You understand the women who testified in this case were not recalling an incident each witnessed. But rather each testified as to a personal experience? Something that happened to each of them."

"Yes, I understand that," Fox said, unable to conceal her anger. "And it doesn't change my opinion on suppressed memory."

"But you acknowledge PTSD exists," Blass said.

"Yes, and I also said it is diagnosed too often."

"And you are aware of studies establishing the link of exposure to a traumatic event to memory loss?"

"More common with PTSD," Fox said in an icy tone, "are flashbacks and not being able to forget the event," Fox said.

Blass stepped closer to Fox. "Did you understand the question I asked you, Dr. Fox?" Blass said, returning the ice.

"I did."

"Then answer it."

"Objection," Chandler said, "The prosecutor is badgering the witness."

"Overruled. Farmington said. "Please answer the question. Do you remember it?"

"I think so," Fox said.

"Christ," a juror muttered, loud enough to draw a stare from Farnsworth.

"I asked if you were aware of studies establishing the link of exposure to a traumatic event to a memory loss?"

"I am aware of them," Fox said.

"Have you ever had a clinical practice, Doctor Fox?? Blass said. "One, where you see patients in therapy."

"I have not," Fox said.

"In fact, you wrote a book saying most of psychiatry is psycho-babble, didn't you?"

"I did, and most of it is," Fox sneered.

"So, you think it's a waste of time?" Blass said.

"For the most part it is," Fox said. She flashed a thin, almost lipless, smile.

"Yet, you choose to get a doctorate's degree in Psychology," Blass said.

"Not all of it is babble," Fox said. "And I thought I'd be in a better position to debunk its theories, if I studied it in depth."

"So, you had already decided you wanted to debunk a subject *before* you studied it at the doctorate level," Blass said.

"That's not what I said," Fox said.

"It isn't?" Blass said. "We'll let the jury decide what you said." She moved quickly to the next question. "Earlier you made a reference to the fact more clinicians believe in suppressed memory than do researchers. You remember that?"

"I do."

"Can you cite any authorities or statistics supporting that statement."

"I wasn't asked to bring any," Fox said.

"Are you saying you have them, or are just being sarcastic?" Blass said.

"They exist, I'm sure," Fox said. "I don't carry them around with me."

Blass smiled, happy to dwell in Fox's anger. "And when you talked about these clinicians who believe in suppressed memories, you also noted they are the ones being paid to retrieve suppressed memories, or words to that effect. Do you remember that?"

"I do," Fox said. "I think it goes to their motive in asserting its existence."

"So, if someone is being paid for their time and work, it makes their motives suspect? Is that what you're saying?" Blass said.

"Well, it's certainly something to consider," Fox said.

"Tell us, Doctor Fox, are you being paid for your time in court here today?" Blass said.

"Objection," Chandler said. "She's implying Doctor Fox's

CHAPTER 5

testimony was bought."

"Overruled," Farmington said. "Your witness opened this door; I'm not letting you close it."

"I am," Dr. Fox said. "For my time, not my opinions."

"Are you suggesting Mr. Chandler did not know your opinions before he paid you to come to court today? Blass said. "Is that what you're saying, under oath, to the jury?"

"Objection!" Chandler shouted.

"Not surprised," Blass muttered. "I'll withdraw the question. I have no further questions."

"No redirect, Your Honor," Chandler said.

"Fine," Judge Farmington said. "The witness is excused."

Fox slid off the chair, made a show of slowly gathering her coat, put it on and picked up her briefcase. She walked through the trial section of the courtroom, passing Chandler and Palfrey, on her right. Fox pushed open the gate in the wooden barrier separating the trial area from the rows of spectators. She slowed as she approached the row with Sister Alicia to her left. Fox kept her eyes straight and briefly touched her left temple area with her middle finger, and continued out of the courtroom.

"The defense rests," Chandler said.

Blass stood. "No rebuttal,"

Farmington nodded and taped her gavel lightly on the wooden block. "Court stands in recess until tomorrow morning at ten o'clock." She faced the jury. "Deliberations should begin tomorrow afternoon. Bring your suitcases."

Chapter 6

Joe McDonald was fifty-seven, six-foot even, and twelve pounds over his ideal weight of one-eighty. He had longish, thick and prematurely white hair with a matching beard. This provided the image and aura of an undersized shopping mall Santa. The image was enhanced by the fact McDonald was a classic bon companion and raconteur. He was a man who carried the hint of a smile, as though perpetually amused.

McDonald was tough, street smart, politically astute, and the local prosecutor for Caleb County, Maine's smallest county. His jurisdiction included Naples, Lake Sebago, Queen's Lake, Gorham, and North Windham. "More fish than people," Joe said when he described Caleb County.

Queen's Lake was close to two thousand acres of water with a thirty-two-mile shoreline well developed with mostly modest homes and camps catering to full-time residents and weekend vacationers. A crooked two-mile peninsula of land running into Queen Lake like a third finger was Jefford Point. While Queen Lake spread across the towns of Harley and Fulton, the residents of J Point pledged allegiance to neither. They considered themselves a quasi-sovereign, and tried valiantly and unsuccessfully, to get their own post office, zip code and telephone exchange. But they were not militant about it. They paid their taxes, obeyed the laws, and every four years the year-round residents voted unanimously for Joe McDonald as the man to prosecute those who did not.

J. Point was home to 19 year-round residents and 20 "seasonal owners." The number of permanent or year-round residents was painted on a large, white sign greeting travelers, who could only arrive over a dusty, narrow road following the curvatures of the third finger and passing private, narrower roads leading to fishing camps and homes on either side. While these narrow paths were named, usually after a breed of fish, the single public access to J. Point was unnamed and referred to as "The Road." It and J. Point ended at a ninety-foot strip of shoreline that served as the public beach and gathering place. The year-round residents of the J. Point gathered at twelve noon, each Memorial Day on the public beach for an informal census and a repainting of the sign. Anyone who missed the count, no matter the reason, reduced the number to be repainted on the large white sign. New year-round arrivals to J Point were informed of this ritual as part of a welcome package of trinkets, fruit and other oddities.

Joe McDonald and his wife, Cassandra Harvey, were born near but not on J. Point. They attended the public schools in Fulton and later Boston University, where after nearly twenty years of ignoring or avoiding each other, they connected at a party, fell in love, and married two weeks following their graduations in 1986.

Joe honed his political skills as a volunteer for the 1988

presidential campaign of Michael Dukakis, then Governor of Massachusetts. As an unpaid volunteer, Joe made the Technology/Science section of Time magazine for showing the Dukakis higher-ups how to use satellites for local TV interviews instead of flying to small studios across the United State. In Joe's case, political was not an adjective, but a noun. Cassandra, more focused and practical, voted for Dukakis, but managed to secure a paid position with the Bush Campaign running Democrats for Bush. George Herbert Walker Bush won and proved to be a grateful benefactor to Cassandra and her husband.

They both landed feel-good paid internship positions with the State Department. Within five months of their appointments, Joe and Cassandra were assigned to PROJECT TEACH, an educational initiative that brought them initially to Bahrain, Qatar and later to the United Arab Emirates. One Wednesday night, Joe found himself playing pool with the Bahrain Minister of Justice. Joe politely let him win. Later, the Minister saw Joe run the table against another American. The Minister dubbed him "Shark" and gave him access to the dark corridors and inner-workings of government.

Cassandra spent her first month teaching English and mathematics to girls ages six to twelve. Then she was assigned to a mapping initiative doing topographical surveys of the area and examining satellite images.

Joe was assigned to a project with the stated mission to cultivate relationships with small and remote villages in order to promote, through education, the principles of justice and self-government.

It took Cassandra and Joe less than a month to conclude each now worked for the CIA.

CHAPTER 6

* * *

The presidential inauguration in 1992 brought Bill and Hillary Clinton to the White House, sent George and Barbara Bush to Houston, and steered Joe and Cassandra to Langley, Virginia. They remained as obscure numbers in the budgetary black hole of the CIA. In the middle of the second year of the Clinton Presidency, Joe and Cassandra were selected for a program providing enrollment at the University of Georgetown Law School. For the next three years, they lived in a brick town house two blocks from DuPont Circle and attended classes. Each received a monthly stipend of seven thousand dollars. Neither ever received a tuition or rent bill.

During their years as law students, a person identified only as Felix periodically contacted Joe and Cassandra. The contact was by email, text or a phone call with the voice distorted electronically. Felix would politely inquire as to their health, happiness and overall well-being. Occasionally, Felix asked them to attend and provide notes of panel discussions at The Elliott School of International Affairs. Less often, their presence and note-taking would be requested at lectures and seminars at George Washington University. The notes taken by Joe and Cassandra on these occasions were mailed to Felix at a post office box in Georgetown. Each call, email, or text from Felix ended with the words, "We've big plans for you, Joseph. And for Cassandra as well."

* * *

The robotic voice belonged to Felix Ketch, a mid-level CIA analyst in Langley, Virginia. Joe and Cassandra had come to Felix's attention early in their stint with the Agency. Felix made them parts of a strategic plan to advance the Agency's interest in the United Arab Emirates. Ketch's own advancement through the bureaucracy was a co-equal priority of the plan. Felix joined the Agency as an analyst shortly after graduation from college. Quiet, unassuming and gay, Felix climbed the rickety corporate ladder with caution and a careful attention to not offending any in competition for advancement. Felix volunteered for a number of teams and was careful to share credit with others no matter how small their contribution. Advancement was slow but steady and Felix now had a small staff in the Directorate of Analysis and an office on the fourth floor with a window providing a glimpse of the Kryptos, the encrypted sculpture on the ground of CIA Headquarters.

* * *

Joe and Cassandra declared and paid taxes on their income, and lived their lives quietly and openly in a style to which they never thought they would become accustomed. Each was simply a speck of dust in the machinery and bureaucracy of an Agency with a public budget in excess of fifteen billion, and an employee count that was classified.

Cassandra became Editor of the Law Review and graduated Summa Cum Laude. Joe made friends, developed connections and graduated in the middle of his class. Following graduation, they remained in Washington in the picturesque townhouse.

CHAPTER 6

Without much effort, Cassandra secured a teaching position at Howard University Law School.

Joe was offered and accepted a position as legal counsel to a congressional sub-committee focused on the Middle East. He expanded his network and made friends on both sides of the political aisle. Joe's knowledge of intelligence issues and his political skills were noticed by the Chairman, who moved him up to the House Committee on Intelligence, and provided him a nice office and a staff of eager interns.

Joe and Cassandra's salaries were more than adequate, and allowed them to bank the stipend checks, which continued to arrive on the tenth day of every month.

* * *

Alan Jonathan Weiss was one of three deputy assistants to the assistant to the Region One Administrator of the Directorate of Analysis at the CIA. Weiss was sixty-three, rail-thin, ex-military with a brush cut, weathered face and prominent nose. He was a bureaucratic pain in the ass. Although several levels above Felix, he enjoyed peering down to the underlings to make certain all was well, and to assert his authority. Without an appointment or warning of any kind, Weiss would strut into Felix's office and ask about projects he cared little about and understood even less. He did this again on the first Thursday in January, 2009.

"Felix, tell me about that project involving Joe McDonald. Where are we on this?"

"Sir, I gave my monthly report on that to Patrick Sullivan,"

Felix said. "I can give you a copy if you'd like." Felix started fishing through a small file cabinet.

Weiss sat on a metal chair in front of Felix's desk. He brushed a speck only he could see from the sleeve of his suit. "Give me the elevator version." He crossed his legs, careful not to do damage to his heavily creased trousers. "I don't have time to read reports."

Or to learn anything, Felix thought. *But plenty of time to fuck up my day.* "I expect in about a year, Joseph will be ready for transfer to Bahrain to implement the plan. If that goes well, and I am certain it will, he will go to the United Arab Emirates. I'm optimistic all the objectives of the mission will be accomplished in three years, four tops."

"Jesus, Felix. I've been hearing about this scheme of yours for close to ten years, we need to move faster, or I'll have to consider dumping it. And you."

"It's been four years, Sir." Felix said. "And Mr. Sullivan seemed pleased with my progress."

Weiss stood and brushed an invisible speck off the padded shoulder of his jacket. "I'm about 3 levels of bosses over Sullivan. Get this started right away. Or you and Sullivan will both be looking for work." Weiss turned sharply and marched out of the room.

Asshole, Felix thought.

Weiss closed Felix's door and walked down the corridor. "Asshole," he muttered to the empty corridor.

7

Chapter 7

On a rainy Monday morning in February 2009. Joe was in his Capitol office, surrounded by law books, legislative reports, and portraits of prior Chairs of the House Committee on Intelligence. Felix called, and told Joe to report to Langley in one week for a nine-week training, after which he would go back to Bahrain on a special assignment. "You have good connections there, Joseph," the robotic voice said. "We need you to establish a special program with their judicial system and in a year or so bring it to the United Arab Emirates." The tone was clear. This was not a request.

Joe resisted.

"Felix," Joe said. "What about Cassandra? I don't want to leave her for an assignment on the other side of the world. Can she at least come with me?" Joe stood and paced his office, careful to keep his voice low and calm.

"No, this assignment is for you," Felix said. "You work for us, and you do not get to question your assignments."

"With all due respect, Felix, I work for the House of Representatives," Joe said. He peered out his window to a side view of the marble steps to the Capitol.

"Don't be naïve, Joseph. You work for us," Felix said. "We pay your rent, and we paid your law school tuition. It is time, Joseph, to put your legal training to our use. I have told you many times, we have big plans for you."

"You always said me and Cassandra," Joe said. "Now you expect me to leave her behind? Be reasonable." A drop of perspiration began its roll down Joe's back. *How many financial disclosure regulations have I violated?* He thought. *Jesus, could I go to jail?*

"We have been good to you, Joseph. It's time for you to do as you are told."

Joe paused. A different strategy came forth. "Look, Felix, I've made a lot of friends. I can do more for you and the Company here than in the United Arab Emirates. Could you speak with your superiors and persuade them to keep me here? I'd be grateful." Joe paused for effect. "And I know Chairman McNiff would be as well."

"You think Brian McNiff will go to bat for you once he discovers you've been on our payroll all these years?" Felix said. "Report to Langley next Monday."

"Felix, be smart," Joe said, hurriedly, before Felix could terminate the call. "Whaddya think Chairman McNiff will do to you when he discovers you put one your operatives on his sub-committee." Joe could imagine the spinning of wheels coming through the phone line. "I know you were instrumental in getting me that job. McNiff will fire me, and I can live with that. *Like hell I could.* But, Felix, your fuckin' career will be over. You'll be a pariah. You'd be lucky to get a job cleaning toilets in the Toledo office. You must know that. Be smart, talk

CHAPTER 7

to your superiors. Please."

"There was a long pause. "I will see that the proper people are made aware of your concerns," the robotic voice said. "Stay where you are until you hear from me." The call was terminated.

* * *

The days came and went. The shadows crossed the room. The phone calls from Felix ceased, but the checks came. Occasionally, Cassandra expressed concern about their mysterious lives and living accommodations. Joe offered reassurance, saying "I think Felix got my message, and will leave us alone, so long as I do my job. Let's enjoy the ride. We know it won't last forever."

And it didn't.

Felix called on the first day of October in 2009, the start of the federal fiscal year. The distorted voice advised Joe that his and Cassandra's services were no longer required. No check arrived on the tenth day.

Joe resigned his position with the House Intelligence Committee. He discouraged efforts to organize a farewell party, concerned any focus on his departure might trigger Felix to alert one or more investigative reporters. His exit from Washington was silent and quick. Thirty days later, Joe and Cassandra were back at J. Point. They moved into a two-bedroom home on the east shore, the second home on Pike Lane, one of the narrow paths running off the unnamed road. It was built by Cassandra's father, acquired by her mother as part of a divorce settlement, and then inherited by Cassandra when her mother died in 2008.

The home was the first in a line of two seasonal homes built on lots directly behind a large house constructed decades earlier by Abner Duffy, an original developer of J Point. Duffy owned a large tract of land, and Pike Lane, the narrow path running off the Road became the driveway to his home. He operated and maintained a still on the land behind his ornate home. When prohibition ended, Duffy concluded it would be more profitable to close the still and sub-divide the land behind his house to allow others to enjoy life on J. Point.

There was a problem with Abner's plan. His large home, designed to prevent anyone from seeing the still behind it, blocked access to the two building lots he wanted to create. Abner removed one of the two side porches to his home and extended Pike Lane so that it ran along the side of his house and back to the two new lots. Since it was on land owned by him, Abner provided a right-of-way across his land in each of the deeds to the new lots. The town approved the new plan and a seasonal home was built on each of the two lots.

Joe and Cassandra accumulated savings during their years with the Company. They decided to keep the property on Pike Lane as a vacation home and moved to Melrose, a community about nine miles north of Boston. Joe did political consulting and eventually became a consultant for the Judicial Council, the lobbying arm of Massachusetts judges seeking judicial reform and pay raises.

* * *

CHAPTER 7

Everything changed six years later, when Cassandra received an unsolicited offer for a tenured teaching position at the University of Maine School of Law in Portland. They moved back to J. Point, renovated the home with heat and air conditioning, added a porch and became part of the year-round J. Point community. Joe did political consulting and found friends in the Maine Governor's Office. After seven months in Maine, he was recruited to accept a gubernatorial appointment as county prosecutor to fill the unexpired term of Paul Brauneis, who accepted an appointment to the state's supreme court.

Two years later, Joe was re-elected Caleb County Prosecutor. Considered now to be unbeatable, Joe is often mentioned as a potential candidate for Congress. He developed good relationships with legislators across Maine and became an effective advocate for all the county prosecutors at budget time. It provided him a statewide network of friends in the event his political ambitions focused higher than a congressional district.

Cassandra became a well-respected professor of law and a popular speaker at legal conferences and judicial gatherings.

Joe and Cassandra became one of Maine's most notable and accessible power couples. They were popular, successful and completely unaware of the intrigue, stress and murder that was about to enter their lives starting the second Friday in January, 2022.

Chapter 8

Friday, January 14, 2022 was the fifth day of the below zero temperatures that descended on J. Point the previous Monday, following what had been an unusually mild winter. It was a barren cold, without wind or spirit. The kind of cold that reached the marrow of your bones and filled your veins with shards of ice. Joe decided the cold snap was a reasonable price to pay for the mild winter that had preceded it. He stomped his feet for warmth and walked across the frozen dirt, expelling puffs of steam, which dissipated in the cold air, to his 2019 black Subaru Outback, its body and windows glazed with ice. Joe elected to keep his thick woolen mittens on, and pushed the button on his fob. Yesterday, his mittened hand had triggered the alarm, sending sharp and loud shrieks into the cold air, waking Cassandra. This time, the mechanical beep signaled an unlocked door. He pulled it open and climbed inside the cold, windless interior. Following a silent prayer, he pushed the start button while his foot gently rested on the brake. The car started without hesitation or any strange noises, as it had since its purchase two years ago. Joe, who knew nothing about cars, regularly brought the vehicle to those who did. He charted oil changes, tire rotations and whatever else the thick book containing the manufacturer's detailed instructions suggested. The vehicle, the mechanics Joe entrusted it for care assured him, was "good as new." Yet, he never failed to recite a quick prayer before each start.

Belts and suspenders.

Joe let the vehicle run and trudged back into his house to retrieve a thermos of hot coffee and enjoy the warmth of his kitchen while the car heated up and the engine prepared for the nine-mile trip to his office. Cassandra was sitting at the oak kitchen table, reading *The Boston Globe* and *The New York Times* on two laptops while grading a pile of papers. A black stove on the far wall threw heat and aroma into the comfortable kitchen with a muted crackling of wood. A year younger than Joe, Cassandra was five foot eight, with thick brown hair carefully styled to frame a squarish pale face. Striking green eyes and a thin cluster of freckles across her nose confirmed her Irish heritage.

"Car start, okay?" She said, without looking up from the computer screens.

"It did," Joe said as he pulled out a chair across from her. "A quick prayer to St. Michelin never fails." He sat and took a careful sip from the thermos.

Cassandra looked over from her computer screen. "Don't you mean St. Michelob?"

Joe frowned. "Not for the car. He only cures hangovers."

Cassandra laughed. She closed the laptop with *The Globe*. "I just read the jury's still out on the Palfrey child abuse case up in Bangor," she said. "Wasn't that supposed to be a slam-dunk?"

Joe shrugged. "That's what the woman trying the case, told me at the state-wide meeting last month. Elaine Blass is the top prosecutor in that office. She's tough, experienced and usually right on these things. Something must have gone wrong." He shook his head. "I guess there's no such thing as a slam dunk."

"*The Globe* said a source claims a psychologist, a Doctor Fox, testified for the defense and may have created enough doubt to hang the jury, if not acquit. Also, one of the victims called her an effing bitch in open court."

Joe shook his head. "That source would be the defense attorney," he said. "Elaine would fire anyone who talked to a reporter. Sounds like the trial got out of hand. I'll call her when I get to the office. Offer some collegial support. Maybe find out what's really going on."

"Well, it's a Friday before a long weekend," Cassandra said. "The jury will figure something out." She spied the confusion on Joe's face and gave a tolerant smile. "Martin Luther King Day. You remember him?"

"I lost track of the calendar and forgot," Joe said. "You looking to go someplace? Get off J. Point? I'm game."

"A day or two in Portland would be nice," Cassandra said. "We can try that hotel on the harbor we keep talking about."

Joe stood. "Call me when you're ready to head out, and I'll come home. I won't be busy. Lakes are all frozen. No fishing-without-a license cases until the spring." He stood and pulled on his mittens. "Maybe we should move up to Bangor. I could prosecute real cases."

"You could get elected up there," Cassandra said. "Maybe this Elaine woman could get you on the staff." She leaned closer to Joe across the table. "The law school has a satellite

CHAPTER 8

campus in Bangor. You wanna head up north, I'll go."

"You'd follow me anywhere? You're that desperate to get off J. Point?" Joe laughed. "No, No. I'm not ready to stop being the boss. Just complaining about a job that's easy, pays well, and I like. Don't listen to me." He took a sip from his thermos. "I'll be home by early afternoon. One-thirty at the latest. Whaddya got going, today?"

Cassandra brushed aside some errant strands of hair that fell over her left eye. "I'm just handing in grades. There's a faculty/student forum at eleven. Probably more information on the move to Portland."

"Can you skip it?" Joe said.

"I plan to," Cassandra said. "Like the Palfrey jury, I want to wrap up my work and get home early."

Joe stood and started towards the door. "I hope you're wrong on a hung jury. I'll call Elaine, and offer my support. Try to find out something about this Doctor Fox."

"Paper says she doesn't believe in psychology," Cassandra said. "Thinks a lot of it is just psycho-babble."

Joe shrugged and opened the door. "I'm not surprised. I know judges that don't believe in justice."

* * *

It was twenty minutes after eight when Joe pulled his car into his assigned parking space in the back lot at the Fulton Town Hall, a two-story white clapboard building with dark green shutters on either side of its eighteen six-over-six windows. The windows provided views of the town green out front, a fire station to the east, a Starbucks to the west and the parking lot out back. Joe convinced the county commissioners to allow him to rent space on the second-floor rear to avoid the longer commute to the county seat. It was not a difficult sell, given the surge in population and arrests during the summer months. Over the years, he had expanded his space to four offices, each with a view of the parking lot and a more distant view of Queen Lake.

He hurried over to the Starbucks, expelling puffs of hot breath into the cold air. Joe usually emptied his thermos by the third mile mark on the trip to his office. He ordered and paid for a large house blend, with one cream no sugar, over the Starbucks app on the ride in, without speaking to a real person. Once again, he wondered how long it would be until humans were obsolete. It was another part of his work day ritual. The coffee was ready, as it always was, when Joe pushed open the door and walked to the counter. He grabbed the coffee, shouted a quick "thanks," and hustled out the door. He wondered, as he always did, exactly who did he just thank and who got the tip?

* * *

Joe entered the reception area of his suite of offices at eight twenty-five. A receptionist desk was centered in this the largest of the four offices. The walls were white plaster with wooden wainscoting, painted beige, running up four feet from the oak plank floor. Four tall, four-drawer oak filing cabinets, were against one wall. A heavy-duty copier

CHAPTER 8

cranked nosily as it spewed out recipes and sheet music into a large gray tray. Jacqueline Brewer, 34, the niece of a former Congressman looked up from her magazine. She had dark hair, blue eyes, firm breasts, world-class legs, and the brains of a clam. "Morning, Joe," she said.

"Hey, Jackie," Joe said. "Could you try to get Elaine Blass in the Bangor Prosecutor's Office on the phone?"

"Who's she?" Jackie said.

"She's the woman in the Bangor Prosecutor's Office I want to talk with on the phone," Joe said. He opened the adjoining door to his office and turned. "That's why you're calling her for me."

"Oh."

* * *

Joe's office was the smallest of the four. It had the same beige wainscotting from the reception room, two windows overlooking the parking lot, and a large walnut roll-top desk with nooks and drawers and a green leather inlay on the writing surface. It had occupied this room since the construction and opening of the then new town hall, and the inlay was weathered with the age and dust acquired over eighty-plus years It and the reception area were the original two offices Joe leased from the town. When the lease was expanded to include an office and a conference room on the other side of the reception area, Joe elected to remain in this office because of the desk. No one was certain how to take it apart to move it to a different office. Joe was afraid any dismantling might damage the desk, so he elected to keep it and the smaller office. He sat at the desk and sipped his coffee, trying not to burn his tongue.

Another workday morning ritual.

The intercom function of the three-line land phone on a small table near his chair, burped.

"I have Elaine Glass on line one."

"It's Elaine Blass," Joe shouted into the intercom. He pushed the button for line one. "Elaine, thanks for taking my call. I know how busy you must be."

"Joe, are you kidding?" Blass said. "Nobody does more to get us better funding every year. Whaddya need?"

Joe laughed. "Nothing, Elaine. I'm just calling to offer collegial support on the Palfrey case."

"I may need collegial prayers more than support, but I appreciate your call," Blass said.

"Any ideas on what's going on?" Joe took another careful sip of his coffee. He put the cup down and reached for a pad of paper.

"I thought the case went in well," Blass said. "The victims were good, believable and likeable. Hell, one's a nun."

"My wife told me a *Globe* source said Dr. Fox might have created enough reasonable doubt to hang the jury."

"Yeah, that would've been Palfrey's lawyer, Trevor Chandler," Blass said. "Asshole, but knows what he's doing. I thought I discredited her enough on cross, but maybe not. Didn't expect deliberations to last this long. Hope I didn't let an asshole and a quack steal the case from me. Maybe I should have gone at her harder."

"Elaine, don't second-guess yourself," Joe said. "Only takes one moron to fuck up a jury. Not your fault if they deadlock."

"Well, it's Friday, so it'll end today, I think," Blass said. "Joe, it was nice of you to call. How's everything on J Point?"

"Quiet and cold," Joe said. "What I need is an asshole like Palfrey to prosecute."

"Be careful what you wish for," Blass said. "Hold on a sec." There was silence on the line for several seconds. "Joe, I'm told the jury's coming back into court at ten o'clock," Blass said. "Usually, I'm told they've reached a verdict. I think this means they have a question or are announcing a deadlock. Shit." She laughed. "I've got 45 minutes to find a bar and a tall Bloody Mary."

"I'll let you go," Joe said. "I'll say a prayer to Saint Perry Mason. All will be well."

"He's the patron saint of defense attorneys. Maybe a prayer to Hamilton Burger?" Blass said.

"He never won a case," Joe said. "I pray to those who win. Text or call me when you get a chance."

9

Chapter 9

At ten o'clock, Cassandra pulled her dark green four-year-old Toyota Camry into her assigned parking space about a hundred yards from the main entrance to what *Architectural Digest* named one of the eight ugliest university buildings in America. The University of Maine School of Law was housed in an eight-story structure that looked like a silo, but wider and with columns of windows spaced between sheets of white concrete. The magazine article bestowing the honor described it as a futuristic version of the Roman Colosseum. Its image was not enhanced by the cellphone towers and antennae sprouting from its roof like the bristles of an angry porcupine.

Cassandra walked to the main entrance and meandered to the elevator through packed boxes, crates and stacked furniture. The University had approved the signing of a five-year lease to move the law school into the Old Port Office Building in downtown Portland. During the five-year lease period, one of the eight ugliest university buildings would be leveled and a new home for the law school constructed. The

CHAPTER 9

in-fighting had begun for office space with water views in the new location in Portland.

Cassandra rode the empty elevator to the seventh floor, unlocked the door to her office and dropped her leather briefcase on her desk. Because of the building's odd shape, faculty and administrative offices were pie-shaped and it was difficult to get furniture to fit. Her office was minimalist with a small square desk and two chairs for visiting students. Her power wall was dotted with degrees and awards received over the years, and the other with a single framed black poster with white lettering announcing WELL - BEHAVED WOMEN RARELY MAKE HISTORY. The curved wall of the pie-shaped room overlooked a square, squat addition to the building. It did little to improve the overall appearance, and was described in one news article as "resembling a child's block placed next to a sand tower."

Cassandra draped her overcoat over the back of her chair and sat at the desk. She pulled her laptop from the briefcase, typed in a password and leaned back in the chair to watch the computer come to life. After a few seconds, she accessed the secure site for the placement of student grades and began typing. She was interrupted by a knock on the door.

"C'mon in," Cassandra said. Her voice sounded hollow in the small room.

The door opened slowly. A narrow man with a gray face, thin shoulders, and an $80 dollar double knit suit, stepped inside. "Professor Harvey, there's a woman here who would like to speak with you. She says it won't take long, and would be much appreciated."

"Harold, who is it?" Cassandra said.

"Dr. Alice Ruth Fox," Harold said. "May I bring her in?"

* * *

Joe sat his computer and scrolled through the police reports from the previous night. Another quiet night in Caleb County. Three arrests for operating under the influence, one attempted larceny of a motor vehicle, and two shoplifting complaints. Joe had one full and two part-time deputies covering the county. He assigned one OUI case to each. The shoplifting cases would be handled by the police prosecutor. The arraignment for the attempted larceny of a motor vehicle would be in a court house less than three miles away. He assigned that one to himself. His promise to be home early was safe. Being the boss had its perks.

"Joe, a Ms. Blass is on line one," Jackie's announced through the intercom, "you said her name was Glass, but it's Blass. Or is two different women?"

"It's one, but she uses an alias," Joe said. He pushed the button to line one. "So, Elaine was it a question, the announcement of a deadlock, or a verdict?"

"A little of everything," Blass said. "Jury came in at 10 o'clock and announced it had verdicts on eleven of the thirteen counts. Said they were hopelessly deadlocked on two counts. Whaddya think Farmington did?"

"I'd guess she questioned the jury on the deadlock issue and polled them. Once each juror said he or she agreed they were hopelessly deadlocked, she'd let them announce the verdicts on the other eleven counts."

CHAPTER 9

"And that's exactly what she did," Blass said.

"Why I make the big bucks," Joe said. He listened to the silence for a second or two. "You gonna make me beg?"

"Guilty on all the other counts," Blass said with no attempt to hide her joy. "The deadlock was on the two child molestation counts related to Samantha Cronin. She called Dr. Fox a 'fucking bitch' in open court. Farmington had her ejected."

"You think the jury punished her for that?" Joe said, incredulity riding with his words.

"I do," Blass said. "We found out later the vote was 9 to 3 for guilty. I think the three jurors liked Fox, or felt sorry for her, and the outburst from Cronin stuck in their craw. They couldn't let the issue go and went to a deadlock on her case."

"Well, congratulations, my friend," Joe said. "Eleven out of thirteen is a good win. Farmington will drop the hammer on that asshole. His parole officer hasn't been born yet."

* * *

Cassandra rose from her chair and walked over to Fox. "Good morning, Dr. Fox, I'm Cassandra Harvey. How can I be of assistance?"

"Oh please, call me Alice," Fox said. "After all, we're about to become neighbors."

"We are?" Cassandra blurted in surprise, then felt childish. "You're moving to J. Point?"

Fox nodded eagerly and with a smile. "Probably won't be a year-round resident, but certainly in the spring and summer. I bought the old Abner Duffy house."

"Well, it's nice to meet you," Cassandra said with a smile that did not hide her concern. She walked back to her chair and sat. "Please sit down, Alice. Do you have a few minutes? Would you like a coffee?"

Fox sat, her feet just touching the floor. "No thank you, I don't have much time. I just wanted to come by and meet the woman who'll be living in my back yard."

A sour blend of uneasiness and anger clutched Cassandra's stomach. "Well, we'll share a road. I wouldn't call it your back yard. Unless you're planning on mowing the grass and doing all the landscape work." She tried for a laugh, but it wasn't there.

Fox stared at Cassandra. "You live on J. Point the full year? Must be awfully quiet."

"The classroom gives me all the noise I need. I enjoy the solitude of J. Point. Something stirred in her mind. "Tell me, when did you purchase the Duffy place? I didn't realize it was on the market. Have you closed, or is under agreement?"

Fox stood. "I'm on my way to the closing. It's set for eleven-thirty. She glanced at her watch. Just wanted to meet my neighbor." She spit out a high-pitched laugh. "See who's camped out in my backyard." She walked to the door and turned. "Have a nice day, Professor Harvey."

"You, as well, Alice," Cassandra said. "And it's not your backyard." Anxiety wrapped itself around her like a body cast.

Fox stuck her head back into the office. "Just having a little fun with you. By the way, during business hours, I prefer Doctor Fox."

Cassandra slumped in her chair as soon as the door closed again. *How'd the hell she find out I was her neighbor, and I worked here?*

Chapter 10

"She kept referring to our house as being in her backyard," Cassandra said to Joe. "Christ, she's an odious little bitch. I wish she'd been there when you texted me on the Palfrey case. Would've loved to shove that tidbit up her tight, little ass. I spent the next hour on my computer doing research the troll."

"Sounds like you two really hit it off," Joe said around a laugh. "Look, Cassandra, she can call it whatever she wants, but we own the lot and we have a deeded right of way across her land to get to it," Joe said. "I wish one of the Duffy heirs had mentioned they were selling. I always thought the property was in trust and they'd never sell."

"Would you have wanted to buy it?' Cassandra said.

"No, but I would have reminded them to make certain the buyer understood the arrangement the three houses have about Pike Lane. Plowing, repairs, etcetera."

"It's still binding, even if there was no conversation," Cassandra said, more a statement than a question.

"It is," Joe said. "It's referenced in the deed and the

agreement was recorded when the two houses behind Duffy's were built. And, I've made sure it's been re-recorded every seven years. It's binding on Fox, whether she's read it or even is aware of it." He shrugged. "It's just a pain in the ass if the new owner doesn't understand everything before they decide to buy. You don't want it to be a surprise at the closing, or even worse, once they move in."

It was two o'clock. They were sitting at the kitchen table in their home. Cassandra could not shake the foreboding doom that had descended upon her after the meeting of Dr. Fox.

"The right of way is still binding," Cassandra said. "I know that much about property law."

"It is," Joe said. "Let's get packed for Portland."

"How'd she find out I was her neighbor, and where I worked?"

"Probably checked the town tax records or the assessor's office. It's all online," Joe said. "She got our names, Googled us and *voila*! There are no secrets, anymore."

Cassandra stood. "Let's get packed. I got us three nights in the Westin Portland Harborview. We can walk from there to several pubs, a theater, a nice restaurant and the Old Port Building, soon to be the law school's new home for five years."

"You don't want to spend the weekend living in Fox's backyard?" Joe said. The first smile in the past hour spread across Cassandra's face.

* * *

The storm began Saturday morning. It was constant, heavy,

and slow moving. Large floating snowflakes fell across J. Point. It would encase the Point in silence so dense it became its own sound. In Portland, twenty-odd miles away, Joe and Cassandra were on the right side of the snow-rain line. Their brightly colored umbrellas rested against the bench seats of their booth in Becky's Diner. The outside wind smacked thickening drops of rain against the large windows facing Commercial Street and the harbor.

"J. Point must be getting creamed," Cassandra said. "How'd you feel if I suggested cutting this short, and we head back this afternoon?"

Joe took a forkful of his corn beef hash omelet. He chewed and closed his eyes in thought. "How about we head home tomorrow morning? We can enjoy today, tonight, and still be responsible adults by cutting our vacation short by a day."

"J. Point could be under two feet of snow by tomorrow morning," Cassandra said. She stuck the pointed end of her triangular cut wheat toast into egg yolk and brought it to her mouth. "How do we know that bitch Fox called Andy to plow Pike Lane?" We could get home and find ourselves walking through waist-deep snow."

"I have another compromise," Joe said. "How about we finish our breakfast, and get the hell home."

* * *

By eleven-thirty, Joe and Cassandra were home and settled into a lazy Saturday mode. Cassandra was at the kitchen table with her laptop reviewing obscure law cases to either discuss in class or turn into exam questions. Joe was reading a Stephen King novel, nestled in a comfortable brown leather chair close to the fireplace.

The sounds of a distant plow reassured them Andy's Towing and Auto Body had indeed been contacted to plow Pike Lane. The company was run by a father and son team, both named Andy. No one seemed to know their last name, so they were referred to by all as Andy Senior and Andy Junior. The arrangement for plowing Pike Lane was specified in the agreement referenced in the deeds. Each property paid a stated percentage of the costs of maintaining Pike Lane. The percentages were based on the amount of footage the road extended across their property compared to the total footage of the road. The house behind Joe and Cassandra was owned by Roosevelt Wilson, a seasonal owner. Joe had agreed with him years ago to pay his share of the plowing costs rather than to have the plow leave a large snow bank at their property line.

"It looks like Fox called Andy's Towing. That's a good sign," Joe said without looking up from his book. He recrossed his legs and adjusted the light on the table beside his chair.

"Yeah, I guess so," Cassandra muttered, her eyes and mind focused on her computer screen. "Still a bitch, though."

Ten minutes later a loud knock brought both of them back to J. Point and their surroundings.

"I'll get it," Joe said around a groan. He got out his chair, walked over to the door, and opened it. "Hey, Andy Junior. Howareya?" Joe opened the door wider. "Come in, come in. Get outta the cold."

Andy Junior stomped his feet to remove excess snow and stepped inside. He was in his late twenties, very tall, well over six feet, with long brown hair draped over both ears and covered with a faded blue Red Sox cap. His face was red and wet from the snow and cold. A large drop of moisture or phlegm hung from his nose. He brushed it aside with a large mittened hand, crusted with snow and ice.

"What's up, Andy? Having trouble with the plow?" Joe said.

"We got a call from an Alice Fox, saying there was no need to plow Pike Lane since she wouldn't be up here until the spring. When my dad said she was required to have it plowed so you and Mr. Wilson could get to your properties, she said he should talk to you guys and hung up."

Cassandra got off the stool and walked over. "I knew that bitch was going to be trouble."

"Hang on," Joe said. "Andy, you want some coffee. Can you sit a minute or so?"

* * *

A few minutes later the three of them sat at the kitchen table, each with a steaming cup of coffee.

Joe reached across the table and touched Andy's thick arm. "Andy, I want you to plow the street as usual and send me the bill with the breakdown like you always do. I'll pay it and get reimbursed from Fox. If we get another storm, plow it and send me the bill. Unless you hear otherwise from me, you are to keep plowing the road and sending me the bill."

"Appreciate it," Andy said. He took a careful sip of coffee and toasted the cup to Cassandra. "Good coffee. Better than the crap I make at the office."

"Another thing, Andy," Joe said. "You have Dr. Fox's

number? I want to call her."

"Thought you might," Andy said. He pulled a piece of paper from his jacket pocket. It was wet, the handwriting a faded blue, but legible. He handed the paper to Joe.

Joe pushed in the numbers and leaned back in his chair. He sprung forward when he heard the voice, and put the phone on speaker.

"This is Doctor Fox," a tinny, high-pitched voice said.

"Afternoon, Doctor. This is Joe McDonald calling. Cassandra Harvey's husband? I'm one of the people living in your back yard."

Fox laughed. "Cassandra told you about that, I see. What can I do for you, Joseph?"

"Well, you can start by honoring the terms of the agreement that runs with your land. It requires you to plow Pike Lane from where it runs off The Road to the end of the Wilson property. He lives behind me. We pay you a percentage of the costs. It's all in the agreement, referenced in your deed."

"I didn't realize this was a business call," Fox said with a hunt of annoyance. "I didn't sign any agreement."

"I know that," Joe said. "The agreement was written and recorded when Abner Duffy subdivided his land and created the two parcels behind the house you just bought. It's referenced in your deed along with the right of way. It's binding on you whether or not you signed it or even knew about it."

"That hardly seems fair. I'm not at the property during the winter," Fox said. A poor me tone replaced her annoyance. "Joe, I don't see why I should have to pay to plow my driveway, if I'm not going to be there."

"Because it's not your driveway, Dr. Fox," Joe said. "It's a private road leading to the three parcels of land Abner Duffy created when he sub-divided his land. And I really don't care whether you think it's fair or not. It's binding, and it's all part of what you just bought. Did you have an attorney at the closing?"

"There was an attorney, but she represented the bank. Nobody told me anything," Fox whined. "I don't trust attorneys."

"Look, Dr. Fox, we're going to be neighbors, at least in the spring and summer, so let's start over and let's be honest with each other."

"Joe, I'm being honest," Fox said. "How do I know this agreement even exists, or you are who you say you are?"

"You're not being honest, Dr. Fox," Joe said, putting a little force in his tone. "You knew about the agreement and your obligations. That's why you felt the need to call Andy's Towing. I know every bank lawyer in this area. It'll take me three phone calls to find the one who represented the bank and I know she will tell me you got a copy of the agreement as part of the closing package of documents. If you didn't know about the agreement, you'd have simply gone home and not called the plowing company. Let's stop playing victim. You called Andy's Towing to see if you could get away with something, save a little money and then play Mickey the Dunce if anyone called you on it."

The silence told Joe he was right. He waited, understanding the human impulse most people have to fill silence with words.

"I'm not a liar," Fox said. "And I'm not a dunce. I'm confused. I'm not a lawyer, I don't understand these things. This call is upsetting me. What are you asking me to do?"

"Give me your mailing address," Joe said. "I'll mail you a copy of the plowing bill, marked paid, and you will send me a check for that portion of the bill that is yours. I'll give you a post office box for you to use to send my check. If I do not have the check by the end of January, I will file suit against you the next day." Joe paused. "If I do receive the check, I will forget all this happened, and we will become good neighbors. Understand?"

"I don't know what I did to make you so angry, but I want to be a good neighbor. I'll send you the check, as soon as I receive the copy of the bill."

They exchanged mailing addresses, and she hung up.

* * *

Ten minutes later, Joe and Cassandra stood at the door watching Andy walk through the snow and back to his plow. Cassandra closed the door and turned to Joe.

"You think she'll send the check?"

Joe shrugged. "Probably, I think she was trying to pull a fast one and got caught. She might try something else, but it won't involve plowing."

"So why do you look troubled?" Cassandra said. She guided him to the kitchen table and sat beside him."

"Something about that call didn't feel right," Joe said. He shrugged as if to shake it off. "Can't figure it out. Probably don't like arguing with my neighbor before I even meet her." He laughed. "I'll get over it."

"Just don't apologize to her. She's a bitch."

"My apologies always seem to work on you," Joe said around a laugh.

"You're not calling me a bitch, are you?"

CHAPTER 10

"Of course, not," Joe said. "Just someone good at accepting apologies."

11

Chapter 11

Spring came early to J. Point.

After a cold January and first ten days of February, warm temperatures descended on The Point like an obsessive parent. By the end of February, the snow banks had melted, crocuses appeared along with buds on the willows and silver maples. The chant of the chorus frogs, like thumbs running across combs, filled the early morning air. Three snow storms in January and one in early February tested the truce between Joe and Fox. In each instance, the snow plow arrived and the bill, including Fox's share, was paid in full without comments or delay. The sour taste of Fox's visit to Cassandra and Joe's contentious phone call her faded with the arrival of warm weather and eternal hopes of spring.

On the first Saturday morning in March, Joe was raking winter's debris along the entirety of Pike Lane, raking leaves, fallen limbs, and litter into small piles he would shift to his wheel barrow and then to his car and a yard waste site in Fulton. It was warm and sunny. Joe's forehead glistened as he continued raking and thought about the cold IPA waiting in his refrigerator. The sound of wheels rolling over the dirt lane brought him back to his chores. He looked over to the brown military-style jeep coming towards him.

It stopped twenty feet away and Roosevelt Wilson, Joe's rear neighbor, jumped out.

"Hey Joe," Roosevelt said. "Good to see ya, how was your winter?" He was a trim black man in his early fifties with close-cropped brown hair, a face lined by bourbon, and a voice roughened by cigarettes. He was wearing jeans and a corduroy barn coat. A retired marine sniper, he walked with the ramrod posture of former military.

Joe walked over and the two hugged. "Roosevelt, you're looking well." Joe looked at the jeep. "You've got the roof off already. You sneaking onto beach dunes somewhere?"

Roosevelt laughed. "I admit to nothing, especially to a prosecutor. I heard someone bought the Duffy house. You met him?"

"I met the new owner and it's a she. Alice Ruth Fox, who likes to be called Doctor Fox, during business hours. We had a bit of a squabble when she first took title, but I think it's okay now."

"What kind of squabble?" Roosevelt said. He leaned forward, his hands balled into fists, prepared for combat.

"Nothing big," Joe said. "She was trying to get out of paying her share of the plowing costs, but it got straightened out. It wasn't an issue the rest of the winter. I think she'll be okay. She's a bit weird, but hell, who isn't? Present company excluded, of course."

Roosevelt laughed. "I owe anything for the plowing?" A question he asked Joe at their first meeting each spring.

"A case of Harpoon will do it," Joe said. The same answer he'd given since the two met nine seasons ago.

Roosevelt smiled and nodded. "Happen to have one in the back seat. Still cold. I'll leave it on your porch. Let you finish up the spring cleaning while you're still sober. By the way, you need a bow saw? Got one you can use on the larger limbs."

"All set, but thanks. Come by later, you can help Cassandra and me make a dent in the case, and we can catch up."

"I will," Roosevelt said. He climbed into his Jeep and leaned toward Joe. "Want to hear more about this Dr. Fox." He started the jeep. "Just what we need. I guess all the geezers on J. Point will be coming around to get a look at her."

"I suspect interest will wane after the first one or two get a peek," Joe said.

"Not a looker, huh? Must be what my mother used to call a gal with a nice personality?"

"I'm afraid she's neither," Joe said. "But we'll let the others make up their own minds."

* * *

Just under 150 miles away, Elaine Blass, the prosecutor in the Palfrey trial and Samantha Cronin, the woman who dropped the f- bomb in court, stood in the doorway to a small, second-floor conference room Elaine used for quiet and solitude. Both of which had been interrupted on this Saturday morning by the sudden arrival of Samantha.

"I saw your car in the lot and figured I'd drop by to see if there was anything new on my case," she said. She wore jeans

CHAPTER 11

and a dark blue pea coat. A woolen knit stocking cap was pulled over her ears and dark hair.

"If there was anything new, I'd have called you," Elaine said. "My car is here on a Saturday, because I have work to catch up on a complicated manslaughter trial starting on Monday." She smiled to soften the hint.

Samantha ignored or didn't get the hint. She entered and sat down across from Elaine and her piles of papers, files and law books. "Have you talked to Chet again?" Chester "Chet" Snow was the County Prosecutor and Elaine's boss.

"Sammy, he hasn't decided whether to retry your complaints on Palfrey. We have a backlog of cases, a tight budget, and Palfrey's gonna be in prison for at least twenty years." She tried another smile. "Even if we convict Palfrey on your two charges, it's unlikely the judge would add anything to the sentence he's serving. Nothing would really change."

"But if he's found guilty, I'll be vindicated. A jury would have believed me and not his bullshit defense. That fuckin' Doctor Fox did this," Samantha said, repeating the mantra, she'd started when the jury announced it was deadlocked on the two charges that involved her.

"No, Sammy," Elaine said. "Dr. Fox didn't do this. It was your outburst at the trial that did this. We've gone over this. I'll ask Chet to let me retry the charges, but it's an uphill fight."

Samantha stood and turned to the door. "Fox is a fucking bitch. No one supports me on this."

Elaine stood. "Hold on, dammit. I've supported you on this since we met more than two years ago. "You've got no complaint. I worked my ass off on this case."

"I know," Sammy muttered without looking at Elaine.

"Look Sammy, how about we try this? I'll call Trevor

Chandler, Palfrey's lawyer. I'll tell him we want to retry the charges, and when he's convicted, we'll ask for the max and that it be served on and after the sentence he's now serving. Then I'll tell him if Palfrey pleads guilty, we'll ask the sentence be served concurrently. Whaddya think?"

"I think Fox is a fucking bitch and Palfrey doesn't deserve any consideration. He should be castrated."

Elaine laughed, trying to gain support. "I agree, but that's not an option. How about my approaching Chandler with the proposal I just outlined? You get your conviction, you're vindicated in terms of filing the complaint, and it avoids the vagaries of a jury and the expense of another trial."

"You think he'll go for it?" Samantha said

"I don't know, but I think it's worth a try."

Samantha shrugged. "Sure, go ahead. But that fucking Fox is still a fucking bitch. I'm not done with her." She walked out without a goodbye, a thank you, or closing the door.

12

Chapter 12

There were no empty seats for the Friday afternoon Psychology 101 class with Dr. Alice Ruth Fox. Attendance was mandatory, and Fox promised and delivered low grades to students who believed they could ace her exams without the benefit of her lectures. As a result, her classes were full and small. Thirty masked students remained from the sixty-five who enrolled in the two-semester course the past September. These students were psychology majors, who did not have the option of looking elsewhere for knowledge. This was a required course and a prerequisite for Freud and other advanced courses waiting their attention in later semesters.

It was March 25th. The extended stretch of warmer than usual weather shortened the incubation period for spring fever. It started its spread two weeks earlier and had reached full contagion in the student and faculty communities. It always spiked on Fridays, as the approaching weekend challenged the attention of even the most serious students.

Doctor Fox was immune from spring fever. She stood erect

wearing dark blue blazer and tan slacks on an 18-inch wooden platform that allowed her to appear taller behind the podium, which was on an elevated platform in front of a wall high chalk board. She did not wear a mask. She called out the name of the last of her registered students, and placed a small check beside her name. Although her focus was on name calling and placing appropriate check marks in her attendance folder, Fox noticed the woman in the last row. The white mask hid her face, but the short, curly hair was unmistakable. Samantha Cronin. She was not a registered student, but the University had a liberal policy that allowed students – and, to her horror even community members - to monitor a class, provided there was space available. Fox decided she would remove the extra chair in her class. She closed the attendance folder and slid it into the space provided under the angled portion of the podium.

She took out a seating chart and placed it where notes or formal remarks might ordinarily go. Fox needed neither. Her lectures were not written speeches, but rather extemporaneous remarks interrupted by questions or comments from students eager to accommodate Fox's demand for attendance and participation at all her classes.

"I want to start today's discussion with something current," Fox said. "Are any of you aware of the new policy that allows a U.S. Passport to be issued to a person other than a male or female?"

A hand shot up. It belonged to eighteen-year-old, Eugene Phillips, a lanky boy with longish dark hair and a pale complexion. He wore tan slacks and a University of Maine hooded sweatshirt. During the first semester, Phillips proved to be a talker and unafraid to take issue with Fox's often provocative prompts. He paid the price with a grade of D. His appeal to an academic panel was pending and included a blistering attack on Fox, calling her "homophobic, racist and a hypocrite."

Fox looked down at the seating chart, as if Phillips was a stranger and of no consequence to her. She looked up. "Yes, Mr. Phillips, tell us what you know about the policy."

"Well, I read it was designed to give non-binary, intersex and gender non-conforming people a marker other than male or female on their travel documents," Phillips said.

"Isn't that what I just said?' Fox said. She shook her head. "Mr. Phillips, you should know by now that participation in this class is more than simply repeating what I said. Participation means adding something new."

Phillips stood and removed his mask. "I thought your description of the policy was inaccurate," he said. "And with respect, I thought it was a bit demeaning to the people it was designed to help."

"Did you?" Fox said, dragging the words to add the wrappings of sarcastic surprise. "And, how exactly was my description inaccurate or demeaning?"

Some students squirmed in their seats either eager or uneasy with the prospect of yet another verbal rumble between Phillips and Fox.

Phillips was undeterred. "I thought you made it sound like passports would be going to inanimate objects or some kind of strange beings who were neither male nor female." Phillips placed air quotes around strange beings. "The policy allows those people who are either gender uncertain or transferring from one gender to another to get a passport, without forcing them to select a gender." He smiled at Fox. "I think my summary was more accurate, less judgmental, and therefore added to the discussion."

Fox smiled back. "I said person other than a male or female, so that certainly does not include an inanimate object, Mr. Phillips, And, I never used the words strange being." Fox returned the air quotes. Her smile dissolved to solemnity. "I can only conclude you were not listening, but felt the need to respond anyway. This, of course is entirely consistent with your narcissistic personality. Your constant clamor for attention. Always trying to make this class about you and not the issue I raised."

Phillips remained standing; his arms crossed. "Dr. Fox, insulting me is indicative of a person who has no interest in discussing the issue *you* raised. How the hell can you help people as a therapist, or train people who are interested in becoming therapists, if your response to anyone who challenges your position is to insult them?" He stared at Fox.

"Is that what you think this is, Mr. Phillips? A therapy session?"

"I don't know what this is," Phillips cut in. "If it's therapy, it's not helpful. And since I'm sure as hell not learning anything from you, if it's supposed to be a class, it's a complete failure." He sat down.

Fox pulled a small note book from the breast pocket of her dark blue blazer and scribbled something in it. She looked to Phillips. "You should consider a career in something more agreeable with your temperament. Something that doesn't require you to understand the mind or to use the one you allegedly have."

There was stunned silence for several seconds. Suddenly, a voice: "May I ask a question?" Emily Harkins, a first-year student and co-chair of the Campus LGBTQ+ Club stood. She wore a tie-dyed sweat shirt with matching hair and round metal rimmed glasses. Like Phillips, she received a D as her first semester grade. She also appealed, but without any accusatory diatribe. Her grade was changed to an A.

Fox made a pretense of consulting the seating chart and looked up. "You just did, Ms. Harkins. You may, however, ask another."

"Thank you," Harkins said. She removed her mask. "I've read your articles critical of the so-called bathroom bills. I think you made some cogent and forceful arguments against those laws, even though I support most of them." Harkins paused, perhaps expecting a reply. She received silence and continued. "It seems to me this passport policy is very different. It doesn't impose a threat, or embarrassment or inconvenience to anyone. It simply allows a person, who is conflicted or confused about his or her gender, or maybe in the process of transferring from one gender to another, not to have to declare a particular sex. Why not allow them to select a box marked X in his or her application for a passport? Where's the harm?"

"Well, first of all, that's two questions," Fox said. "But in any event, you answered your own question by saying his or her gender and his or her application or passport, didn't you? You see, Ms. Harkins, it's one or the other. You're either a male or a female. You're not an X or both male and female."

"I didn't answer my own question," Harkins said, some heat coming into her words. "I asked where's the harm? I'm not denying it's either male or female, but there are people who are genuinely confused about their gender. Males trapped in female bodies and vice versa. Why not accommodate these few people? Do you think they should be punished? Or ridiculed? Or denied passports?"

"Because we don't pass laws or make policies just because they don't hurt anyone. Laws are supposed to be grounded in reality or science," Fox said, returning some heat. "As I stated in the articles you just claimed to have read, but clearly haven't, we should not be making laws or policies based on delusion. You are either a male or a female. Transgender is a delusion. We should create laws pretending to accept it as reality."

"I did read your articles. You think transgenderism is a delusion?" Harkins said. "I have good friends who are tormented by the fact the gender assigned at birth does not reflect their reality. Some will undergo difficult surgeries, and others are in therapy."

"You defined the very nature of a delusion when you use words like 'gender assigned at birth does not reflect their reality,'" Fox said. "It's as if reality is something personal and not factual." She gave a hopeless shrug. "I resent policies and laws that are not grounded in science or reality. Laws that are passed because it's fashionable or in vogue," Fox said. "Anyone else have something to say?"

"I do," Harkins said, shutting down the effort to silence her. "Vogue? Do you think anyone wants to be transgender? You think they want to be stared at, laughed at, ridiculed? I can't believe you said that." Do you think people undergo these operations, and doctors perform them because it's fashionable?"

"Doctors performs surgeries because insurance companies now pay for this craziness," Fox said. The hint of anger was gone, replaced by a tone of impatience. She was tired of the discussion. Fox took a breath. "I suppose you think a man who likes to dress in women's clothing should be allowed to use the women's bathroom." She pulled out the small notebook and starting writing.

"We're talking about passports not bathrooms," Harkins said. "I don't think a man who likes to cross dress has the right to use the ladies' room, but maybe a transgendered person does. And I don't think it's delusional to try to help these people. I don't think they should be punished or ridiculed. Or, denied a passport."

Fox returned the notebook to her breast pocket. She looked at Harkins. "Well, of course, you feel that way, Ms. Harkins," she said. "You rushed out of the closet, and slammed the door behind you. You celebrate your own non-conformity. Indeed, I suspect you relish it. So, it's hardly surprising you'd expect society to bend over backwards for every delusional A-hole who demands a new right no matter how it might impact the rest of us."

This produced loud gasps and murmurs from the students. A stage whispered, "Jesus Christ, floated above the white noise and rustling.

"The rest of us?" Phillips shouted through his mask. "You mean all us white, straight, normal folks, Doctor Fox? "Who are the rest of us? What kind of psychologist are you?"

Samantha Cronin stood up in the last row. "I'll answer that." The heads of students turned towards her. "She's the kind that supports child abusers and demeans their victims, calling them liars, delusional and saying their claims of abuse are made to excuse their own failings in life. That's the kind of psychologist she is."

Fox remained calm. "Young lady, you are allowed to monitor, but not participate. I'm afraid I must ask you to leave." She pointed to the door. "Please go, and without any further comments."

Samantha sauntered to the door, her mask still in place. She turned to the other students and pointed at Fox. "Ask her about her friend Robert Palfrey."

"Please leave," Fox said firmly, but without anger or any emotion.

Samantha left, leaving the door opened.

"Who's Robert Palfrey?" A voice asked from a middle row.

Fox glanced at her watch. Thirty minutes left. "Give me a moment, please." She stepped off the small platform and put on a mask. She turned to the students. "I'll be right back. I want to be sure she leaves the building."

Chapter 13

Samantha Cronin leaned against Dr. Fox's sleek, gleaming, silver Lexus with shiny black tires, smoking a menthol cigarette. She looked over to her faded, maroon 2013 Mini Cooper, with a dented front fender and a rusty bumper at the end of the student parking section. It looked like it belonged to a student. *This fuckin' Lexus*, Samantha thought, *looks like it belongs to a college president. Maybe I should key it.*

Samantha had spent the past two weeks learning Fox's teaching schedule and where she parked her car. She'd followed Fox home and now knew where she lived. Samantha was assembling a dossier on Fox. When completed, it would list the cases where Fox testified on behalf of child abusers, the instances where she opposed proposed laws or policies advanced by the LGBTQ communities and others, and instances of her using her class to insult or bully those who disagreed with her.

Samantha planned to become Fox's worst nightmare.

Samantha taped today's class, and decided to enlist Emily

Harkins and Eugene Phillips in her effort to persuade the University to terminate Doctor Alice Ruth Fox. Samantha closed her eyes and imagined the scene. *I'm going to destroy that fuckin' bitch*, she thought. She dropped the cigarette and crushed it with the heel of her boot.

"Samantha, I'm glad I caught up with you," Fox called from a door to the building some thirty feet away.

Samantha looked up from the crushed cigarette. Fox was hustling over to her, a wide smile on her face. "What the fuck?" She muttered and straightened up as Fox drew closer.

"I owe you an apology." Fox said. "And I have something for you. I hope it will help you forgive my insensitivity towards you and the other victims at Palfrey's trial." She brushed past Samantha to the trunk of her car. Fox reached in her blazer pocket and pulled out a fob. She pushed a button, the trunk opened, and Fox disappeared behind it. Her voice cut through the mild air, from under the trunk's lid. "I hope you can give one of these to each of the others. I have forty dollars for you to pay any postage or delivery expenses." Fox stepped away from the trunk carrying a large package, wrapped in bright yellow and white stripped paper. "There are gifts inside for each of you." She stepped closer. "Just because I don't believe in the theory of suppressed memories, doesn't excuse my callousness and insensitivity to you and the others. It was rude and unprofessional. I'm sorry." She handed the package to Samantha.

"Samantha instinctively took the package with both hands. "I'm not sure any of us want anything...."

Fox jabbed Samantha just below her left ear with the stiffened fingers of her right hand. She dropped like a bag of wet laundry. The package bounced off her knees and cushioned her fall to the black asphalt. Fox was strong for a woman her size. She dragged Samantha to the back of her Lexus, and hoisted her into the trunk, lined with plastic. Fox wrapped her wrists and feet with gray duct tape. She pinned Samantha's arms to her side with still more rolls of tape, and placed a plastic bag over her head. and cinched it around her neck. Fox picked up the package, and threw it into the trunk. She stared at Samantha's unmoving body. "You think I don't know you've been following me? That I don't know what you're up to?" Samantha's eyes suddenly opened. Terror gripped as she struggled to breath. Fox raised her right hand, smiled and wiggled her fingers goodbye. She pushed a button on the fob, and the trunk slowly closed bringing darkness to the last moments of Samantha Cronin's life.

* * *

Fox strode into the classroom and stepped onto the wooden platform. "Couldn't find her." She said aloud and shrugged. "Hope she gets the help she needs." She glanced at her watch. Twenty-three minutes to the end of class. "Okay, now where were we?"

* * *

At five-thirty that afternoon, Pete Reynolds, a member of the University's facility management team walked out the same door Doctor Fox had exited three hours earlier. Reynolds was mid-forties in good shape, and partial to jeans and boots. He had longish brown hair with a thick ore mustache that drooped along the sides of his mouth. Reynolds looked like a gunslinger. He knew and enjoyed the fact he looked more student or faculty member than custodian. He ambled over to the nearly empty student parking area and stopped to study the maroon Mini Cooper parked next to his blue pick-up truck. There was no student parking permit on the window. Nor was there a one-day visitor parking permit hanging from the rearview mirror.

One of Reynold's duties was to periodically check the parking lot to ensure all cars had a student, staff or faculty parking permit. When he did this at noon, the Mini Cooper was not here, next to his truck. "Huh," Reynolds muttered to himself. He looked around to see if anyone was approaching the car. Nothing. *Fuck it,* he thought. It was Friday. If the car was here on Monday, he'd have it towed. That was the plan. He gave the car a quick, two finger salute. "TGIF."

Reynolds got into his truck and drove out of the parking lot.

* * *

On Sunday of that weekend, Reynolds woke with some congestion, a runny nose and an irritated throat. He purchased a home kit at a local pharmacy and tested positive for Covid-19. Because he was fully vaccinated, his symptoms were mild, but company protocols required he remained at home, in isolation for the next ten days. Reynolds returned to work on Wednesday, April 6th. He parked his truck in the lot and walked towards the door he always used. On his mind was the pile of work slips he knew would be on his desk. Repairs to be done, areas to clean, supplies to order and pick up. The work that fell to him, the only worker in facilities management that did not wear a suit coat to work.

The maroon Mini Cooper was still sitting in the student parking area now covered with a thin film of dust, grime and dirt. Reynolds parked three rows behind it. Out of sight and mind. He began a slow jog to the building and the work load awaiting him.

He never noticed the little car.

Chapter 14

At four o'clock, the afternoon of the day Pete Reynolds returned to work, Alice Ruth Fox made her first appearance on Pike Lane at Jefford Point. She drove the silver Lexus up the long driveway – she would not call it a road, or a lane – to her home. She drove past her parking area and left the vehicle on the road. The fact it blocked access to the homes of Joe and Cassandra McDonald and Roosevelt Wilson was of no concern to her. *This is my driveway not a public road,* she thought. She unlocked the side door to her house and stepped into a large kitchen. *Besides, there's no one here but me.*

* * *

An hour later, Fox, nestled on a sofa her feet up on an oak coffee table, and admired the large stone fireplace in her living room. She'd purchased the couch from the previous owners

CHAPTER 14

at the closing. She brought the glass of vodka on the rocks to her lips and could see it was a swallow away from requiring a third trip to the kitchen to make another.

Shit.

The blast of an odd-sounding horn startled Fox. Some drops of her drink spilt onto her pale silk blouse causing dark blotches to surface. "Dammit," Fox shouted. Her voice sounded odd in the large, sparsely furnished room. The horn blared again. Fox got up and strutted to the side door. She opened it. A Black man stood beside an open-aired military style jeep, his hand extended into the vehicle and on the horn.

"Whaddya want," Fox said. She noticed the glass in her hand, and dropped it to her side and out of view.

"I want you to move your car," Roosevelt Wilson said. "You can't park here. I have a right of way along this road to get to my property."

"This is my driveway," Fox said. "You should have bought a home with its own driveway."

Roosevelt stepped around his jeep and towards Fox.

She stepped back, one foot now in her house.

"I've talked with Joe and Cassandra," he said. "I know all about you trying to get out of snow plowing, and the BS that we're living in your back yard. Don't play that game with me. Get your fucking car off the road. You've got enough room for 3 cars. You don't need to block me. Move it!" Roosevelt got back into the jeep and waited.

Fox went into her house and reemerged seconds later waving her fob. She moved her car to McDonald's property and pulled aside to let the Jeep pass. She gave Roosevelt the finger, but kept it out of sight, as he passed. She turned the car around and drove back to her property, and parked it along the side of the road cutting its width by several feet. *Fuck him*, Fox thought. She went into her kitchen and poured herself a large vodka on the rocks.

* * *

Fox woke on the sofa. The room was dark, and she knew she had passed out and would now have to travel home in darkness. The inside of her mouth felt dusty. She glanced at her watch: twenty after seven. She got off the couch, splashed water on her face at the kitchen sink and went outside. She saw it immediately. The tires in her line of sight were flat. She walked around the Lexus and saw the other tires were flat. "That sonofabitch," she shouted into the cool night air. She turned. The lights were on in Joe McDonald's house, but only darkness beyond that. Fox trudged off to McDonald's house.

He's some kind of sheriff. He can do something.

* * *

Joe and Cassandra were at the kitchen table, the meal eaten, the dishes cleaned, a glass of chardonnay poured for Cassandra, a bottle of Harpoon opened for Joe. They'd arrived home shortly before six, and within fifteen minutes of each other. Both had squeezed by Fox's Lexus and both had noticed the flattened tires. Since Fox's house was in darkness Joe and Cassandra assumed she'd called someone for a ride to her permanent home, and left the tires as a problem for tomorrow.

"You think Roosevelt flattened the tires?" Cassandra said. She took a sip of her wine.

"She didn't drive here on four flats," Joe said. "Roosevelt's a good guy, but he can get hot. If he couldn't get to his place because of how she parked, I can see him doing something like that."

"Jesus, why not knock on her door and tell her to move the car? I know she can be a pain, but the two of them haven't even met. Have they?"

Joe shook his head. I don't think so. Maybe he did knock, and the two of them argued." He took a swallow of beer and wiped his mouth with the back of his hand. "We got by her car. What if Fox told Roosevelt there was plenty of room to get by, and slammed the door in his face."

"We're gonna be in the middle of a war between those two," Cassandra said. "I knew she'd be trouble."

"They'll be no trouble if she honors the obligations of the right of way," Joe said.

A sound distracted him. He looked to the window. "Oh shit, here she comes." Joe got up and headed for the door. He opened it before Fox could knock. "Doctor Fox, howareya? Come in."

Fox looked tired and disheveled, as if she'd just got out of bed. The smell of alcohol surrounded her like a cloud of smog. She stepped into the kitchen. "Joe, call me Alice. Her face brightened at the sight of Cassandra's wine and moved towards the table.

"Would you like a glass of wine?" Cassandra said. She stood to retrieve the bottle from the refrigerator.

"Anything stronger?' Fox said. "Vodka? It's been a difficult afternoon."

* * *

Joe and Cassandra were wine and beer folks, but Cassandra found a quart of Grey Goose at the back of a kitchen cupboard. A gift from Roosevelt Wilson, more than six years ago. The bottle carried the dust of time and neglect. Joe used a small set of pliers to twist off the cork and brought it to the table along with a glass of ice and a wedge of lime. "I'm afraid we don't have any mixers."

"Rocks are the perfect mixer," Fox said. She spoke with the slow, careful diction of a person nearing or at intoxication. But her hand was steady and accurate when she poured a heavy dose into her glass. She emptied it with a long swallow. Then picked up the bottle and refilled the glass, while it was still in her other hand. She took a small sip and put the glass down with a careful, deliberate movement. "Joe, I want you to arrest that Black sonofabitch who lives behind you. That nig... bastard slashed my tires."

"You saw him do that?" Joe said.

Fox nodded and took another swallow of vodka. "Damn right I saw him," she said. "But I was afraid to come out of my house. He threatened me earlier. I was afraid he'd use the knife on me."

"He had a knife?" Joe said. "You're sure he had a knife?"

"Yeah, I'm sure. A big one," Fox said. Her tongue now thicker. "I want that bum arrested."

"I'm not a police officer," Joe said. "Tomorrow morning,

I'll drive you to the police station and you can file a complaint. I can help you with the wording. But you can't lie or exaggerate what happened. You understand?"

"Course, I do." Fox said. It sounded like: Horse, I do. She emptied her glass and reached for the bottle.

Joe took it away from her. "Doctor Fox, do you understand what I just said about not lying?"

"I'm not lying," Fox said. "Can a lady get a drink around here?"

"So, if I walked down to your car right now, I would see slash marks on each of your tires?" Joe said.

"Can I have a drink?"

"I think we're done with drinking, Joe said. "Let's do this. I'll get a flashlight, and walk you back to your house. Then I can take a look at the tires. How's that sound?" Joe stood and walked over to his coat hanging on a large pewter hook.

"No electricity in my house," Fox muttered to no one in particular. It sounded like: no leck-triss-a-tree.

Joe's shoulders sagged. He turned and looked to Cassandra.

"You want to sleep here, Doctor Fox?" Cassandra said, still looking at Joe. "We have an extra room. Tomorrow you and Joe can go to the police. How's that sound?"

Doctor Alice Ruth Fox was asleep, her head cradled in her arms. The soft murmur of her snore floating in the air.

Chapter 15

Joe and Cassandra decided it would be easier if Fox slept in their bed. Cassandra drew down the sheet and blankets and Joe carried her from the kitchen and placed her in the center of the bed. Cassandra removed her shoes and pulled the bedding over her. They took out clothing each would need in the morning, turned off the light and closed the door.

"Jesus H. Christ," Cassandra said. "She better not make a habit of this."

Joe extended his arms. "Give me your tired, your poor, your huddled masses yearning to breathe free."

"Yeah, and there's nothing in that about an intoxicated pain in the ass. That woman could piss off St. Francis of Assisi."

Joe laughed. "I have an idea to discuss with you. Let's get our drinks and move this horror show to the living room."

* * *

CHAPTER 15

Joe started a fire and Cassandra brought in the glasses and a bowl of white cheddar popcorn. They moved to their usual chairs and for a few seconds enjoyed the sounds of the fire taking hold.

"Your idea?" Cassandra said.

Joe had a mouthful of popcorn, and held up a finger. He chewed and took a swallow of beer. "It's more a thought than an idea, but it's given me a plan on how to stop a war between our neighbors. Of course, for it to work Fox's tires will have to be flattened, but not slashed."

"She said she saw Roosevelt with a knife." Cassandra said.

"Yeah, but we both know Fox is a liar and can't be trusted. The plowing incident taught us that." Joe reached for more popcorn, but changed his mind. He leaned towards Cassandra. "You know, it's not easy to slash a tire, and it's dangerous. If you're not careful, the tire can explode. I think Roosevelt knows that."

"You said earlier you thought it probably was Roosevelt who flattened her tires," Cassandra said.

"Flattened, not slashed," Joe said. "I think he let the air out with one of those screw in tire deflators. You can get them on the Internet."

"Why would Roosevelt, or anyone else for that matter, have one of those?"

"One reason people have them is to deflate the tires for riding on beaches. That's something Roosevelt likes to do. There's another gadget, a portable air compressor tire inflator. You plug one end into the cigarette lighter attach the other to the tire valve and boom, the tire get inflated."

"It's still vandalism," Cassandra said. "Fox ain't riding any dunes. Roosevelt needs to grow up. He's acting like a juvenile delinquent."

"I agree," Joe said." But, if the tires weren't slashed, then the problem can be fixed and maybe a criminal complaint avoided."

"Get the tires re-inflated and use the leverage Fox lied about the knife to persuade her against filing a criminal complaint." Cassandra nodded her head. "Not bad. So, what's next?"

"I'm going to call Roosevelt, and suggest he re-inflate the tires."

Cassandra chuckled. "Be careful. You said, yourself, he can get hot. Use those diplomatic skills you're always bragging about."

"Watch and learn my dear," Joe said. He pulled out his phone. "Of course, everything goes to shit if he's not home or doesn't answer his phone."

"Or if he did use a knife and slashed them."

"Don't even think that," Joe said. "We're trying to stop a war."

"I'm gonna need more wine." Cassandra got up and rushed to the kitchen.

***

Roosevelt was home and answered his phone. Joe gave Cassandra the quiet signal and put Roosevelt on speaker.

"Hey, Roosevelt, it's Joe McDonald, what's up?"

"That's what I was going to ask you?" Roosevelt said. "This is your call."

He's nervous, Joe thought. *He did it, and he's been waiting for a*

CHAPTER 15

call from me or the police. "Fair enough," Joe said. "Roosevelt, I want you to listen carefully to what I am about to say, and do not say anything or interrupt me. I want you to remember that I'm a friend, but I'm also the local prosecutor, and depending upon what happens next, I may have to testify as to what you say to me. Okay?"

"Jesus, Joe," Roosevelt said. "Do I need a lawyer?"

"Not if you just listen and don't talk," Joe said. "No more interruptions, Roosevelt. Just listen to me. I'm trying to be a friend." Joe paused and heard only silence. "Okay, Doctor Fox came by my house and said you threatened her sometime this afternoon. She said later she saw you with a knife slashing the tires of her car, which was parked half on her property and half on the right of way."

"She's a fucking..."

"Quiet," Joe shouted into the phone, startling Cassandra who was hunched over, close to the phone trying to listen. Joe paused. "I have reason to suspect, Dr. Fox is not being entirely truthful, but she wants to file a criminal complaint against you. If she alleges a threat and a knife, etcetcetra, it'll be messy, and you will have to get a lawyer. Expensive and messy. On the other hand, if the tires were not slashed, and if they could be re-inflated between now and say seven tomorrow morning, I think I can persuade Doctor Fox to forego any complaint. In fact, given her present condition, I think I could convince her, the tires were never flattened. Finally, you should know Doctor Fox is asleep in my house, where she'll be the rest of the night. So, she will not see or hear anyone who might come up to re-inflate her tires." Joe paused and heard only silence. "You have a nice evening, Roosevelt." Joe terminated the call.

"You think he'll do the right thing?" Cassandra said.

Joe swallowed the rest of his beer. "We'll know tomorrow morning." He stood to return the empty bottle to the kitchen. "Cassandra, we need to remember three things. One, we never noticed any flat tires when we drove by Fox's car. Two, we only have her word on everything, and she was drunk. Three, this phone call never happened."

"What call was that?" Cassandra said.

16

Chapter 16

A cold front came in overnight and snapped the stretch of warm weather like a dead twig.

After coffee and a breakfast of bacon, eggs and toast, Joe loaned Fox one of Cassandra's heavy jackets, and the two of them walked back to her house. He acceded to her request to take the vodka bottle when she promised (twice) to bring him a bottle on her next trip to J. Point.

"I could've used another cup of coffee," Fox complained. "Christ, it's cold." Her voice scratchy like a rusty gate.

"It's past eight," Joe said. "Our days usually start earlier than this. Let's check your car."

"You check it," Fox said. "I need to get some warmth." She took the bottle from Joe, pulled out her keys and started towards her house.

Joe did a quick prayer to St. Michelin and walked over to the Lexus. The tires were fully inflated, sitting proudly on the now frozen road.

* * *

Five minutes later, Fox, now wearing a pair of jeans, boots and a wool sweater under the borrowed jacket, stared at the tires. "They were flat. I saw them up close. All of them were flat."

"Last night, you said you were in the house watching Roosevelt Wilson slash them with a knife," Joe said with a practiced stern look across his face.

"Well, yes," Fox said. "But once he left, I came out and the tires were flat."

"But these are not flat. Or slashed with a knife."

"Well, maybe it wasn't a knife," Fox stammered. "But it looked like one. I wasn't lying."

"Doctor Fox, you never saw Roosevelt do anything to your tires. You thought they were flat and then assumed he did something to them because the two of you argued earlier, when you say he threatened you."

"I still want to file a complaint."

"Not a good idea," Joe said. "Because when I'm asked what I know about this, I'll have to tell them you came to my house last night, full of vodka and lied to me about seeing Roosevelt slash your tires with a knife. Then you passed out and Cassandra and I had to put you to bed. You really want that in an official court record? Where nosy reporters and others can see it?"

"Why are you taking his side? I thought we were friends," Fox said.

"I am a friend," Joe said. "I'm trying to stop you from making a big mistake. You bring this to court, and everything comes out. Cassandra and I don't care if you had one or two too many. We've all been there. But reporters and the University might care." Joe paused to let his words take hold.

"Maybe one too many," Fox said. "But I was traumatized by that black man."

"You let it end here, and no one will be the wiser." He smiled at her. "I'll talk to Roosevelt and tell him you and I are friends. It'll be like none of this ever happened. Okay?"

Fox sniffed with mild indignance. "I guess so," she said. "You know more about these things than I do, I suppose. I'll take your advice, although I don't like it."

"One more piece of advice," Joe said. He pointed to the large dirt area near her house. "Park your car there. Right now, it's blocking the right of way. You keep doing that, you'll keep having problems, and you will end up in court. I'd be grateful if you'd move it now, so Cassandra and I can get out without worrying about hitting it."

"I still think it should be my driveway," Fox said. She pulled her keys out and walked to her car. She turned to Joe. "Are we done?"

"I'll need Cassandra's jacket back once you've moved your car."

* * *

Joe got back to his house in time to hold the door for Cassandra and give her a kiss goodbye. "Have a great day," he said.

"What I need is a great nap," Cassandra said. "That guest room bed is awful. Oh, by the way, I found something next to your car, when I went out to warm mine up. I left it on the kitchen table."

"Fox is moving her car. The tires weren't flat after all." He winked at her.

"I know," Cassandra said. "As I said, there was something near your car this morning."

Joe went into the house. He shrugged out of his coat and hung it, along with the one he took back from Fox, on one of the pewter hooks. He turned.

On the kitchen table was a case of Harpoon, its bottles gleaming in the sunlight from the kitchen window.

* * *

While Joe was admiring his beer bounty, Elaine Blass was in her Bangor office getting prepared for a cross-examination scheduled to begin in less than an hour.

"Elaine," a voice called from just beyond her office door. "There's a sister Alicia calling from the New Beginnings Orphanage in New York. She's on line one."

"Got it," Elaine called back. She pushed in the button to the line. "Hello, Sister Alicia, howareya?"

"I'm fine, Elaine. I hate to bother you this early."

"This is the best time, but I'm due in court in..." She glanced at her watch. "...forty minutes. What's up?"

"I'm worried about Samantha, have you seen or heard from her in the past week?"

Elaine flipped the pages of her desk calendar. "She was here on Saturday, March 5th. I haven't seen or spoken with her since, which is unusual for her." Elaine scribbled a note to remind herself to call Palfrey's defense attorney as she promised Samantha several weeks ago. "Tell me why you're worried."

"Samantha calls me every Tuesday and Thursday evening, promptly at seven. She's been doing it for years. We spoke on Tuesday, March 8th. She told me about meeting with you on that Saturday. I haven't heard from her since. I've called her several times, and every message goes to voice mail. I think her phone is off, or missing. This is not like her. I'm worried."

"Do you have an address for her?" Elaine said. "I can have someone go by for a wellness check. She's in Bangor, isn't she?"

"I don't have an address or any contact information other than her cell," Sister Alicia said.

"Not a problem, there'll be something in the case file. She have a car?"

"I think so, but I've never seen it."

"That'll be in the file, as well." Elaine said.

"Give me Samantha's cell." She jotted down the number as Sister Alicia repeated it. "You have anything else you can tell me?"

"I don't think so," Sister Alicia said.

"What'd you two talk about on your last call? Any hints there?" Elaine said.

"She was still pissed at that Doctor Fox. Blamed her for the hung jury."

Elaine smiled at the word *pissed*. "I know. She was mad when I saw her on that Saturday."

"She told me she was building some kind of dossier on Fox. She mentioned maybe monitoring one of her classes."

A place to start, Elaine thought. "Was this in your last

conversation? Did she give you a time frame for doing this?"

"I'm not sure when she mentioned it. It might have been the last conversation, or the one before. I'm just not sure. Sorry."

"No need to apologize, Sister. Let me do a few things at this end. I'll get back to you the beginning of the week. If you hear from her, let me know right away."

After a few pleasantries and another expression of concern from Sister Alicia, they said goodbye. Sister Alicia promised to pray for Elaine and Samantha.

Elaine took another look at her watch. Twenty minutes to court. A vertical worry line appeared between her eyebrows as she jotted a note. She pushed a button on the desk phone.

"Bill, I need you to get everything we have on Samantha Cronin. She was one of the victims in the Palfrey case. She could be missing, so get anything that would help locate her. You know, known associates, hangouts, blah, blah, blah. Email me whatever you find. When you get her address, ask the police to do a wellness check. Use one of the officers from the Palfrey case. They're both good guys. I'm off to court. Thanks."

Elaine rushed out of her office and towards the elevator. She managed to push Samantha out of her mind and shifted her focus to the court proceeding now ten minutes away.

17

Chapter 17

Joe sat at the roll top desk in his office staring at his computer screen, which was filled with a law review article on the creation, rights and responsibilities of rights of way. Dry as dust, the article confirmed what Joe knew and brought a smile to his face. He hit the print button and knew it would take at least twenty minutes for the seventy-page treatise to come out of his ten-year old printer. It would go into a file he had created on his new neighbor. A file he hoped he'd never use, but one he wanted to have ready.

Earlier, he had spoken with Karen Ferrick, the attorney who represented Gorham Bank and Trust, at the closing when Doctor Fox purchased the property on J. Point. The bank lent Fox the money to purchase the home and now held a mortgage on the land. Karen confirmed to Joe she had given Fox a copy of the documents creating the right of way, as well as the agreement on maintenance and improvements to the road. "I explained everything to her in detail, answered her questions and had to deflect all her complaints about having to share the road with the people living in her back yard," Karen said. When Joe asked if she had any doubts as to Fox's understanding of the documents, Karen became agitated. "Joe, watch out for that SOB. I made her sign a separate document stating I had explained everything to her, and that she fully understood the right of way and her obligations under the agreement. I suspected one day she'd claim I hid all this from her. That was my CYA." Karen agreed to send Joe a copy of the "cover your ass" document. It was destined for the file, along with a detailed summary of Joe's telephone conversation with Fox at the time of the plowing dispute and copies of her subsequent reimbursement checks to him for paying her share of the costs. A voice snapped Joe back to his office.

"Joe, Elaine Blass or Glass is on line one."

"Thanks, Jackie." Joe pushed in the button. "Hey Elaine, howareya? Kicking ass?"

"I did today, Joe. Had some piece of shit in tears before I was through cross this morning. Don't mean to brag," Elaine laughed

"Yeah, you do," Joe said. "You know the only trial thrills I get are vicariously through you. Thank you for the call."

"Actually, I need your help on something," Elaine said.

"Name it."

"One of the women, a Samantha Cronin, who testified in that Palfrey case back in January seems to be missing. No one has seen or heard from her since a phone call to her friend, a nun, one Sister Alicia in New York, on March eighth."

"Shit, that's almost a month," Joe said. "We're getting a late start on this."

"I know, and I appreciate your use of we," Elaine said. "The Bangor Police did a wellness check on the L-K-A we had on her,

CHAPTER 17

a boarding house. The house manager says she left without paying rent. He bagged up her clothes and has them in a basket in the basement, but she hasn't come by for them."

"What can I do, to help?" Joe said.

"This Sister Alicia told me Samantha said she was going to monitor one of Doctor Fox's classes at the University of Southern Maine. She's the psychologist..."

"Yeah, I know who Doctor Fox is," Joe said.

"The Bangor Police put out a BOLO on Samantha's car. I asked them to send it to the Campus Police at USM. I don't know if she ever went to one of her classes, but I'd like someone to speak with Fox. I don't want to send uniforms. Fox is a shrewd sonofabitch, and I think it could turn into a confrontation. We're just trying to set a timeline of where Samantha's been and when. Maybe say her family's worried, creditors are angry, etcetcetra."

"Speaking of which, any tracers on her credit cards?" Joe said.

"We only know of a VISA. No activity on it since March 25th," Elaine said. "Samantha used it for everything, gas, a cup of coffee, a newspaper. It's not a good sign."

"I've got a friend with the Campus Police at USM. I can make sure their parking lots are checked," Joe said. "You want me to talk with Doctor Fox?"

"That'd be great," Elaine said. "I don't know if she's at the University today. I'll text you a home address. She lives near Portland. I have a university number I'll text, but no cell number."

"I have her cell number from a call I made in January," Joe said. "She's my seasonal neighbor on J Point. I have her on speed dial."

"I didn't know you were friends," Elaine said. "Look, Joe I can get someone else to do this. I don't want to put you in an awkward situation."

"Elaine, trust me on this," Joe said. "Doctor Fox and I are not friends. And we never will be. As soon as we're finish with this call, I'm going to USM."

Chapter 18

Joe pulled into the student parking area at USM and spotted the 2013 Mini Cooper almost immediately. He stopped his car in front of it and got out. He tried the doors of the Mini Cooper.

Locked.

There was a notebook on the passenger's seat and two large black trash bags stuffed behind the front seats. Joe got back into his car and pulled out his phone. He pushed the button for Sam Baldwin, a friend and a sergeant with the Campus Police. In one of those rare miracles of modern life, Sam answered after the first ring.

"Joe howareya? What's up? This isn't an election year, is it? Where you want the check sent?"

"I'm about to make you a hero, Sam," Joe said. "Sometime today, you guys got a BOLO from the Bangor Police on a 2013 maroon Mini Cooper. My guess is it's collecting dust in a basket on somebody's desk."

"I'm afraid it's in my basket," Baldwin said. "I was going to head over to the parking areas, but I got caught up in something else."

Joe laughed. "Well, shut off the solitaire game and get over to student parking lot G. The vehicle is there in the third row about ten spaces from the main aisle."

"Jesus, Joe, how'd you know that?"

"Because I'm standing next to it. Get over here before some other hero finds it and gets your citation of achievement."

"I'm on my way," Baldwin said. "Thanks, Joe."

"I'll leave once I see you coming into the lot. I'll keep people away until you arrive.

Sam, when you get here, secure the car. Use yellow tape or whatever you guys have. Treat it like a crime scene. Stay with the car until Bangor PD shows up or tells you what they want done with it."

"Roger that," Baldwin said. "I'm already in the car, just a few minutes away. Christ, what a rush. I've got a boner like a hockey stick."

"Another thing," Joe said, suppressing a laugh. "Make notes on the locations of all security cameras, and once you get the okay from Bangor to leave the scene, tell them you'll start the process for getting footage from the security cameras. It shows initiative. Last thing, be polite with Bangor when they show up, but remember this is your Campus. Don't get pushed around. Or ignored."

"Roger that. Coming into the lot, Joe," Sam said.

"I see you. Take your third right and you'll be on top of me. I'm going to move away, but I'll check back with you later."

Joe looked around. A silver Lexus was parked at the other end of the lot, close to a side entrance to the building. He drove his car over and parked next to it.

CHAPTER 18

* * *

It was a few minutes before two when Joe reached the open doorway to Doctor Fox's office. She was behind a small desk, cluttered with papers, books, a laptop, a container filled with pens and pencils and a telephone. Fox's head was bent over, her nose almost touching a piece of paper while her right-hand scratched notes onto an index card. He lightly knocked on the door frame. "Doctor Fox, could I have a minute or two of your time?"

Fox looked up abruptly. Annoyance briefly flared then vanished when her eyes met Joe's. She waved her arm. "Joe, Joe, please come in. Grab that chair and sit down. This is an unexpected surprise. What can I do for you?"

Joe moved a wooden chair from under a window to the front of Fox's desk and sat down. "Thank you, Doctor. I won't be long. I learned an hour or so ago that Samantha Cronin appears to be missing. Her family is worried. Samantha was one of the women in the Palfrey case..."

"I know who Samantha is," Fox interrupted. She reached for her desk calendar and flipped a few pages. "In fact, Samantha showed up at my Psychology 101 class on March twenty-fifth. It ran from two to three. She interrupted a discussion I was having with my students, so I had to ask her to leave. Which she did."

Joe pulled out a reporter's notebook from his suit jacket. "She interrupted your class? Was she hostile? How'd she appear to you?"

"Well, you probably know she called me a fucking bitch in open court during the Palfrey trial," Fox said. "She was uncomplimentary to me in class. She told the other students to ask me about Palfrey. Fair to say she was agitated, but not out of control. She left when I asked her."

"What happened next? After Samantha left your class?"

Fox smiled. "I actually went after her to make sure she left the building, but I couldn't catch up with her. I was relieved. No telling what might have happened if I confronted her in an empty corridor."

"But you said she was not out of control," Joe said. "Did you really think she might hurt you?"

"Not sure what I thought," Fox said. "But I remember being a bit relieved when I didn't see her. I assumed she'd left the building." Fox paused. "That's the last time I saw her. You say she's missing? How awful for her family. They live around here?"

"Samantha lived in Bangor," Joe said, avoiding the question. "Why do you suppose she was at your class? Instead of coming to your office, for example."

"I don't know," Fox said. "If I had to guess, I'd say she came here to give me a hard time and to embarrass me in front of my students. She blames me for the hung jury on those charges against Palfrey that pertained to her. Of course, it was her own actions that caused it." Fox thought a moment. Then added. "The hung jury, I mean. Not the sexual assault." She shrugged and smiled. "But then again, who knows what really happened between her and Mr. Palfrey?"

Joe didn't take the bait. "When you went to follow her, did you go outside?"

"No, I wanted to be sure she wasn't in the building. When I didn't see her, I went back to my class. I wasn't looking for a confrontation."

"Why follow her out of the class?" Joe said. "I mean, if you don't want a confrontation, why not stay in class?"

"I guess I felt it my responsibility to make certain she didn't stay in the building."

"So why not look outside? Wouldn't that have been the best way to see if she'd left the building?"

"Perhaps in retrospect," Fox said. "But that's not what I did. I checked the inside to make she wasn't there. Then I went back to my class."

Joe stood and offered his hand to Fox who grabbed it, but remained seated. "Thanks, Doctor Fox. You've been helpful and generous with your time." He moved towards the door and turned back. "Would you mind doing one more thing for me?" Cassandra would call this his "Columbo move."

Fox grimaced, but it quickly dissolved into a smile. "If I can," she said.

"Could you take me to the classroom, where you last saw Samantha Cronin?"

"What on earth for?" Fox said. "Besides, I'm sure it's in use now." She turned back to her papers.

"I don't need to go inside," Joe said. "I just want to see where it is, and where you went trying to find her."

"Go to the end of the corridor take the elevator on your left..."

"Doctor Fox, I want you to go with me and show me the route you took when you tried to find Samantha."

"I don't see the need for that. Good God, she's not hiding here. I've got things to do."

Joe walked to the front of her desk and leaned towards her, his hands on top of papers and a book. "Doctor Fox, I can send some uniformed officers and have them walk around the University with you? I can do that, with a phone call."

"Are you threatening me?" Fox stood and gave out her coldest stare."

Joe straightened. "No, I'm trying to get your cooperation in what is an official investigation. This girl's been missing nearly two weeks. You're the last person we know of who saw her. I want to see where that sighting took place. It's how I work, and I need you to accommodate me."

Fox gathered her purse and the blazer draped over the back of her chair. "I didn't know it was this important to you. C'mon, follow me."

* * *

They exited to what the elevator designated lower level. Joe stepped out and looked to his left. Ten feet away, four wide, cement steps with an iron hand-rail in the middle led down to an area with trash barrels and a large yellow door. To his right was a corridor. Straight ahead, two large concession machines, one for soft drinks, water and juice, the other for snacks, stood like sentries on either side of an oak door to a class room. Through a sliver of glass running nearly the length of the door the blank faces of students fighting off sleep appeared.

"That's the classroom I was using when I saw Samantha," Fox said. "There's a second door to access the room, a bit further down that corridor.".

"Is this the door you came out of when you followed Samantha?' Joe said.

"Yes," Fox said. "I went down that corridor about twenty or

CHAPTER 18

thirty feet, didn't see her, and came back to class."

"Let's walk to where you turned around," Joe said. "Mind?"

"Of course, not," Fox said. "I have all night to correct those papers upstairs." She headed down the corridor.

Joe followed. His eyes captured the one door on his right, which appeared to be a janitor's closet. They went twenty feet past the second door to the classroom on the left and Fox stopped.

"I think this is where I turned around," Fox said. "At this point you can see a good distance down the corridor. I didn't see her, so I decided to turn back. You want to follow me back to where I re-entered the classroom?"

"I do, and then I'll be out of your hair."

Joe followed her past the other door to the classroom and back to the elevator. Fox stopped and turned to him. "I went back into the classroom through that door. My memory is there was twenty odd minutes to the bell. So that would make it about twenty before three."

"She probably went through that door," Joe said. He pointed to the yellow door at the bottom of the stairs. "It's not alarmed, is it?"

"I doubt it, certainly not at this hour," Fox said. "I think it's used more for hauling out the trash barrels. Are we done?"

"Any reason why you came all the way back here to re-enter the classroom?" Joe said. "You could've used the other door. The one we passed walking back here."

"That door would have put me at the back of the room, behind the students." She pointed to the door in front of them. "That door brings me to the lecture platform in front. Now, are we done?"

Joe stared at the door and nodded. "That makes sense,

111

Doctor, I can see how the room's positioned." Joe pushed the elevator button and waited with her. "I need to ask a lot of questions, Doctor. If I don't whoever reads my report might think of one, and ask me, or someone else, to come back here and ask it. Better to get it all done in one visit."

"Are you coming upstairs with me?" Fox said.

"No, just being polite."

A few seconds passed. The loud mechanical sound of the old elevator coming to a stop broke the silence and the doors slid open. Fox stepped in and turned towards Joe. "Have a nice day, Joe. I hope this helps to find that poor girl, although I can't see how it possibly could." She smiled and wiggled her fingers goodbye just as the doors closed.

Joe turned and walked down the stairs to the yellow door. He opened it and stepped outside. He was about thirty feet from his car and the one he suspected belonged to Dr. Fox. He went over to the Lexus and jotted down the plate number. He examined the faculty parking decal and added its number to his notebook. Before getting into his car, Joe looked back to the building for security cameras.

One looked back at him; its red light shined like a beacon of hope.

* * *

Back in her office, Fox replayed her conversation with Joe and gave herself an A. She tilted back in the chair, stared at the ceiling, and tapped her bottom teeth with the eraser end of a pencil. *No surprise someone would come by asking about*

CHAPTER 18

Samantha. Why Joe? Has an investigation really opened up? How many young ladies go missing every year? Must be hundreds if not thousands. No body, no case.

The chair snapped back to attention. Fox looked at the pile of exam booklets on her desk. She picked one and read a few lines of the scratchy handwriting. She couldn't concentrate.

Am I suspect?

Am I being followed?

Chapter 19

"Security camera was of no use?" Cassandra said to Joe.

"The cameras are on a forty-eight-hour cycle. Sam Baldwin, my friend with the campus police, is getting me a copy of whatever's there, but I don't expect anything." They were at their kitchen table in the same seats as when Fox passed out the evening before.

"Nothing about this feels right," Joe said. "Fox said the doors were used mostly to take the trash out, but when I went through them, her car was parked just thirty feet away. My guess is she parks there every day and uses the doors to get in and out of the building. She never told me that."

"You're sure it's her car?"

"Checked the parking permit number with Sam. He says it's hers."

"Still pretty weak, Joe," Cassandra said.

Joe waved his hand as if to brush aside her comment. "I know, I know. It's my gut that's talking to me, not the evidence."

CHAPTER 19

"Wasn't there a study that said most people go to the right when they walk out a door? Fox should have gone right and out those doors."

Joe shrugged. "Yeah, but there are other studies that say lefties go to the left and if you drive on the left side of the road, you'd go left."

"Well Fox drives in America, and I'm pretty sure she's right-handed," Cassandra said. "She'd have headed to the doors after she came out of the classroom, not left and down a dark corridor."

"Now who's talking about weak," Joe said.

"Well, I've come to know and trust your gut," Cassandra said.

* * *

Dinner was from a general store that sold everything from tools to toys, newspapers, canned vegetables, and the best pizza in southern Maine. Joe grabbed a slice and placed it on a paper plate in front of Cassandra. He grabbed a slice for himself, sprinkled some Parmesan cheese, and took a bite from the pointed end. He chewed thoughtfully.

"Another reason my gut feels off is that Samantha's car was still in the student parking area." He took a long swallow from his bottle of water. "Sam said it's been there since the day she showed up in Fox's class."

"He knows this how?" Cassandra cut a piece of pizza from the crusted end of her slice and brought it to her mouth on a fork.

"Sam talked with a maintenance guy, a Peter Reynolds." He took another bite, chewed and swallowed. "Reynolds says the car was there on Friday, March 25th. He remembers, because that was his last working day before he tested positive for Covid. He didn't get back to work until yesterday."

"Long time for a car without a parking sticker to still be on campus," Cassandra said.

"Yeah, somebody should talk with the campus police, but that's a separate issue," Joe said. "It shows that whatever happened to Samantha happened after she left Fox's class. She never got to her car. She'd have taken it if she was going back to Bangor, or anywhere else."

"No chance she was using the campus lot as her own parking area?' Cassandra said. She cut another piece off her slice, working her way to the pointed end.

"Reynolds told Sam the car was exactly where he last saw it on the 25th." He shook his head. "Something happened in the parking lot after Samantha crashed Fox's class."

"Not necessarily," Cassandra said. "She could have left the car in the lot and took a walk around Portland. Plenty of pubs, nice shops, places for a young woman like Samantha to go. Maybe she met someone, went off with him and boom, she's missing. Anyone looking at security cameras in Portland?"

"I put a request in to the Portland Police. Elaine was going to send them a recent picture. Problem is it's been so long. I'm not sure we'll get any footage from back then." Joe shrugged. "I suppose she could've left the car and walked around Portland, but Elaine told me her charge card hasn't been used," he said. "And she used it for everything."

"Maybe John Doe was paying for her drinks or dinner, or whatever."

CHAPTER 19

"Okay, then what?" Joe said. "Think it through. Why didn't she go back to get her car? Why hasn't she called her friend, Sister Alicia? Where is she? Did John Doe kill her? Where's the body? What happened to her?"

Cassandra cut another piece of pizza. "Under my scenario, she must be dead, or she'd have gone back for her car. I mean. Even if she met Mr. Right, there's no reason to leave the car in the lot."

"Unless, Mr. Right didn't know she had a car," Joe said, his mouth full of pizza. "And he's killed her before she mentioned it."

"I suppose," Cassandra said, dragging the word as she searched for a thought, "it doesn't feel right."

"Nothing about this feels right," Joe said.

"What'd the police say? You talk with them?"

"No. I'll call Elaine in the morning. Sam told me they sent a tow truck to get her car, so he hasn't any information, other than what he gathered from his own initiative."

"Bangor's not as concerned as you," Cassandra said.

"Not yet," Joe said. "That'll change after I talk with Elaine. I'll ask her for a copy of the inventory from the car. I saw a notebook and some of those large black trash bags like the ones we use. Everything that poor girl owned was in that car."

* * *

Later, in bed they returned to the subject.

"If something bad happened to Samantha, how'd the perp get rid of the body? I mean, you've always told me it's not that easy," Cassandra said. "He must've had her in his car, so he could drive away."

"It's not easy to dump a body," Joe said. "Particularly if you're not a pro, or someone who's done this before. The first timer panics, takes off, dumps the body in a parking lot or a park. Someplace that might be isolated after dark, but busy in the morning, and the body's discovered."

"Doesn't that ague against anything happening in USM's parking lot. The body would've been found quickly," Cassandra said.

"Yeah, that's true," Joe said. "I think. Christ, nothing about this feels right." He reached for the lamp on his bed table and the room went dark.

* * *

A minute later, Joe snapped on the light.

Cassandra sat up. "What's up?"

"I've got close to ten thousand dollars in an account for miscellaneous expenses for investigations. Some might call it a slush fund." He shifted his body to face Cassandra. "I'm thinking I might call Connor McNeill. He has a friend who's a former cop and another who's a P.I. He used to play for the PATS. I could ask them to look into this. I don't think it's gonna get a lot of attention from either Bangor or Portland, and I don't have the staff to give it the attention I think it deserves."

"Makes sense to me," Cassandra said. "You guys were good friends, and we haven't seen him for a long time."

CHAPTER 19

"I'll call him in the morning, thanks." Joe turned off the light.

* * *

Less than a minute later, Cassandra turned on the lamp on her bed table. "Hey, you've got a ten-thousand-dollar slush fund, and we had pizza for dinner?"

"But it's great pizza. And I let you have the last piece."

"Both good points," Cassandra said and turned off the light.

20

Chapter 20

Joe called Elaine Blass from the car, on the way to his office. He left a message on her cell. His next call wasn't actually a call but a mobile order for his coffee *via* the Starbucks app. Elaine called back as he was walking from his car to pick up his coffee. Turned out she was pulling into her parking spot, and wanted time to get her coffee, get to her desk, and get settled. The two agreed Joe would call her at ten after nine.

They reconnected and after a few pleasantries got down to business.

"I had to get a warrant to break into the car," Elaine said. "It was easy enough, and I had it in hand by the time the tow truck got to it the police garage." Her voice softened. "As I prepared the affidavit for the warrant, I became convinced she's dead."

"I know," Joe said. "We need to move on this."

Elaine wasn't ready. "God, I feel awful. I promised her over a month ago I'd work on getting Palfrey retried on her charges, maybe even bluff him into pleading guilty. Then I promptly forgot my promise and moved to more pressing matters. Christ, more pressing. Now she's dead."

"Not your fault, Elaine," Joe said. "We need to focus on finding out what happened. Anything with the car? I saw a notebook."

"She was doing research on Fox. There was a list of the articles Fox wrote in opposition to transgender bills, along with a scattering of juicy quotes. You know the bathroom bills, shit like that. Also, some articles where she argued against gay rights. She's not a fan of gay marriage, either."

"Her opinions on those issues are hardly a secret. Whaddya think was the point of the notebook?"

"No secret there," Elaine said. She wrote that she was making the case that Fox shouldn't have tenure or be teaching at a public university or college. Parts of the notebook are like a diary where you fill pages as if dictating from a stream of consciousness. No question, she wanted to destroy Fox."

"Anything that shows planning or working with others?" Joe said. "Something beyond venting her anger?"

"She wrote that she planned to recruit current or former students. And she knew where Fox lived," Elaine said. "She followed her home. I found that a bit disconcerting."

"Anything else?"

"There is no indication she ever telephoned or confronted Fox, other than going to her class on March 25th. That was her last entry. On the day before she went to the class."

"Can you send me a copy?"

"I've got someone making a pdf. He'll email it to you today. He'll include the inventory list. That covers the contents of the trash bags."

"Anything helpful there?"

"Oh God, those were sad. They were full of old clothes, some shoes. No jewelry, or anything nice. Did you know she almost made the US Olympic Gymnastics Team? Missed by less than one tenth of one percent or something like that. However, they do it. Never was a gymnastic fan. Sister Alicia told me this. I was on the line with her when you called this morning."

"That couldn't have been a fun call," Joe said. "Anything else? Mail? Shopping receipts? Something to tell us where she was before…" Joe let the words hang

"Nothing on the inventory list, but I'm having an investigator from my office inspect the car today. "Look under the seats, behind the visor, in the spare wheel well. The places a cop in a hurry doesn't check. We've subpoenaed phone records and hope to have them by the end of today. I'll keep you in the loop."

They talked a few minutes more and agreed to touch base Monday morning, unless something broke earlier.

* * *

After her one class on Fridays at eleven o-clock, Cassandra had a leisurely lunch at a Souper Salad in Portland, and decided to surprise Joe by doing the food shopping, a task they usually suffered through together and reserved for Saturday morning. It was just after two, when she drove up Pike's Lane and found Fox's silver Lexus blocking access to her house.

"You fucking pain in the ass," Cassandra screamed in her car.

She got out, walked up to the front door and knocked. There was no answer or sound of any movement in the house. She knocked harder. "Doctor Fox! It's Cassandra, you need to move your goddamn car."

No answer or movement.

Cassandra went back to her car and retrieved the bags with perishable items. She trudged to her house unlocked the door and place them in the refrigerator. She walked back to Fox's door and knocked.

This time it opened quickly and Fox appeared, as if she'd been waiting. "Cassandra, how nice of you to drop by. Would like tea? Perhaps a glass of wine?"

"You're blocking the road. I had a car full of groceries, and couldn't get to my house. I knocked and shouted for you. Didn't you hear me?"

"I'm afraid I was in the toilet and didn't hear you. She gave out a smile that begged for understanding.

"Why do you do this?" Cassandra said. "You have plenty of places to park. You enjoy irritating people?"

"I did some shopping myself," Fox said. "I parked where it would be convenient to bring things into my house," she said in a tone as if this excused everything. "There was no one around, so I didn't think it would be a big deal. It took me some time to unload and put everything away. I guess I forget it was there. It's my driveway. You get to drive over it, but it's my driveway."

"It's not your fucking driveway," Cassandra hissed. "It's how the rest of us get to and from our properties. Why is it so hard for you to understand that? What you find convenient is a king size pain in the ass for the rest of us."

"You don't have to be rude about it," Fox said.

"I'm not rude, I'm angry," Cassandra said. "You don't want to be near me when I'm rude." She took a deep breath and leaned closer to Fox. "This isn't the first time, you've done this. Stop being so selfish. Use your parking area instead of the road. Now, move the car so I can go about my day."

"I made an honest mistake," Fox said. "I don't like your tone. Am I gonna get my tires slashed again?"

"Don't play victim with me. Your tires were never slashed. You've been nothing but a pain in the ass since the day you arrived. If you'd act like an adult and a neighbor, you'd find all of us are friendly neighbors. Keep this shit up, and you'll have more than flat tires to worry about."

"Is that a threat?" Fox said.

"I'm asking you to act like a goddamn adult."

Fox took a vodka bottle off the counter. "I bought this for Joe to replace the one he opened for me." She handed it to Cassandra.

Cassandra took the bottle. She took another deep breath, an effort to calm herself. "Look, I'm sorry if I overreacted. It's just we've been up here for a lot of years, and there's never been any problems with the road or the right of way. Everybody's been nice and we all get along. Since you've come, we've had issues with the plowing, flattened tires, and now I can't get to my house because you've blocked the road and couldn't hear me knocking."

"I was in the toilet."

"Yeah, I know. You told me," Cassandra said. "My life shouldn't have to pause because you needed to take a crap."

"That's not fair," Fox said.

"Use your parking area, you won't have to remember to move it and *you* can go to the toilet any time *you* want, and *I* can get to my house, when *I* want." Cassandra waited a second or two for a response that didn't come. "Then we can all be

CHAPTER 20

friends and get along. Okay?"

Fox took the vodka bottle back. "I want to give this to Joe myself, the next time I see him." She closed the door.

Cassandra stood on the step waiting. After a minute passed, she banged on the door and shouted, "Hey! You still need to move your car." Another thirty or forty seconds passed. Cassandra banged on a pane of glass while kicking the bottom panel of the door, all to make the noise louder. "Doctor Fox, if you don't move your car in one minute, I'm having it towed."

She backed down the steps and walked back to her cabin.

***

Twenty minutes later, Andy Junior fastened the chains to the Lexis, pulled a switch and the car began to roll backwards up the ramp of his flat-bed tow truck.

Cassandra watched from her car and began to worry. "One second Andy, I need to make sure the old bitch didn't drop dead, although that would solve a lot of problems." She went up to Fox's front door. It opened before she could knock.

"What is that tow truck doing here?" Fox screamed. She pointed to Andy Junior. "Young man, get off my property, or I'll call the police."

"You didn't move your car," Cassandra said. "I told you I'd have it towed if you didn't move it. I shouted it through your door."

"I was in the basement. I didn't hear you. You can't have my vehicle towed. It's on my property. I'll sue you."

"It's blocking the right of way. Don't you remember us

talking about this?"

"You have no right to have my car towed," Fox said. "I'm calling the police.

Cassandra looked at Andy. "Andy, tow it over to her parking area. Send Joe and I the bill." She turned back to Fox. "I'm suing you for the towing bill."

Fox screamed: "Wait, this is my car and my property, you can't tow it. I'll sue both of you," Fox tried to step down her steps, but Cassandra blocked her.

She leaned into Fox putting her head within inches of her. "Listen to me, you fuckin' bitch. You do this again, or force me to have your car towed, I'll fucking burn your house down, with you in it. Do you hear me? Do you understand?"

Fox backed into her house and slammed the door.

Cassandra looked to Andy Junior. "One second." Cassandra pulled out her phone and took several pictures of Fox's car from different angles. "Tow it over to her parking area. With a little luck, you can be outta here before the police arrive."

* * *

The police never came. Fox left J. Point about four o'clock and by six o'clock, over a glass of red wine, Cassandra told the tale of the afternoon's events and vented her anger to Joe, who nursed his bottle of Harpoon.

"You threatened to burn down her home with her inside?" Joe said around a laugh. "Where is my soft-spoken, erudite wife, and what have you done with her?"

"Not my finest moment, but I've never been so pissed in my

life," Cassandra said. "I think she loves pushing my buttons. I'm sure she heard me banging on her door. I can picture her hiding behind the door laughing at me, reveling in my anger and frustration." She drained her glass. "That bitch is sick. I knew it from the day she walked into my office."

"I'll go to her office on Monday," Joe said. "If she comes up this weekend, I'll corner her in her house. This shit has to end. Life's too short to put up with assholes."

"Bring Roosevelt with you. He'll break her in two. That'll end it."

"I don't want to use gasoline to put out this fire," Joe said. He got up and walked to the counter and brought the wine bottle and another Harp to the table. "Let me tell you about my conversation with Elaine. Oh, and I called Connor McNeill."

Chapter 21

It was close to four-thirty when I received Joe McDonald's text asking me to call him at five o'clock. I was relaxing in a large, plush, seat in what used to be the second row of the balcony at the Signet Movie Theater in Everett, about five miles north of Boston.

The Signet was an old-styled theater revamped to suit new-fashioned movie goers. Originally, a 950-seat auditorium-style theater, its capacity was reduced to 600 large comfortable swivel seats positioned around sleek tables and bright orange containers filled with small bottles of wine, beer, vodka, bourbon and other beverages. A compadre of young, pleasant and attractive waitresses were there to fetch and provide more elaborate drinks to patrons not satisfied with the choices they found in the refrigerator assigned to their seats.

The chairs were equipped with earphones and a sophisticated sound system to accommodate the hearing requirements of all patrons. There were also small discreet fasteners to each chair to accept sturdy trays (with linen table cloths) of hot and

CHAPTER 21

cold food, the patron had selected.

The napkins were cloth and the cutlery heavy and silver.

In the past two weeks, I went to the Signet eight days, at different times and counted the attendees on each occasion. I texted the numbers, dates and times to a colleague, who went to the Signet on the days I didn't. Neither of us were movie buffs. We preferred the commercial-free films on TV and at home, where we could watch in a comfortable chair and pause everything to take a leak or to get a beer. The Signet didn't have the pause feature, but it had everything else. It was nice enough to tempt me to become a member. The annual fee of one thousand dollars allowed the privilege to attend movies for $40.00 per showing and have all the alcohol and food you wanted. Also, you could bring a guest for an additional $50.00. The temptation was easy to resist for two reasons: I couldn't afford it and, the Signet would soon be closed.

Management didn't know it, but I did.

The Signet would close because the revenue it reported to the IRS and paid taxes on was too large. A six hundred seat theater with three showings a day, would have to be running at better than a two hundred percent occupancy, or have a membership that could fill Gillette Stadium and Fenway Park to generate the revenues it reported. It's a common mistake greedy or inexperienced money launderers make. A theater is a nice place to launder money, but you need to keep it real and not report an obscene amount of gross revenue from an operation averaging less than fifty patrons at its daytime viewings, and just over 200 in the evening. I felt bad. This was a terrific theater. Once the indictments came, it would close and never come back. Probably end up as condominiums, or a parking lot.

Today was Friday. I knew my office on State Street would close promptly at five. My boss, Malcolm Butts, a former forensic accountant with the FBI, was taking ventriloquism lessons on Monday, Wednesdays and Fridays. He told me he wanted to add to his repertoire of tools for meeting women and scaring young children. Malcolm was now a federal contractor with a client list longer than the Nile, seeking his expertise to detect criminal activity. I've suspected a few of his clients are off-book, and purchase his expertise to avoid detection. Malcolm Butts has a carefree disposition and demeanor that hide a razor-sharp mind that could detect the criminal activity behind a sidewalk lemonade stand.

Malcolm hired me two years ago, at the urging of Anthony Novello, Head of the Homicide Bureau for the Massachusetts Attorney General. I was tangentially involved in two high-profile criminal cases Novello and Butts had been investigating. Butts discovered the law practice of an attorney on the Cape, where I was a paralegal, was a laundering scheme for a New Bedford gangster. Novello suggested Malcolm hire me to make amends for shutting down my source of employment.

Last year, Butts got me involved in an investigation centered around three mob bosses fighting for control over the Encore Casino, just a mile or so from where I now sat. If movie theaters are desirable for money laundering, then casinos are the Holy Grail.

If you ignore the murders of a crooked US Attorney from Maine and a moron on his payroll plus the disappearances (and presumed murders) of the Massachusetts US Attorney and a Rhode Island mobster, the Encore investigation was a success. After all, no law-abiding citizens were killed, the Encore ended up no worse than where it was when the mobster bash began.

CHAPTER 21

And I ended up with some new friends and business contacts. One of them was Calvin Washington, a former offensive guard for the New England Patriots now an attorney and a licensed private investigator. I also met Patrick Murphy Muldoon who has a live-and-let-live relationship with Paul Cunningham, a Southie mobster who became the last man standing, and now has more authority and respect in the New England crime family than the Pope has in Vatican City. I haven't seen "Murph" or Cunningham since last year, but I sent both of them a Christmas card.

You never know when you might need a Godfather.

I drained the last of my Jameson on the rocks, gathered up my coat, baseball cap and gloves and headed out with ten minutes left in a George Clooney directed movie that had been filmed in Massachusetts last year. This was my third viewing of the film, so no surprises were left.

My wife, Abby, and I spent four hours watching Clooney and Ben Affleck film a four or five-minute scene inside a bowling alley in Wakefield. Abby actually appears in the background for a millisecond as Affleck rolls a ball down the alley. Abby fell in love with both of them, but decided she'd leave me only for George because he came over to say hello to Calvin and gave her a smile and a nod. Affleck did not.

More than ten years ago, Calvin and Clooney connected through a sports agency, and Calvin became a source of Superbowl tickets for half of Hollywood during the Tom Brady era. As a result, whenever the film industry came to Boston, Calvin got a contract. Sometimes it was arranging security or schmoozing with local officials to secure filming locations. Calvin's a six-foot-three, 270-pound black man who can flash an affable smile or a death piercing scowl. A good man to have around a crowd. He was our ticket into the alley to watch the filming. As I said, the investigation I worked on last year ended well for me.

I walked through the lobby and to the door. A tall kid in his late teens in a maroon jacket with a white shirt and maroon bowtie opened the door for me. "Have a nice evening," he said.

I stopped, one foot inside the theater the other on the sidewalk. "You work here long?"

"First day," he said. "I'm a student at Emerson in Boston. "Helps with the books and fees." He smiled.

"Whaddya studying at Emerson?"

"Film production, screen writing and theater management."

"They pay you well here? You get any benefits?"

His eyes rolled. "Minimum wage, and a reduced price on the popcorn, but not the candy, cola or ice cream."

"You're shitting me," I said.

He smiled and shook his head.

A fat, bald guy, also in a maroon jacket, and a white shirt with a soup stain and one popped button near his waist walked over to about ten feet of us. "Ben! You're letting the heat out. For Chrissakes, close the door. Get in here and find something to do."

"Find another job," I whispered to Ben. "No future here." I looked over to loud mouth. "He was helping me with directions to the Encore," I said. "Don't be such an asshole."

I walked out, no longer bothered by the prospect of closing the Signet.

* * *

CHAPTER 21

I called Joe from the car as I travelled home to Melrose. By the time I reached the driveway to our ranch home on a quiet, tree-lined street, I knew all Joe knew about the disappearance of Samantha Cronin and his strange neighbor, Doctor Alice Fox. I told him I'd get back to him as soon as Calvin Washington and I connected and came up with a plan.

I joined Abby in our office/den and told her what Joe and I had discussed. Joe's been a friend long enough to know I tell Abby everything. Everybody has somebody they tell everything. For me, that's Abby, and fortunately I'm that person for her. It makes life easier. Also, it takes a memory and organizational skills I don't have to tell lies or keep secrets from a person you live with and love. I also do it because she's smarter and usually has better ideas than me.

I called Calvin, told him I had a paying client, and we needed to meet as soon as possible. Calvin said he heard although small, Melrose was a food-eating Mecca with three Mexican restaurants, one seafood, two Spanish, two Italian, some pizza joints and an English-style Pub. He said he'd meet me for the best breakfast in town.

I gave him the address to my house and told him to be there tomorrow morning at ten.

Chapter 22

I stood in the sunlight spilling though the kitchen windows and chopped celery on a small cutting board. Calvin knocked on the door at the top of our driveway just seconds after I cut the third stalk for the tall bloody marys on our kitchen island. Abby opened the door and gave him a hug.

"Calvin howareya?" she said. "Quick, get in here before someone sees you and calls the police."

Calvin laughed and returned the hug. He stepped inside. "Wouldn't want that. They might discover an ex-felon lives here."

"Careful, or I might accidentally spill your bloody mary," I said. I walked over and joined the hug parade.

The 7-foot Walnut, farmer's table in the eating area was set, so we had our drinks there. Calvin was immaculate in pressed slacks, crisp blue, button-down collar, dress shirt and a blue blazer. Abby looked, as she always did, amazing, in tan slacks and a green sweater. Her auburn hair was freshly cut, one side tucked behind her left ear, the other hung loosely to the top of her shoulder. I was the discordant note in my clean jeans, white golf shirt and a gray Boston College sweatshirt. But I did the cooking and made the drinks.

Breakfast started leisurely with a lot of catching up, laughter, and promises to see more of each other. I served Calvin and myself three-egg omelets with sausage and Cheddar, some corn beef hash and grated and grilled potatoes. We both eat like we suffer from CDD, Cholesterol Deficiency Disorder. I made Abby a bowl of fresh berries with a dollop of yogurt. I'm worried she might have a nutrition obsession disorder. On the other hand, she can eat three times a day, every day, while I won't be able to digest anything until Wednesday.

As we ate, I told Calvin about the call from Joe and consulted a short pile of scrap paper to tell him everything I learned. Calvin took just a few notes and used a small device he pulled from the inside pocket of his blazer. I knew he ran a paperless office, so I wasn't surprised.

"Whaddya think?" I said when I finished talking about the Palfrey case, Samantha Cronin and Doctor Alice Ruth Fox. Outside a car horn blared and a dog barked.

"I think Samantha's dead. And, I think she was killed by somebody who knew what he was doing," Calvin said. "You got anymore coffee?"

* * *

I brought a large Thermos-type coffee pot to the table along with fresh cups for the three of us. "Don't hold back or sugar-coat it, Calvin," I said. "Tell us what you think."

Calvin smiled and grabbed the coffee pot. He lined up the three cups. Abby and I answered yes to his raised eyebrows and he started pouring. "Connor, don't tell me you and Joe haven't reached the same conclusion. Does anyone think she decided to run away, but left her car because she prefers to hitchhike?" He speared the last piece of sausage on his plate and pointed it at me. "You said Joe told you he thought everything she owned was in that car. No way is she leaving that behind. Even if she hooked up with someone, she'd come back for the notebook and the bags."

"Joe sent me a copy of the inventory sheet from that car and the notebook I mentioned to you. I've got copies for you," I said. "I think we all suspect she's dead, but Joe and I didn't talk about what we thought might have happened. He was anxious to get something started and was afraid of losing more time."

"Yeah, because he knows, or seriously suspects, that young lady is dead," Calvin said. He looked to Abby. "Any thoughts?"

"I agree we have to assume she was murdered," Abby said. "We won't learn anything if we just run around putting up pictures of her asking have you see this girl? As if she was a lost cat."

"So how would you start?" Calvin said to me. He took a cautious sip of his coffee.

"We need to dig into Samantha's past. You think this was done by someone experienced because the body hasn't been found. That means there's probably something in her past that caused someone to want her dead. We find whatever that was, we might find the person involved. Part of that is digging through whatever's in her car."

Calvin looked to me. He moved uneasily in his chair, as though afraid it might break under his weight. "Christ, we

CHAPTER 22

don't have a body or a likely crime scene. Can you get Malcolm Butts to work his magic on Samantha Cronin's background?"

My boss had access to a network of connections and computers that could tell you Samantha's whole life. What she ate, drank, where she shopped, who she wore, who she dated and the name of her goldfish. Some of it involved hacking into areas where a mistake could get you into jail.

"Malcolm has taught me enough of his tricks that I could make a start. If we find we need to go deeper, I can ask him. Not sure I want to involve him this early."

"Fair enough," Calvin said. "I'm glad Joe's pushed this Elaine person to start a full-scale murder investigation. All we can do is pick around the edges, maybe go in a direction different from the cops. Her credit card hasn't been used; she's not showing up on security cameras. I assume they've pinged her phone with no results."

"Joe didn't know everything Bangor or Portland has done. He's getting a copy of the telephone records. He'll send them to us. As for the security cameras, most of them are on a 24-to-48-hour cycle, so not surprising she'd not show up there."

"There's no way a young girl like Samantha would not use her credit card or phone for over two weeks," Abby said. "What about family?"

"No help there, I said. "Elaine told Joe Samantha was estranged from her mom and stepfather. She said her mom told the police she was used to Samantha not calling or being in contact for months."

"Did the cops ask her mom when's the last time *she* reached out?" Abby said. "Christ, it's always the kid who's supposed to reach out. What the hell kind of mother did Samantha have?"

"Might want to take a look at that stepfather," I said. "God forbid, but maybe Samantha's anger at Fox over her testimony for Palfrey has its roots at home. I'll get his name from Joe and add him to my check-out list."

"Have either of you considered Samantha might be gay?" Abby said. "Joe told Connor Elaine said there were no boyfriends in the picture, and her one and only friend is that nun in New York."

An awkward silence descended. "Gives us more to look at," I said. "Nothing's off the table."

"Tell Joe, we're happy to help," Calvin said. "Ask him to send whatever standard government contract he uses for this kind of situation, and I'll sign it. I assume it'll be on paper, so I'll have to buy a file folder."

We laughed and drank our coffee while silence reasserted itself.

Calvin stirred and his chair creaked. "We know enough to start in a particular direction." He raised his index finger. "One, Samantha would not have voluntarily left her car and its contents, particularly the notebook, in the parking lot." Another finger popped up beside the first. "Two, she had some kind of obsession with Doctor Fox." A third finger appeared. Three, Doctor Fox chased her when Samantha left the classroom, and four, Samantha hasn't been seen or heard from since."

"You think Fox killed her?" Abby said.

Calvin shrugged. "It doesn't do us any good to wonder if Samantha might have been walking around Portland and met someone. Since the security cameras are no help, we can't rule it in or out. And the fact is, we're not equipped to walk into the bars, stores, or coffee houses with her picture and ask have you seen her?" He looked to Abby. "The lost cat approach."

CHAPTER 22

He took a sip of coffee and leaned back. I heard another squeak. "Since her credit card wasn't used, I think we assume she never left the parking lot. We let the cops figure out if she was in Portland. Let them look for the lost cat. My guess is next week her picture will be on TV with a story."

"Former star gymnast and near-Olympian missing. News at eleven," I said, in my best TV anchor voice.

"Exactly," Calvin said. "The only scenario that explains no use of her credit card, even for a cup of coffee, and the fact her car has been in the parking lot since the day she went to Fox's class is that something happened to Samantha before she could get from the building to her car. And rather than chasing shadows, we should focus on Fox. I think the two of them had a confrontation and Fox killed her. Fox dumped her into her car and got rid of the body. That's the direction we need to start. Connor, that means a heavy snoop into both Fox and Samantha."

"And you'll be...?" I let the words hang.

"I'm gonna start with the students in that class where she confronted Doctor Fox. Maybe she said something to one of them that'll help." He shook his head at the hopelessness of it all. "It's been so long. We'll need luck to pick up any traction."

"What'll I tell Joe? Hey, we think your neighbor did it."

Calvin smiled. "We're not the police. We don't have to follow the evidence and we can start wherever we want. Besides, I think the evidence points to Fox. I think your friend Joe suspects her, and that's why he called you. We can do things Joe and Elaine Blass can't. So, let's do them."

23

Chapter 23

Doctor Fox didn't come to J. Point the day after her confrontation with Cassandra. Joe went to her home on Perch Lane several times, knocked on the door and peered through her windows.

She was not there.

Three calls to her cell over the morning hours went immediately to voice mail.

Connor McNeill called him at noon. Joe learned Connor and Abby had had breakfast with Calvin Washington. All of them believed Samantha was dead, and their initial focus would be on Doctor Fox. Connor gave Calvin's contact information to Joe so he could send whatever forms were necessary. Calvin would bill at $300.00 per hour and he'd split it equally with Connor. Joe suggested Calvin meet him Monday morning at Southern Maine University where he could speak with the students in Fox's class. Connor told Joe he was heading to his office to hack into some computers.

CHAPTER 23

"You're my friend, Connor," Joe said. "But don't tell me shit like that."

Joe briefed Cassandra on his conversation, and the fact everyone seemed to believe Samantha was dead. "Connor and Calvin are going to focus on Doctor Fox," he said.

"Don't act surprised, Joe," Cassandra said. "That's why you asked Connor to get involved. You wanted a fresh set of eyes to confirm what you already thought."

"You know me too well," Joe said.

"That bitch wouldn't dare come up here today," Cassandra said. "I'd stuff her in a box and throw it in the lake."

"I'm meeting Calvin at Fox's office on Monday," he told Cassandra. "That should be fun." He took her hand. "No more talking about Fox. Let's spend the rest of the day celebrating her absence and enjoying this fabulous weather."

And that's what they did.

***

Roosevelt Wilson arrived early and spent the morning cleaning and pruning his property. He scraped and painted away the rust on some outdoor furniture he never used, a task he did every other year. He came by Joe and Cassandra's house, as he often did, mid-afternoon with a grand smile and a six-pack of ale.

He and Joe stacked twigs, branches, and logs in the fire pit on Joe's property. Roosevelt struck a match and began the proceedings, and Joe retrieved three lawn chairs from his porch. Cassandra followed him out with a glass of white wine and a small cooler, filled with ice and Roosevelt's Harpoon. Joe went back to the house and came out with a plastic bowl of white cheddar popcorn. He placed the popcorn on a tree stump, which had been shaved and preserved for this very purpose. Two months after they purchased the property, Joe had the tree cut down and constructed and positioned the fire pit to take full advantage of the remaining nature's table.

The flames flickered and danced noisily as the sun filtered through the thin bent trees that wore the wind off Queen Lake. The ambiance and comfort were familiar and welcomed by the three, who enjoyed each other's company and the solitude of J. Point. These Saturday sessions went for hours, often deep into the evening, interrupted only by the arrival of pizzas or sandwiches for dinner. The three gossiped, laughed and talked about the weather, politics, the Patriots, Bruins, and Celtics. Some days it was everything, other times, a singular subject. Five or six years ago, Roosevelt surprised them with a comment about a book of poems he was writing. Joe thought it was a joke, and had to suppress a laugh when he realized Roosevelt was serious. He recited a short piece he had written on the death of his partner, a victim of AIDS. Both Joe and Cassandra had teared up. Later, Cassandra chided Joe it was probably racist, perhaps homophobic, that he never considered it possible that a black, military man with a quick temper could also be a gay, sensitive poet.

"I'd have been just as surprised to learn Robert Frost was a gunfighter," Joe responded.

These afternoons were treasured and were repeated most Saturdays until early October, when Roosevelt would drain the water from the pipes, close his home and head to a small town

CHAPTER 23

ten or so miles to the north.

"I ran into Andy Junior at the market on the way up here," Roosevelt said to Cassandra. "Said you and that Fox gal had at it yesterday."

"Please don't ruin a perfect day," Cassandra said around a smile. "She blocked the road. I had to carry some grocery bags to my house. Claimed she was in the bathroom and didn't hear me knock. Then she closes the door and still doesn't move the car. I called Andy to tow it."

"Andy said he'd never seen you so mad." Roosevelt shrugged and smiled. "Can't blame you, Cassandra. I've had my own problems with her." He turned to Joe. "But we won't talk about that, will we Joe?"

Joe smiled and saluted him with a bottle of Harpoon.

"Don't look like we'll need a fourth chair for these sessions," Roosevelt said.

"If she'd stop being an asshole, she'd be welcomed," Joe said. "But I don't think Doctor Fox wants anything to do with us. Except to aggravate us."

"She's good at that," Roosevelt said.

"I'd bury her under this pit before I'd sit around it with her," Cassandra said.

They discussed the peculiarities of Fox and debated if she would ever "come around," as Roosevelt liked to call people who changed and became friends. That conversation evolved into speculation as to why the family of Abner Duffy would have sold the property to anyone, let alone Doctor Fox, which, in turn, led to stories about the Duffy family members. Joe continued to think about Samantha and the fact Fox could be a suspect. He struggled to stay in the moment, and contributed stories to the conversation. But his mind returned to Samantha and Fox. *Was Fox missing too?* He dismissed the thought. One day and a few unanswered calls, meant nothing. He returned to the conversation and offered a Duffy anecdote, generating laughter and a toast. But his mind continued to return to darker matters. *Fox would never return any calls from me. Avoidance behavior. I'll confront her in her office. Samantha's missing, probably dead. Fox is alive and well,* he shouted silently.

Or is she?

Chapter 24

After the goodbyes were exchanged and the dishes cleaned, I made a call to update Joe. Then, a quick hug from Abby, and I headed to Boston and my office on the second floor of 92 State Street. It was in a suite of three mid-size rooms and one large room filled with computers, printers, and some machinery, which Malcolm never explained. The gold-leafed lettering on beveled glass on the entrance door to our suite read: Malcolm Butts and Associates. No hint as to who we were or what we did. Malcolm often said we were safer if people don't know.

The offices were in an old stone building with large arch-shaped windows on the corner of State and Merchants Row. The latter is just a half block long and ends at the Southern entrance to Faneuil Hall. While most known for its American Revolutionary-era protests, others including abolitionists, women's suffragists, as opposed to the more militant suffragettes, and labor unionists have held protests, meetings, and debates at Faneuil Hall since its construction in 1742. Today, it is more often used by candidates preaching to supporters and announcing candidacies for governor or the U.S. Senate, while jugglers, street-grifters and musicians garnered more attention outside. As it has been for generations, the building is a centerpiece of a busy marketplace. Gift shops, clothing stores, restaurants, pizza and ice cream shops have replaced the cattle, poultry, fish and corn of previous generations.

While I liked Faneuil Hall and its marketplace and often spent time wandering through its crowds, the real attraction of the office space was the Starbucks across the street and the Dunkin' less than one block away.

It's good to have options.

Today, I chose expediency. As a result, a large, black, house-blend coffee in a recyclable cup emblazoned with the familiar green logo of a mermaid with long braids and a crown and star over her head, sat beside my computer, while I hacked into other computers to get information on Samantha Cronin and Alice Ruth Fox.

I feel safer hacking a computer if I'm at my office. Malcolm told me if I followed his guidance, I'm just as safe at home, but I always come to 92 State to do the deed. I could go to a parking lot near the John Joseph Moakley Federal Courthouse in South Boston. There, I could work off a laptop that operated off a WI-Fi system in the courthouse, across the street. Butts had taken the precaution of building what he called *a repeat* into the building several years earlier. How he did this, or what it meant is still a mystery to me. It didn't matter, I'd never hack while in shouting distance of federal authorities.

Butts was part of a hacking network that the FBI and the National Security Agency tried to destroy a year ago. His weekly routine was to monitor the feds to see what they were doing. As part of this effort, Butts tapped into the City of Malden's Police Department's computer systems. This gave us useful access to several federal systems. The federal systems had safeguards, but since the basic design of their system was to encourage access by local law enforcement agencies, the safeguards were relatively weak. Once you had unrestricted access to a few big federal systems, you could get to some amazing places. Butts told me he avoided the Boston and Cambridge Police Departments out of fear they would be sophisticated with strong safeguards. Malden was a large enough city to need access to the federal websites, but less likely to pay for the safeguards to keep us out.

I decided to start with Samantha Cronin. Joe gave me her name, Bangor address and the plate number on her car. That was enough to get me into the Maine Registry of Motor Vehicles, which gave me her birth date. That got me into the National Crime Information Center Records. Samantha had a single encounter with the criminal justice system: a trespassing and open container charge six years ago on St. Patrick's Day in South Boston. She must have mouthed off to an unfriendly cop to earn that charge on the High Holiday. In any event, she'd been law-abiding since, or skilled enough not to get caught.

Samantha briefly attended Plymouth State University in New Hampshire, where she'd majored in sociology, marijuana, and vodka. She dropped out after a semester and bounced between two community colleges in Maine. She didn't graduate from either. Her longest employment stint was as instructor at a gymnastics academy in Bangor for just under two years. Her credit score was weak and of no significance. Joe gave me her cell number and that of Sister Alicia. A quick check disclosed nothing out of the ordinary and confirmed Sister Alicia was her most frequent contact. Samantha's last call had been to her on Thursday evening March 24th, the evening before she crashed Doctor Fox's class.

Samantha's life had been, I thought, sad and unfulfilled. I said a quick prayer to St. Jude for her soul. Like Calvin, I was certain she was dead.

I shifted my attention to Alice Ruth Fox.

I had her Maine car registration number from Joe, but little else. I decided to try the employment records at the University of Southern Maine. It took less time than picking a lock, and I soon had her social security number, date of birth and home address.

Since getting to the site was so easy, I decided to stay awhile. Fox received her Doctorate Degree from Georgetown University in 2008. Her undergraduate degree was from Penn State in 1989. She started at an Assistant professor at the University of Southern Maine in 2012, became an Associate Professor with tenure in 2019. She was making close to $130,000.

There was no evidence of disciplinary actions against Fox, but there were many appeals to an academic committee filed by students seeking a review of their grade. In all but two instances, the appeals resulted in higher grades. I wandered around for several more minutes, but found nothing that piqued my interest, or warranted further review.

I went to the National Military Records Depository and punched in her date of birth and social security number. The screen went green and then black.

"Shit," I shouted and turned off my computer. I waited several minutes and tried to restart. The computer came on and I was back at my start menu and the Windows page. I shut down the computer. I would leave Doctor Fox to Malcolm Butts. I grabbed my coffee, turned off the lights and walked out of the office.

Riding the Orange Line home, my stomach was queasy, and I felt out of sorts. Had I jeopardized Malcolm Butts and the entire operation by called attention to myself? I was nervous, a bit afraid and embarrassed. I felt as if I had set off one of those air blast horns in the middle of a quiet church service.

Chapter 25

Joe and Calvin Washington talked on Sunday afternoon. Although they'd never met, the conversation was casual and free from any hesitancy or "feeling out" process. Calvin suggested they meet Monday morning at ten at the Holy Donut, a short drive from the Portland Campus of the University of Southern Maine. When Joe cautioned the shop had no inside dining, Calvin brushed aside the objection. "I heard they make bacon and cheddar donuts," he said. "I have to try those. We can eat in my car."

"How'll I know you?" Joe asked.

"Look for a two-hundred-and-eighty-pound black man with a box of eleven donuts in his left hand and one in his mouth." Calvin said before hanging up.

* * *

CHAPTER 25

Joe arrived a few minutes before ten. Calvin stood at the front door, a wide smile on his face and with an empty left hand. The Holy Donut was popular and its policy was to close once its morning supply of donuts was sold. Joe knew the absence of a line could signal the shop was closed, but Calvin's smile told him it only meant the morning rush was over. They exchanged greetings and handshakes and headed inside. "Whaddya like here?" Calvin asked Joe. He held the door open.

"I'm getting two glutton-free plains and a black coffee," Joe said.

"I'm going with a mixed dozen," Calvin said.

"No longer focused on just the bacon and cheddar?" Joe said. He ordered his donuts and coffee and stepped aside to give Calvin the counter.

"I got here early," Calvin said. "I discovered they have a maple bacon donut and a bacon cheddar. I felt like Pavlov's dog." He smiled at the young woman behind the counter. "I'll have six maple bacon and six bacon and cheddar." He turned to Joe. "A mixed dozen."

* * *

"All of a sudden my computer screen went green and then black," I said to Malcolm Butts. It was just after ten on a sunny Monday morning. We were having coffee at the conference table in our office at 92 State Street. I explained what happened when I tried to access information on Doctor Fox the past Saturday.

"Don't worry," Butts said. "Someone put a block on her file

to deny access to everyone. It's a routine security device."

"Can they trace it back to me, or us?"

"No, it's sounds like basic run-of-the-mill security. If they'd let you into part of her file and then blocked you, I'd worry about a track. But that's not what happened."

"You're sure?" I said.

"If you were tracked, they'd have been here waiting for you this morning," Butts said.

"Connor McNeill, open up. This is the FBI," a high-pitched voice shouted from the other side of the room.

I pretended to be startled and looked at Butts.

He laughed. "You have to admit, I am getting better at this."

I nodded agreement. "The ventriloquist lessons have taken hold. Much better than your efforts a few weeks ago. In a year or so, you'll fool me. If we're not both in jail."

Butts toasted me with his coffee. He stood up. "Give me the information you have on Fox. I can work around the security. I'll also check on her credit card usage."

I handed him the file I created. "Be careful."

"I will," said a high-pitched voice now coming from under the table.

* * *

At ten-thirty Joe and Calvin sat in upholstered visitor chairs in front of the ornate walnut desk of Associate Vice-President Margaret Barnhill, a long-time friend of Joe and a serious Patriots fan. She was a stout, light-hearted woman with white hair, neon-blue rimmed glasses and a small mouth.

CHAPTER 25

Joe easily secured permission for Calvin to briefly address the students in Doctor Fox's eleven o'clock psychology 101 class. For ten minutes Calvin answered questions about Tom Brady, Bill Belichick and the new overtime rules changes, which she enthusiastically supported.

"You don't think Doctor Fox will object to this intrusion?' Joe said, trying to steer the conversation away from football.

Barnhill's smile and shrug told Joe she recognized and would accede to his effort. "I went to her office this morning. Doctor Fox is usually in early, but not today."

Uneasiness grabbed Joe stomach. He dismissed it and shifted in his seat. "Should we try again? Or perhaps go to the classroom and wait?"

"Oh, it more comfortable here," Barnhill said. "I'll take you down to the classroom about ten to eleven." She shifted her eyes to Calvin. "How long do you think, before the Patriots get into another Super Bowl?"

* * *

The three of them stood outside the classroom at eleven o'clock. It was the same room where Fox and Joe had gone on April 7th. Fox had not appeared. Barnhill called her office and was told Fox had not called in sick or otherwise indicated she would not be in class today.

"This is most unusual," Barnhill said. "I can't remember Doctor Fox not being here for a scheduled class." She guided Calvin towards the door. "You may as well go in and make your announcement. If she's not here by ten after, the class is dismissed, and you'll be run over by a stampede of students."

Calvin stood at the lecture podium. The rumble of class nose subsided. He went to the whiteboard and wrote his cell number. He turned back to the students and smiled. "Good morning, I'm Calvin Washington. I'm helping in the search to find Samantha Cronin. She's the young woman who came to this class on Friday, March 25th. She spoke briefly and Doctor Fox asked her to leave the room. Samantha did, and Doctor Fox followed her out and returned in about twenty minutes." Calvin saw nodding heads and decided no description or further information on Samantha was necessary. "Samantha hasn't been seen since that day. I'm here to ask if Samantha said anything to any one of you, no matter how insignificant it might seem to you, please call me at this number." Calvin pointed to the whiteboard. "All calls will be in strict confidence. I don't even need to know your name." He paused to let the message absorb. "Any questions?"

A hand shot up in the back. "You think Doctor Fox had anything to do with Samantha's disappearance?" There was a gasp. Calvin sensed the movement of Barnhill towards the podium. He shook his head. "No, I do not," he said in a firm voice. "Any other questions?"

Another hand came up. "How long before the PATS get to another Super Bowl?"

* * *

It took a few minutes, but Joe convinced Barnhill to allow them into Fox's locked office. They looked through her desk appointment book, desk calendar and a small leather-bound journal they found in her desk. Nothing provided a reason for today's absence.

Barnhill called the employment office to get Fox's home address. She gave it to Joe, who was holding his cell phone. "I'm calling a friend with the Portland Police," he said to her. He pushed a button. "Jackson? Hi, this is Joe McDonald.... Yeah, yeah, it's been awhile. listen, I need you....yeah, yeah, I will. Hey, shut up a second. will you? I need you get a wellness check ASAP. Yeah, yeah. Alice Ruth Fox." He gave him the address. "ASAP. And call me back at this number. Thanks."

While Joe was talking on the phone, Calvin kept searching through papers and folders scattered on Fox's desk and on a chair by the window. Margaret Barnhill, now consumed by the frenzy of Joe and Calvin, hovered near the door as if afraid to touch or see anything. Calvin pulled out his cell and called Connor. He asked him to check Fox's credit card use.

Suddenly, a man, fifty or fifty-five, weathered, stocky, with a sandy three-day beard and dishwater blond hair worn long from a balding head, stepped into the room. "What's going on?" He asked in a voice trying to be authoritative, but sounding tentative.

Calvin dropped his phone to his side. You are?" Calvin said.

"Harlan Perkins, I'm Chair of the Psychology Department. Why are you searching Dr. Fox's office?

Margaret Burnhill came to life to assert her authority. "Dr. Fox is missing. These men are trying to find something that might tell us where she is. Do you know if she had any meetings scheduled that would have prevented her from being at her class this morning.?"

"Missing?" Perkins said, failing to stop the thin smile

spreading across his face. "Why are you looking?"

"You're not a fan of Dr. Fox?" Calvin said.

Perkins stepped closer to Calvin. "Ever have a stone in your shoe?" He didn't wait for an answer. "Dr. Fox was like that. A constant annoyance that you'd do anything to remove, but couldn't. And she was a big, sharp, pointed stone."

* * *

Thirty minutes later, Jackson called back to announce the house was empty, although her car was in the driveway. There were no signs of any disturbance. They entered through a bathroom window at the back of the house. Jackson told Joe he'd check all the closets and found the clothes hangers full, and several pieces of luggage, empty and in place. Jackson found a medium size safe in the basement. "If she's missing another few days," he said, "we'll try for a warrant to get it opened. "She's not on the run. Her car was locked, but appeared clean. No signs of blood."

"Thanks, Jackson," Joe said. "I owe you. Don't let me forget it." He looked at Calvin. "What's next?"

"Your place," Calvin answered. Outside of Barnhill's hearing, he added: "We need to get into Fox's house."

26

Chapter 26

By twelve noon, Joe and Calvin were standing in the living room of Fox's house on Perch Lane. Calvin picked the locks to get them inside. Before he did, he texted a report to Connor. Joe rationalized the break-in was really a wellness check being organized by a concerned neighbor. The house had the dead air smell of a strip motel room or a hospital corridor. Sunlight came in from a bay window facing the road and played on a faded oriental rug. Joe thought he detected the faint odor of perfume. The smell he remembered from the night Fox came to his house and ended up spending the night. It was as if her presence was still here, floating through the stale air like a ghost.

"Place looks like she never moved in," Calvin said. "I'll go upstairs, you check this floor, and we'll do the basement together."

"Afraid of spiders?" Joe said around a laugh. "Scary things in dark places?"

"Yeah, like a body in a dark corner," Calvin said. "I've got a bad feeling about this."

"Shit," Joe said. "Me too. Let's search together. We'll start upstairs."

* * *

The upstairs, two large bedrooms separated by a Jack and Jill full bath, was empty except for dust motes floating in the air and at rest in the corners. They checked the closets and the bathroom and found nothing. They headed downstairs.

"You ready for the basement?" Calvin said.

"Yeah, "Joe said. "But we do it together. I don't think she's down there, but I'm beginning to worry she's dead. Changes my thinking on everything."

"I've a bad feeling as well," Calvin said. "We're getting way ahead of ourselves, but if Fox killed Samantha, we may start thinking her friend the nun took revenge on Fox. How crazy is that?" He looked around the first floor as they headed to the kitchen and the door to the basement. "This is nice house. Too bad, she'll never get to use it."

Joe shrugged and opened the door to the basement. "I never thought I'd say this, but I hope you're wrong about that."

* * *

The basement at Fox's house had no bodies in dark corners or anything that could provide a clue on Fox's whereabouts. It was clean and empty except for several cartons of garden tools, canned goods, empty jars and rags. Joe and Calvin couldn't tell if they'd been left by the Duffy family or were part of an early arrival of Fox's stuff. They headed upstairs to the main floor. They decided to do it together and room by room, and started in the kitchen.

The refrigerator had plastic squeeze containers of ketchup and mustard, a bag of coffee, a pound of butter, two cans of peaches and several gallons of water. The kind of contents you'd expect to find in a seasonal home before the season started. The freezer held a quart bottle of vodka and two bags of ice. The refrigerator door was clean and free of any pictures, notes, or personal items. "Don't think I've ever seen a refrigerator without a single postcard, picture or reminder of your next dental appointment," Calvin said.

The seldom-used theme carried forward to the kitchen cabinets, which held an array of dishes, glasses, cups and several pans. There was an electric frying pan and a two-slice pop up toaster from the 1950s. They were clean, free of crumbs, dust, and dead bugs. Joe opened a pine door to a small pantry that was empty except for a broom, a dust pan and a large empty wastebasket.

They moved to a small bedroom and anther empty closet. Then, back to the living room, which was cluttered with furniture that had not been staged or placed. The exception was an old sofa placed against the bay window. It looked like one you'd find along a street abandoned to whoever wanted to deal with it. A pile of clean sheets, blankets and pillows rested in the center of it. "She used the couch as her bed," Calvin said. "Couldn't find anyone to assemble the bed frame we saw leaning against the wall in that small bedroom on the first floor."

"It's sad," Joe said. "She buys a nice big house and then has no one she can ask for help to move in and enjoy it."

"You reap what you sow," Calvin said. "You said she was a pain in the ass."

"She is, or was," Joe said. "Still sad."

They spent the next hour opening drawers, rummaging through a small desk, a night table in the bedroom, empty closets and a large bathroom. They found luggage that was empty, and three boxes of clothes with hangers waiting to be unpacked. There was nothing that signaled Fox planned to take a trip or even that she was prepared to settle into the home on Perch Lane.

"Maybe got something," Calvin said. He pulled a leather briefcase from behind the sofa. He dumped the contents on a maple coffee table. There were copies of medical journal articles on psychology, brain development and gender identity. There was also a five by eight journal book with a gold embossed 2022. Calvin picked up the book, and they took it to the kitchen table.

"We need to be quick," Joe said. "Hard to say we're doing a wellness check if anyone barges in while we're reading this at her kitchen table."

"You want me to put it back?" Calvin said. "Your call."

"Just want you to be quick. We've been here over an hour."

Calvin thumbed through the journal. "This'll be quick. It's a diary for this year. He scanned the first several pages, muttering, "nothing," with the turn of each page. "First entry is Tuesday, January eleventh. Just says 'Palfrey trial. Testimony went well. Hoping for a hung jury.'"

CHAPTER 26

"Well, we know how that went," Joe said.

Calvin turned some more pages. "Cassandra is mentioned on Friday, January fourteenth. Fox says she went to Cassandra's law school office to introduce herself. She described Cassandra as 'rude and unwelcoming.' This is the day she closed on this property."

"Jesus Christ," Joe muttered. "She's like a mean girl from junior high."

Calvin laughed. "Hey, you're mentioned on the next page, Saturday the fifteenth. According to this, you 'bullied her into paying for snow removal.' She says she's 'not looking forward to having you and Cassandra as neighbors.'"

"Well, that feeling's mutual," Joe said. "Feels creepy reading someone's diary. Even a shithead like Fox."

Calvin kept turning pages. "Most of this just describes the weather or personal things. "Went to the hairdresser, rainy, sunny, went to bank, cold. That sort of crap." He turned some more. "Hold on, here's the page for March twenty-fifth. That's the day Samantha crashed her class. Says 'Samantha Cronin interrupted my class today, but left when asked. No further issues.'" Calvin looked at Joe. "Pretty tame."

"You expected she'd tell us she killed Samantha and where the body was buried?" Joe said.

"Well, if she had, we'd have a serous search and seizure issue," Calvin said. "I assume we were never here?"

"We're here for a wellness check," Joe said.

Calvin flipped more pages. "On Wednesday, April sixth, she says your neighbor, 'a negro' – she used that word – 'threatened her with a knife and slashed her tires.'"

"That's bullshit," Joe said. "Did she mention spending the night at our house because she was drunk and passed out?"

Calvin laughed. "No, but she said you 'invited her to stay, but she felt uncomfortable with the invite and declined the offer.' She never mentions Cassandra." He looked at Joe. "You dog, you." He flipped another page. "Next page, April seventh, she says you went to her office and asked questions about Samantha. She says and I quote: 'Joe always makes me nervous. I think he does it on purpose. Probably knows about my heart condition.'"

Joe groaned. "Not sure she has a heart. Next, she'll be blaming me for her hemorrhoids."

"She also wrote: 'I'm sorry Samantha's missing. I hope I was helpful.'"

Calvin turned the next page. "Oh, here we go. April eighth. Doctor Fox says 'Cassandra yelled at me and called a tow truck to move my car. Later she threatened to burn down my house with me inside. I am afraid of that woman. She's crazy. I think buying up here was a big mistake.'" He flipped some pages. "That's the last entry."

"Let's get out of here," Joe said. "You got time for a beer?"

"Of course." He held up the diary. "Whaddya want me to do with this?"

"Put everything back where it was," Joe said. "We came here for a quick wellness check. That explains being inside and checking every room and the basement. But we never saw that."

"Okay with me, but I'm taking a picture of every page," Calvin said. "Just in case."

* * *

CHAPTER 26

Ten minutes later, Calvin exited the side door to Fox's house. He squinted and looked downward waiting for his eyes to adjust to the light.

"Hold it right there," a voice hollered. Calvin looked up. Roosevelt Wilson, holding a shot gun aimed at Calvin's chest, stepped forward.

Chapter 27

Calvin's arms shot up over his head. "Hey, hey, relax, I'm here with Joe McDonald, the County Prosecutor."

Roosevelt kept the gun pointed at Calvin's chest. "So, where's Joe?"

"Behind the guy you're pointing the gun at," Joe shouted. "Jesus, Roosevelt put down the gun. Let Calvin step aside and I'll come out."

Roosevelt lowered the gun a few inches. "Go ahead."

Calvin kept his arms high and moved from the small landing of the steps into Fox's house. Joe emerged. "I hope that gun's registered."

Roosevelt lowered it to his side and smiled. "Sorry Joe. I saw movement in Fox's house when I drove by. I got my gun and came back. When I saw this giant coming out...." He shrugged as if it was all self-evident.

"Okay if I lower my arms?" Calvin said, anger and annoyance fused into every word.

"Sure, sure," Roosevelt said. "I'm sorry. Didn't know who

CHAPTER 27

you were or what you were doing."

"You always grab a gun when you're not sure?' Calvin said with a bit less heat. "Damn near gave me a heart attack." He followed Joe down the steps.

Joe stayed between the two men. The tension of the moment still more raw than forgotten. "Roosevelt, say hello to Calvin Washington. He's a friend helping me with the search for Dr. Fox. Calvin, this is my neighbor and friend Roosevelt Wilson."

"I didn't know the bitch was missing," Roosevelt said. "Why the fuck are you looking for her?" He stepped towards Calvin and extended his hand. His eyes traveled up and down Calvin "Holy shit, you're *the* Calvin Washington. I was a big fan of yours. Sorry, about the gun. If it's any consolation, it's not loaded."

Calvin laughed and grabbed his hand. "Nice to meet you, Roosevelt. You named for Franklin or Theodore?"

"Neither," Roosevelt around a laugh. "My Dad was huge fan of Roosevelt Brown. He played..."

"Offensive tackle for the New York Giants," Calvin interrupted. "All Pro nine times, in the Hall of Fame. He and John Hannah are probably the best offensive lineman ever to play the game."

"Yeah, and you're up there in the top three," Roosevelt said. "You'll be in Canton as soon as you're eligible."

"If you think flattery will make me forget the gun, you're absolutely right.," Calvin said. "That, and the fact it wasn't loaded."

The three men laughed. "Okay now that we're all friends, let's go to my porch and have a beer," Joe said.

"You're the Boss, white man," Calvin and Roosevelt said almost in unison. They bumped fists and fell in behind Joe, who trudged ahead and waved his arm in defeat.

"How long before the PATS get into another Super Bowl?" Roosevelt said to Calvin.

* * *

Ten minutes later, the three men sat around a metal table on Joe's screen porch. A large bowl of white cheddar popcorn was centered on the table, and each had a cold Harpoon IPA. "Nice spot," Calvin said with a nod to Joe.

"Even nicer if that bitch Fox is gone," Roosevelt said with a toast of his bottle.

"When's the last time you saw her?" Calvin said to Roosevelt.

"The night I let the air out her tires," Roosevelt said with a wink to Joe.

"Sounds like a story," Calvin said.

Joe gave Calvin the elevator version of the night. It still took almost ten minutes with excited and defensive interruptions from Roosevelt.

"You never saw or heard from after that day?" Calvin said.

Roosevelt shook his head. "Nah, but I realize it was stupid of me to do that. I'm in debt to Joe for getting me outta that mess." He smiled. "Good God, she was a king size pain in the ass," Roosevelt said.

"Another person we talked to today described Fox as like having a sharp rock in your shoe," Calvin said. "He was the chair of her department at the college."

Roosevelt laughed. "That's pretty good. Accurate, too. Is he a suspect?" He paused a second or two and said. "Hmm, am I

CHAPTER 27

suspect?"

"We don't have a body or a crime scene," Joe said. "At this stage, we don't even know we have a crime, let alone suspects."

"True, but nobody's been cleared either," Calvin said.

Chapter 28

When Abby and I owned property in Falmouth, our favorite haunt was The Flying Bridge, a restaurant on the harbor. It provided good eats with fabulous views. We never dined at night since we wanted our cheese burgers, scallops, salads, or fried claims served with views of sea gulls, sail boats, and other sea-faring vessels of varying sizes and values come in and out of the harbor. Every hour or so, the Island Queen, a passenger ferry, would pass us as it headed towards Martha's Vineyard, or as it came back to its dock. On more than one occasion – always in August - we saw Air Force One fly over us on its way to the Vineyard. All in all, it was a great place to have lunch and a few cold Tanqueray and tonics after a round of golf, some yard work, or just to enjoy an afternoon on Cape Cod.

When we moved back to Melrose, there were nice restaurants in walking distance, but no ocean or harbor. We set about the task of finding another Flying Bridge. We started in Gloucester, a working-class fishing town, just over thirty miles away. The

City's been featured in a number of movies, most notably *The Perfect Storm* and *CODA*.

After several trips, we settled on three restaurants. One, The Seaport Grille, is in what we called Gloucester Mainland. It has ocean views, but not quite the feel we were seeking. But every Wednesday they serve all the oysters you want, all day for one dollar each. Plus, it has a large parking lot with no charge. Seaport Grille became our Flying Bridge, but only on Wednesday afternoons.

The other two, The Studio and The Rudder, are on Rocky Neck, a crooked peninsular of land and home to Gloucester's venerable art colony. Originally developed as a hybrid neighborhood in the post-Civil War era, Rocky Neck had a paint factory and the Gloucester Marine Railway at its opposite ends. Artists set up studios among summer homes and a handful of Victorians. The Rockaway Hotel offered nearly 100 rooms in the era of Gloucester's great summer hotels, which came to an end with a chain of mysterious fires in the 1950s and 60s.

Today, the arts community, seasonal and year-round residents and restaurants are all alive and well. The Rudder and The Studio, are within walking distance of each other and both provide outside and inside dining and great views of Smith Cove and the Gloucester Mainland. What neither has is a parking lot. Which is why The Studio is a stop on the Water Shuttle, and The Rudder has a dock for those arriving by boat.

On this sunny afternoon in April, Abby and I arrived by car and met Malcolm Butts at The Studio. Because it was April, street parking for both cars was available and free. All that would change in less than thirty days. When he left the office at ten-thirty that morning, Malcolm suggested "luppa." a term he coined (adding a Boston accent) for a late lunch or early dinner. He promised me information on Doctor Fox and he suggested Gloucester. Malcolm, or somebody hiding in a closet in his office, said, "My ventriloquist lessons are in Gloucester. Bring Abby. Maybe we can have lobstah."

* * *

We had our drinks outside, but by the time our food order arrived, we elected to move indoors to the low ceiling, wood paneled bar area to escape a persistent breeze that negated the warmth of the sun in a cloudless China-blue sky. We had a window table so not all was lost.

"Your Doctor Fox is an interesting woman, and one that should not be taken lightly," Malcolm said. "Of course, that assumes she is alive."

"You think she's dead?" Abby said. She used her folk to roll a cherry tomato off her salad with grilled salmon to the side of her plate.

"Let's start with what you know and then we can move to what you think or what you assume," I said. I glanced at Abby, who nodded agreement.

"Fair enough," Malcolm said. "I will tell you what I know, but not how I came to know it. And, I will tell you only after I devour these fried clams."

I put my lobster roll down and saluted him with a tall Tanqueray and tonic. "Fair enough."

* * *

CHAPTER 28

We engaged in small talk and eating over the next twenty minutes. My lobster roll was gone in ten minutes. I ordered a second Tanqueray and tonic and watched Malcolm savor each clam and Abby cut her salmon into small pieces, each of which she ate with a slice of lettuce, a piece of Swiss cheese and a dab of tartar sauce.

At precisely three-forty, Malcolm dropped his fork, wiped his mouth with a paper napkin, and bent down to pull an iPad from his briefcase. He fired it up, studied it for a few seconds and announced, "your Doctor Fox has a Massachusetts gun license. She owns three handguns, a Walther .380, a Ruger .57 and a Glock .44. She has two rifles. A Remington Air pump and a Colt Carbine. The Colt's an AR-15.

"Jesus," I said. "All registered and licensed?"

Malcolm nodded and smiled at me. "I'm good, but even I'm not gonna find unregistered guns in a two-hour search. I know she has a safe in the basement. Perhaps the handguns are there. Never saw the rifles. Might be in her garage, or the trunk of her car."

"How'd you know about the safe?" I said. "I only learned about it from Calvin an hour or so ago." I told Malcolm what Joe learned in his telephone conversation with the police who had entered Fox's house for a wellness check. "Did you get into her house?"

"In a manner of speaking," Malcolm said. "Remember our agreement, what I know, not how I know it."

"You hacked through one of those doorbell security systems," Abby said. "The more security cameras a house has, the more you can see once you get in. She must have a camera in the basement."

Malcolm smiled. "You should come to work for me."

Abby laughed. "Thanks, Malcolm, but you couldn't afford me."

Our waiter, a tall, thin, twenty-something with a gelled spike haircut that gave him a permanent look of surprise, approached to take our plates and dessert orders. Malcolm ordered coffee and a slice of apple pie with ice cream. Abby still had half of her drink and ordered a dish of coffee ice cream. I got a cup of black coffee.

Malcolm looked down to his iPad and scrolled to a new screen. "Fox was in the Navy and did a short stint – four months - with naval intelligence. She had a moderate to high security clearance, which, I suspect is standard for naval intelligence. She got an honorable discharge in 1989.

"You think naval intelligence or her security clearance is what caused my screen to go blank when I was poking around?" I said.

"Possible, but I doubt it. I think it was just a routine security system, set up to protect records," Malcolm said. He looked and scrolled some more.

"She never married. She has three credit cards, Master Card, Visa, and Shell Oil Company. She has not used any of them since the morning of April eighth. The last one used was the Shell for forty-seven dollars."

"That's the day Cassandra and Fox got into it over her blocking the road," I said. "She had Fox's car towed."

"Aha!" A voice said from under the table. "We have a suspect."

Abby laughed. "Hey, that wasn't bad."

"Thank you," the voice said. "Brains, beauty and a sense of humor."

The waiter arrived with drinks and dessert. He looked even

more startled. I wasn't sure if it was from the voice under the table, or if he had added gel to his head.

"Any more information?" I asked.

Malcolm held up his hand while he digested his first bite of dessert. He looked down at his iPad. "Fox owns a modest home in Langdon, Maine. That's about nine miles north of Portland. No mortgage. There is a one hundred sixty-five-thousand-dollar mortgage on the property on Perch Lane. She's on the enemies list of the three LBGTQ organizations that admit to having one on its website. Fox is mentioned on social media, but she doesn't respond, at least by name, and she does not maintain a website site, or a Facebook, Twitter or Instagram account."

"Unusual for someone who seems to relish being controversial," I said.

"I agree," Malcolm said.

"Probably deliberate," Abby said. "Fox is smart enough to know if she offers her opinion on everything, it won't matter on anything. She saves it for academic journals or trials. It's how she got her reputation."

"Makes sense, I suppose," Malcolm said. "Doctor Fox makes a hundred and thirty grand at USM. She lists a modest sum for speaking fees, less than ten thousand, and no other sources of income. She has several IRAs and is a member of the retirement system at the university. She started there in 2012, got tenure in 2017. No disciplinary actions at the university, but she's had multiple appeals by her students to an academic board, which reviews disputed grades. All the appeals resulted in a higher grade for the student."

"I could have used one of those committees my first year at BC," I muttered.

"Fox has a high credit score, uses credit cards appropriately, appears to live within her stated means." He put the iPad back in the briefcase.

"You said earlier that Fox is a woman we should not take lightly," I said. "Why?"

"It's unusual, but not unheard of, for a woman to own multiple weapons," Malcolm said. "And her experience in the military with some naval intelligence adds some drama, I think, to her background." He shrugged. "Of course, maybe she was a file clerk or a secretary."

"With a high security clearance?" I said.

"Moderate to high," Malcolm said, "which the janitors probably have, as well."

"You think she's dead?" Abby said.

"I don't know," Malcolm said. "But I'm not sure she's alive. Her car is in the driveway, and according to the police office Joe spoke with, her clothes were in the closet. She didn't appear to be running. Police have checked local hospitals. No one has heard from her and the credit cards are not being used. Fox doesn't impress me as being the type of person who would suddenly go out on vacation without telling the university." He took another bit of his pie and took a sip of coffee. "It doesn't feel right." She's either been abducted or is dead."

The silence around the table thickened the space between us.

Chapter 29

On the drive back to Melrose, Abby was silent. I knew she was mulling over what we learned from Malcolm. We are both comfortable with silence, whether in a car, or watching TV. As we entered Grant Circle, and onto Route 128, the silence broke.

"If both Samantha Cronin and Fox are dead, we should rethink everything," Abby said.

"Agreed," I said. A large white, wind tower loomed over us, its three blades cutting slowly through the wind that had chased us off the deck at The Studio.

"And even though coincidences do happen, I have to believe the deaths are connected," she said.

"Fox's death was to avenge Samantha's?" I said. "It seems the only friend Samantha had was that nun, who was with her at the trial." Several years ago, Abby and I had been involved in an investigation that exposed wrongdoing by a Catholic priest. "You think we have another investigation involving a religious? Talk about coincidences."

"I think the connection may be deeper," Abby said. "Maybe

somebody wanted both Samantha and Fox dead. I think maybe there's something between the two of them that we haven't found or figured out yet. Maybe we never will."

"We'll figure it out," I said with more confidence than I had.

"Maybe the police will find one or both of them," Abby said.

"That assumes the police will do a serious search," I said.

We drove home in silence and thought. It would be easier to find Fox, I decided. She was, after all, a public and controversial figure. We'd use media connections to get publicity on her disappearance. It would put some pressure on the police. Another item on my mental list was to contact the attorney who used Fox in the Palfrey case. He probably knew more about her than most of her faculty colleagues. And I needed to check the title on her property at The Point. Was she a joint owner? Was title in a trust? Always better to know the answers than not to know.

I internally debated whether to ask Ed McGonagle, a friend and second in charge of the Massachusetts Homicide Bureau for advice. Not his jurisdiction, I said to myself. On the other hand, Ed was loose on formalities, and he enjoyed chatting over coffee and donuts at the Capitol Coffee House, across the street from his office. I added his name to my mental list.

"We'll figure this out," I said to Abby. "I guarantee it."

"And that's that," she said around a laugh. A few seconds passed and Abby said, "Maybe the police will find them sipping wine in a pink, heart-shaped tub in the Poconos."

"Well, there's always that," I said.

* * *

CHAPTER 29

The days and months passed quickly and seamlessly. Our investigative punch list grew to five pages, each item was checked off and followed up at least twice. Calvin and I took a trip to Troy, New York to visit Sister Alicia at the New Beginnings Orphanage. We learned nothing new. But we did discover the Thirsty Shamrock, an Irish pub less than a quarter mile away, where we made friends over pints of Guinness, and Calvin predicted the Patriots would be in another Super Bowl before either the New York Giants or the Jets. Turned out most of the patrons were Buffalo Bills fans. We all agreed the Bills would beat the PATS in a race to the Super Bowl.

Ed McGonagle used his connections to talk with the state prison, where Robert Palfrey, notwithstanding Dr. Fox's testimony on his behalf, was spending the next thirty years. Palfrey was in protective custody with the other sexual offenders to protect him from the general population. He had had no visitors and received no mail or packages, McGonagle said even within the protective custody population, Palfrey was considered a piriah and avoided.

The news media, the public, and the police began to lose interest in Dr. Fox within six weeks of her disappearance and it appeared no one other than Joe, Calvin, and us ever wondered, or cared, what happened to Samantha Cronin.

Calvin returned the balance of the retainer in mid-September. We agreed to take up the investigation if anything developed. I told Abby I would never stop using the hacking skills I acquired from Malcolm, along with her ideas and brains, to search for clues or new directions to find out what happened to these two women.

Then it was Halloween, Thanksgiving, and the interminable Christmas season. A new year arrived and 2022 became like a forgotten dream.

*　*　*

Almost a year passed from the lunch we had with Malcolm and when I pledged to "figure it out" on the ride home from Gloucester, when it finally happened .

II

Part Two

Chapter 30

The third Wednesday in March 2023 was rainy and cold. Joe trudged across the frozen dirt; his arms full of split logs. He looked to the lake. There was no separation between the water and sky, and the lake, cold as ever, was the color of rolled steel. Joe laid the logs on the back steps and opened the door to the kitchen. Cassandra was at the large table with her two lap tops and the *New York Times*. Joe brought two of the logs into the house and carefully tossed them into the fire, bringing it to life. He walked back to the door, shrugged out of his overcoat, and hung it on one of the large pewter hooks.

"Cassandra, why is it the three months of summer are gone in about six weeks, while winter is with us for six or seven months?"

Cassandra's eyes never left her computer screen. "Because God is punishing you for something or other. Maybe you should drop the subject, or I might find out what it is."

Joe walked over to the counter and poured himself a coffee. He turned to Cassandra. "So, why is He punishing you?"

Cassandra looked over and smiled. "I'm not being punished," she said. "For me, summer was a pleasant, warm, and leisurely interlude of maybe three, three and a half months. Spring will be here in six days ending a typical winter on J. Point." She closed one of the laptops. "I'm not the one complaining about the weather."

A brief gust of wind caused the old windows to rattle. The rain spat against them like the sand carried by a stiff breeze at the beach.

Joe walked over to the table and sat across from Cassandra. "You're right, it was a great summer."

"And too short," Cassandra said, around a laugh. The two toasted their coffee mugs and Cassandra shifted her eyes to the *NY Times*.

"I think the fact Fox wasn't around is what made the summer both great and too short," Joe said to his coffee mug.

Cassandra looked up. "That's because you were so busy trying to solve her disappearance that you didn't have time to enjoy the calm, peace and tranquility it brought to J. Point and to us."

Joe nodded. "So, God isn't punishing me?"

"I suspect right now She's punishing Doctor Fox," Cassandra said. "I certainly hope so."

* * *

"Connor called yesterday," Joe said, interrupting the silence that had descended for several minutes. "He's been checking the real estate taxes and mortgage payments on Fox's two properties."

"You mean he's been hacking into real estate and mortgage records," Cassandra said.

"Whatever," Joe said with a dismissive wave of his hand. "Connor's been working Fox's disappearance on his own time, and checks in with me every week or so. He told me they've been no payments on her Langdon home or the house next door since she disappeared. No real surprise. We've been convinced from early on that she's dead."

"You think they'll be a foreclosure? Will the towns do anything?"

The towns will put a tax lien on any property within its jurisdiction. I suspect each town will just let the lien sit there. When the properties are sold, they'll get any back taxes, plus interest and penalties at the closing."

"What about the mortgages?" Cassandra said. She glanced at her computer.

"Banks are not as patient as municipalities," Joe said. "Not an area of the law I know a lot about, but I'm sure they don't have to wait until Fox is declared dead. They'll go into court and have some kind of receiver or guardian appointed or other person to protect her interests. She doesn't appear to have had any next of kin. They'll be a foreclosure, bank will get the balance due on the mortgage, plus interest, and what's left will be held in trust for Fox or any heirs that are found." He took a sip of his coffee. "You interested in buying the property?"

"Anything new with the police?' Casandra said.

Joe stared at her and smiled. He knew she'd answer his question, but only after she'd ask all the questions on her mental punch list. "Elaine told me the case was assigned to a new investigator last December. Supposedly, this guy specializes in cold cases involving missing persons. Elaine checked in with him last week and was told there was nothing new on either Fox or Samantha."

"Who's your lawyer friend at the bank that financed Fox's purchase of the Duffy house?"

"Karen Ferrick," Joe said.

"I'm gonna call her," Cassandra said. "I'd like us to consider purchasing the property if it goes to a mortgage foreclosure."

"You serious or playing with me.?" Joe said.

Cassandra shrugged. "Maybe a little of both, but I really don't want another asshole moving in. Remember how great the summer was?"

"I remember it was too short," Joe said.

* * *

The rain the weather forecaster promised last night arrived about eleven o'clock this morning. I was in the office/den of our ranch home in Melrose. Abby was off to a seminar to pick up the educational credits she needed to renew her registration as a nurse. It'd been years since she'd hovered over a body in a hospital bed, administering an IV, or an enema, or checking blood pressure, but the registration was important to her and to her health care consulting business. She had developed an expertise in Medicare and Medicaid reimbursements, which not only put food on our table, but also paid for the table, the refrigerator, the oven and just about everything else in our home. As my friends often reminded me, the smartest thing I ever did in my live was to marry up. Not sure what Abby's friends tell her.

The office/den was a large rectangular room running front to back along the right side of the house. The table ran along the far wall and served as a joint desk for Abby and me. We had our lap tops at either end of the table Since Abby worked from home most days, she controlled a larger portion of the desk. A plaid sectional couch in a corner of the opposite wall provided viewing space for our flat screen TV. A round faux-antique clock hung on the wall over the sectional couch, its black metal hands positioned at twenty-five past five. We changed it from its original position (twenty-five before five) because we sometimes like to have Tanqueray and tonics while working.

Today, I had a steaming coffee mug and a three-ring notebook on the Fox and Cronin cases. Harry Bosch would call it a murder book, but that seemed presumptuous, so I use case book. Calvin ran a paperless office, but I still liked the feel of paper and the ability to use a pencil or pen to jot notes and underline certain paragraphs. I felt the same way about the Sunday newspapers, although I rarely jotted notes or made underlines.

I had gone through the book several times; front to back, back to front, and picking random pages. Each time I ended up feeling we needed more information, but with no idea where to go to get it.

From the beginning, Calvin said he thought Samantha was dead and that Dr. Fox had killed her. But why? Why would Fox be afraid of Samantha or her intention to create a dossier on her teaching methods? Fox knew she was disliked by students and her peers. She knew she was controversial. Christ, she built her career and secured tenure being controversial. Our research disclosed no scandal, or even hints of a scandal. It was hard for us to imagine Samantha was blackmailing or threatening to blackmail Fox.

When Fox went missing, we tried to find some connection between her and Samantha. The only one we found was the easy one. Robert Palfrey.

We spoke with Trevor Chandler, the defense attorney that hired Fox as a defense witness in the case that charged Palfrey with sexual molestation on Samantha, when a minor, along with several other female minors. The jury convicted Palfrey on the charges pertaining to the other minors but could not agree on a verdict on the charges of assault against Samantha Cronin.

Trevor told us he learned of Dr. Fox from colleagues. She was considered the witness to use on impossible cases. He had contacted her through the University of Maine. He told us her fees were reasonable and her testimony could be shaped to create reasonable doubt on almost any case. He described Fox as, "a criminal defense attorney's wet dream." Beyond that, he had little useful information. He told us he had had no contact with either Fox or Samantha since the trial.

Ed McGonagle, our friend at the Massachusetts Homicide Bureau, got us visitor logs and phone records from the Maine Bureau of Prisons. Palfrey remained in protective custody with no record of any visitors or telephone calls. In any case, why would Palfrey want to kill (or get someone to kill) Samantha? She got him a hung jury. But, it's always better to know than not to know.

Of course, the hung jury would have provided Samantha a motive to try to hurt Fox, either financially or physically. If Fox had killed Samantha in self-defense, why wouldn't she have reported it as such? Why dispose of Samantha's body?

And, if Fox killed Samantha who the hell killed Fox? Her only known friend? Sister Alicia? A fucking nun?

McGonagle got us copies of the police reports on both Fox and Samantha. The Fulton Police seized the computers in Fox's office and at her home in Langdon. There was no computer at her J. Point property, but Fulton PD did find the diary/journal Calvin told me he and Joe had found when they searched the house, as part of their "wellness check." The police, as did we, interviewed Samantha's mother and stepfather. Although stated more politely in the police reports than my case book, they reached the same conclusion we did: the mother was a timid, frail, alcoholic and Kevin Hart, the stepfather, was a sleaze-bag of the highest order. Samantha's biological father was somewhere in Alaska, and completely out of Samantha's life. Malcolm had done a deep dive into Kevin Hart's background. He found a lifetime of public assistance, misdemeanors (check bouncing), and failed attempts at a few small business endeavors: a pawn shop, a check cashing business and a laundromat. All were in Lowell, and according to Malcolm, all were money laundering operations for Hector Munoz, a small-time neighborhood hood, and part of South Boston mob boss Paul Cunningham's organization.

We thought that looked like a potential clue, so we decided to learn more about Kevin Hart. One of Calvin's associates, Patrick Murphy Muldoon, had a relationship with Cunningham. Patrick spoke with him about our interest in Samantha's disappearance and any possible connection to the activities of Kevin Hart. A few days later, Cunningham assured "Murph" that Mr. Hart had nothing to do with his step daughter's disappearance and knew even less about it. Murph reminded us that Cunningham had several proven methods to get the truth out of people.

That brought us back to Calvin's original thought – Fox killed Samantha. And it brought me back to my questions: Why, and who the hell killed Fox? And do not tell me it was a fucking nun.

I drained my coffee and closed the book. "We've missed something from the very beginning," I said to the emptiness around me. I got up to get more coffee.

Somebody or something is not who or what we think it is, I thought and walked into the stillness of the kitchen. I walked over to the coffee pot. "Something has to break," I muttered to my cup as it filled with black steaming coffee.

And, about two and a half months later, it did.

31

Chapter 31

Memorial Day was overcast, but with a strong hint of the sun that would soon break through the gray sky. It was warm for late May and the air carried a noticeable touch of humidity. It reminded Joe of a stale, high school locker room without the odors of boys racing through puberty. Today was Census Day on J. Point. Joe loaded the cooler into the back seat of his Subaru Outback. He stretched his back muscles, closed the door to the car and walked back to the house.

"What's the weather like?" Cassandra said? Feel like rain?" She was folding towels on the kitchen table.

"Feels like the sun's about to break through," Joe said. "I'm afraid it's gonna get hot." He sat down and shook his head. "I'll be sweating like a pig in Miami."

Cassandra laughed. "I'll bring an extra towel."

"Car's all packed. I told the Dean I'd get there by eleven-thirty and help him set up." Paul Racine was the oldest living permanent resident on J. Point. As such, he carried the title: Dean of J. Point, and oversaw the census count.

"That'll take you about five minutes. Then the two of you can gossip and have a couple of beers before the rest of us show up at noon," Cassandra said. She patted the last of the folded towels, picked up two and placed them in dark blue canvas beach bag with "Georgetown" printed in white block letters across one side. She tossed a third towel to Joe. "Here you can use this while you're working hard - helping the Dean to set up."

Joe draped the towel around his neck. "You're welcome to join us."

Cassandra smiled. "Thanks, but no thanks. I'll be there by noon. There's plenty of time for beer and gossip. Give the Dean my best."

"Okay, see you then," Joe said. They embraced and Joe turned for the door.

"Remember whatever gossip you get from the Dean," Cassandra said. "His is always the best."

Without turning back, Joe waved his hand in acknowledgment and closed the door.

* * *

At eleven twenty-five Joe was at the end of Perch Lane and took a left onto The Road. He was less than two minutes from the beach, where the census would be held, when his eyes were drawn to what appeared to be the carcass of an animal, perhaps a young deer, up ahead just off the left edge of the dirt road. He brought the car to a stop and got out. The carcass turned out to be a dark woolen blanket draped over something. Joe

CHAPTER 31

approached it cautiously, concerned something might leap out from under the blanket. He reach down and lifted a corner of the blanket.

"Jesus Christ," Joe shouted. He dropped the blanket and hurriedly backed away. "Shit," he shouted and took another look.

The skeletal remains of a head stared back with empty eye sockets and protruding brownish teeth.

***

A Fulton Police Department cruiser arrived less than ten minutes from Joe's call. He stood to the side of the road as the vehicle came to a stop. Joe recognized both uniformed officers and groaned inwardly. Sergeant Peter Romano, a mid-fifties burly and gruff man climbed out behind the driver's seat. Romano had the dull eyes of a mule and the lines in his face suggested a permanent skepticism.

"Okay, Joe," Romano said. "What the fuck you dragging us into now?"

Joe smiled. "Nice seeing you as well, Sergeant." He turned his head to other officer, "Hey, Danny, Howyadoing?"

Danny Cassidy was a tall, slim mid-twenties man with soft skin with bright red hair. "Doing great, Joe. How's everything on J. Point?"

"Can't be good if he's calling us," Romano barked.

"Found some bones," Joe said. He turned and waved his arm. "Over here." He walked over to the blanket and stepped aside, hoping Romano would do the honors.

Sergeant Romano did not disappoint. "Fuckin' bones?" He bent over and gabbed a corner of the blanket and lifted it.

The skeleton head, ugly as it was ten minutes ago, stared back.

"Mother fucker!" Romano shouted. He stumbled backwards, tripped on a small shrub, and landed on his back side in The Road. He scrambled to his feet and looked at Joe. "You Cocksucker! You could've warned me," He dusted off his dark blue trousers. "Prick." He turned to Cassidy and pointed. "You tell *anyone* about this, you'll be buying the coffee for the rest of the fucking year. I mean it."

Danny shook his head slowly the way nuns did when they caught you in a lie. "I won't tell anyone." He walked over to Joe and gave a wink.

"I'll get you a Dunkin' gift card," Joe said.

* * *

The three gathered to take a careful second look. They stood shoulder to shoulder on The Road staring at the pile of bones with the head now pushed on its side by the pull of the blanket.

"You think this might be that Fox woman?" Romano said.

"I didn't look close enough to see if it's a woman." Joe said. "Not sure I want to."

"Right, Romano said. "Cassidy, get the tape. Set up a perimeter thirty feet around the bones."

"It's Census Day," Joe said. "Folks will be driving or walking down The Road..." He glanced at his watch. "For the next ten minutes."

CHAPTER 31

"Fucking census?" Romano shrugged. "Okay, we won't block The Road, but we don't want a bunch of yahoos tramping through the woods to get a peak."

"I'll let the Dean know," Joe said. "We'll keep the yahoos on the beach until you're work is done."

"I'll call the Chief. He'll love this. A fuckin pile of bones on Memorial Day.

Chapter 32

The sun broke through the gray overcast, and brought blue sky, heat, and humidity to J. Point. While the Dean was going through the rituals of Census Day, with his wife keeping the count, two additional cruisers, one with two cadaver dogs, and a black SUV with the white block letters; FBI on the two front doors, arrived. Joe was there to greet the police officers after securing a dispensation from being present and raising his hand in order to be counted. Joe knew next year was an election year and honoring the traditions of J. Point was more important than kissing babies. Well, at least as important.

The dogs, Lewis, and Clark, both black short-haired pointers, were pulling two female officers through scrub pines and a swampy marsh area that appeared each year, after the snow melted and before the warmth of July and August. One officer was photographing the bones from different angles. Cassidy and two other officers, with the detached neutrality of postmen sorting mail, were poking shrubs and clumps of grass with long poles, searching for additional bones or markings.

CHAPTER 32

Romano was in his cruiser staring at his cell phone.

Joe walked over and introduced himself to a sixty-something hulking man with gray hair in a military brush cut. He was wearing a white dress shirt, dark gray tie, knotted tight to his neck. The charcoal gray trousers matched the suit coat draped over the passenger seat of the SUV. "Sir, I'm Joe McDonald, county prosecutor. Hope I didn't ruin your Memorial Day." He extended his hand.

The man paused a full second and grabbed Joe's hand. "Special Agent Jake Horan, FBI. You have any ID?"

"Just my word, and the uniforms here all know me," Joe said. "Why are you here?" He added a smidge of bite into his voice.

Horan sensed it and raised his hands. "I'm sorry, Joe. Sometimes, I'm an asshole." He shook his head. "Part of the training I got at Quantico almost forty years ago. I've purged most of it, but it stills flares up. Let's start over." Horan extended his hand.

Joe laughed and grabbed it. "Works for me."

"Anyway, I was here near J. Point with my family for what I thought would be a long weekend. Got a call from my boss." he said. "There no federal interest, other than we were asked to help with skeletal identification."

"You know by whom?" Joe said.

"We have a high-tech research laboratory in Bangor, with a small contract with the New England Consortium of States. My Boss is a friend of the Consortium's Executive Director. When you called this in to the Fulton Police, someone called someone who called the Consortium. We've helped all the New England States with issues like this over the past ten years or so. You want my bosses name? He probably knows who contacted the Consortium."

Joe waved his hand. "No, I'll be getting briefed on everything eventually. "You work in the laboratory? You're a forensic scientist?"

"No, I'm a retired agent and now one of the Bureau's bureaucrats. I got called because they knew I was in the area. They'll send someone down to collect and bag the bones. I'm here to make certain nobody touches or moves them. I have some experience in this area, but not like the folks at the laboratory."

"Can you tell anything from what you've seen?"

"Pretty sure I saw part of a pelvic bone, so it's a woman," Horan said. "And I'd guess she was small."

"Will they be able to determine an approximate age or cause of death?" Joe said.

"Probably," Horan said. "Once everything gets to the lab, they'll get started quick and you'll know more than me before the end of the week." Horan smiled. "Not that I want to know. Like I said, now I'm a bureaucrat."

"End of the week," Joe said with an approving nod of his head. "We don't get a lot of bodies in this county, but I talk with the other prosecutors. They tell me the state lab is good, but slow."

Horan showed several "I understand" nods of his head. He glanced over to the bones. "Well, we could get an ID through dental records. And the lab gets DNA tests quicker than most."

"That was my next question. Can you get DNA from skeleton bones?

"Yup, they can get a lot from not very much." He looked over to the bones. "And it appears we have more than not very much, including that woolen blanket. That's probably got more DNA on it than a West Texas whorehouse."

CHAPTER 32

***

An hour later a black van with the FBI lettering on the front doors arrived. Two men and a woman came out. The woman walked over to Jake Horan, who was sitting in the black SUV with the air conditioning on full blast. The men, both tall and slim with closely cropped hair, immediately put on pale blue, full-body protective clothing. They put similar material on their shoes and donned goggles and rubber gloves. Danny Cassidy wandered over to Joe holding the long pole he'd used to search for other bones.

"What the fuck, Joe? These guys are dressed like astronauts, and we're walking around like assholes in our uniforms?"

"Well, you're real cops," Joe said. "These guys are feebies." He shrugged. "Not up to me, but I think you guys can cool it for a while and let them pack up the bones."

Cassidy nodded towards Romano in the car. "Yeah, time to follow our leader's lead."

***

A few minutes later, Special Agent Jake Horan approached Joe with the woman a half-step behind. "Joe, say hello to Doctor Dorothy Kincaid, one the forensic pathologists associated with our lab in Bangor."

Dorothy smiled and extended her hand. "Hello, Joe." She was a fiftyish, hard-faced woman, pale from a life under fluorescent lights, on concrete floors cutting up and examining the organs of dead bodies. She wore a blue blazer over a pale pink dress shirt, dark gray trousers, and sensible shoes.

"Nice to meet you, Doctor," Joe said. "Jake speaks highly of the lab and the people who work there. I hope you can help us with our Memorial Day puzzle."

"I'm sure we'll be of some assistance, Dorothy said. "Tell me, what time did you first see the body?"

Joe liked the fact she referred to the pile of bones with the more respectful term "body." He sensed the bones would be in good hands. "About twenty-five before noon, today."

"Do you have any recollection of the last time you traveled or walked in this area before today?"

"Hmm," Joe said. "Probably not since last summer, perhaps Labor Day. Not much reason to come down here unless you're going to the beach, or on a run. I'll give it more thought and hopefully come up with a more accurate time frame."

Dr. Kincaid nodded thoughtfully. "Perhaps you or one of these officers, could ask the same question to the people gathered on the beach. It might give us some help on a time frame as to when the body was placed here."

Christ, Joe thought. *I should've told Romano and Cassidy to do that instead of hanging around gawking at the head.* "Good suggestion. I should've done that earlier. I'll send two officers now."

"Don't beat yourself up, Joe," Kincaid said. She nodded towards Romano. "That was his job. Besides, we're probably not going to get anything useful, and it was a higher priority to secure and protect the body from any disturbance."

"Thank you, but I should've either done it, or asked him to do it." Joe walked over to Romano and Cassidy and made the request suggested by Dr. Kincaid.

CHAPTER 32

Meanwhile, Kincaid and Horan walked over to the officers dressed like astronauts, and watched as bones were photographed and carefully placed in plastic bags. Horan numbered and dated each bag and handed it to Kincaid for her signature. Once signed, each bag was placed in a large temperature controlled thermal bag. They both turned when they sensed Joe's presence nearby.

"Do you have any idea who we might have found?" Kincaid asked. She peered into a bag, and Joe saw a suspicious wrinkle cross her face.

"We had two women go missing last year. One, a young college age woman, hasn't been seen since Friday, March 25th when she disrupted a class held by Dr. Ruth Fox. Dr. Fox, fiftyish hasn't been seen since she had an argument with my wife on Friday, April 8th. Fox has a summer place on J. Point. She's our neighbor and has been anything but neighborly since she bought the place in January 2022. We don't know if they're dead or alive, or even if their disappearances are connected."

"You have a remarkable memory for dates," Special Agent Horan said to Joe. "She had an argument with your wife?" Formality had pushed away the conversational tone.

"I've been working and thinking about the two women, along with some associates, for about fourteen months," Joe said. "Not hard to remember the important details. They must have taught that at Quantico. Right?"

Horan smiled, but his face reddened with anger, or embarrassment.

Kincaid placed the bag she was holding into the large thermal bag. She fished a business card from her pocket. "Could you text or email the information you just told me? I don't have your memory. If I don't write names and dates down, there gone forever. If you can get the date of birth for both woman, that would be helpful, as well."

"I'll do that," Joe said. "Appreciate getting any information as soon as you have it."

"Well, I'll certainly know more once we get the bodies to the lab."

"Bodies?"

"Again, I can't be certain of anything until tests are run. That said, I am quite certain there is part of a pelvic bone in one of these bags, and I'm pretty certain I just signed a bag that contained a second left hand."

Joe eyes shifted to the thermal bag.

"Joe," Dr. Kincaid said. "I suspect we have the partial remains of two people, at least one of whom is a woman."

Chapter 33

"Two women?" Cassandra said when Joe recounted his conversation with Dr. Kincaid.

"Two bodies," Joe said. "At least one of them a woman."

It was close to four in the afternoon. The two were sitting on their porch, Cassandra with a wine cooler, Joe with two bottles of water, trying to hydrate before pulling a Harpoon from the cooler at his feet.

"Can she determine the approximate age of the bones?" Cassandra said. She shook her hands as if to wave away her question. "I mean the age of the person the bones belonged to at the time of death."

Joe drained the first bottle of water and opened the second. "I knew what you meant," he said. "I made the same mistake when I asked that question. Kincaid said it's easier to get a fairly accurate AAD - that's age at death – with an immature skeleton. Once a person is over thirty-five, or so, it becomes a little trickier to distinguish between say the bones of a person in their forties and another in his or her fifties, or even sixties."

"Samantha was what twenty-five?" Cassandra said.

"I think so," Joe said. "I called Elaine and asked her to send me the date of birth for both Samantha and Fox. The FBI Agent, Horan, said they'd get dental records, so that should get us one ID, and they can get DNA from skeletal bones, and the blanket that covered the bones so I think we'll know pretty soon."

"What's your gut telling you?"

Joe took a long pull of water, and wiped his brow with a red and white striped beach towel. "I think it's both of them," he said. "I don't think it's a coincidence to have a pile of bones show up on J. Point and on Census Day. And to have them off The Road, where everyone going to the beach or to the census count will see them. It's too convenient. It's as if the person who dumped them wanted them found."

"So, you're thinking the person who dumped them at least knew about Census Day, and Doctor Fox's connection to the Point. Right?"

Joe drained the second bottle and leaned towards Cassandra. "And if it is both of them, it means either one killer killed both, or the killer knew Fox killed Samantha and killed Fox in revenge."

"But, under the revenge scenario, how'd Fox's killer get Samantha's bones?"

"Hmm, good point," Joe said. "Maybe, Fox hadn't disposed of the body. Maybe she had it hidden, or in a freezer in her house in Langdon."

"We know she was alive on the day I had her car towed," Cassandra said. "And, we know the police searched her home the day you and Calvin went into her house next door. So, she must have buried it somewhere."

"She might have had help disposing of the body," Joe said.

CHAPTER 33

"A couple of weeks pass, and the two of them get into an argument. He or she, kills Fox and takes her body to wherever Samantha is buried or hidden."

"But why dig them up and bring them to the Point?"

"I don't know," Joe said. "Too many questions at the end of what's been a long day. Let's wait until we at least know who the bodies are before we go nuts trying to figure it all out." He reached into the cooler and pulled out a Harpoon. He lifted it towards Cassandra. "Here's to Memorial Day and the start of summer."

Cassandra lifted her glass. "God forgive me, but I hope one of them is Fox." She took a sip of her wine cooler.

Joe plunked off the cap with a church key from his college days. "You're still interested in our buying her house?"

"That reminds me," Cassandra said. "I think that friend of yours at the bank, Karen Ferrick? She's ducking my calls." She took another sip of her cooler. "Besides, if those bones belong to Fox, it's not *her* house, anymore."

***

Abby and I spent most of Memorial Day at a Melrose Block Party, meeting neighbors, eating hot dogs, and drinking cold beer. There were more kids than adults, more dogs than cats, and by six o'clock everyone was getting a little tired of everyone. It was a lot of fun, but the trouble with Monday holidays and parties, is Tuesday and work are always there passing through your conscience like a small dark cloud carrying rain and the reminder the long weekend was over. It's one of the reasons I've always thought the July 4th fireworks should happen the evening of July 3rd.

In any case, by seven o'clock we had carried our cooler, lawn chairs and assorted leftovers and beverages back to our home. Five minutes later, we were settled in our office/den enjoying the "last drink of the weekend" (Tanqueray and tonic) and a play list of *The Eagles, America,* and *Simon and Garfunkel.* That lasted until almost eight o'clock, when the telephone rang and the caller ID read: Joe McDonald.

By eight-thirty, I had briefed Abby, Calvin Washington, and Malcolm Butts on all I had learned from Joe's call. There was really nothing we could do, but wait for more information. But, when Malcolm told me he was taking tomorrow off to recover from the long weekend, and suggested I do the same, I immediately made two more calls. By ten minutes after nine, Calvin, Joe and I agreed we should meet for lunch tomorrow, along with Abby and Cassandra, at some place convenient to exchange ideas and to plan whatever our next steps might be.

"God Bless, Malcolm Butts," I said. "He believes every long weekend needs an extra day to recover."

"Want to go back to the block party?" Abby teased

"No, but I'll make us another 'last drink of the weekend,'" I said.

34

Chapter 34

Abby and Cassandra selected the River House Restaurant on Bow Street in Portsmouth, New Hampshire. Calvin, Joe and I knew it was not up for discussion and quickly agreed. Abby and I arrived twenty minutes earlier than the twelve-thirty reservation to ensure a nice view of the Piscataqua River and the tug boats. Yesterday's heat had dimmed and we elected to enjoy the soft breezes on the outside deck. Joe and Cassandra arrived ten minutes after us. It gave Abby and Cassandra time to catch up. They did not see each other as often as Joe and me.

Calvin showed up at exactly twelve thirty, turning the heads of the five or six other diners. At two hundred and eighty pounds and six-foot six inches tall, he often did that. Today, he was in an untucked Caribbean blue shirt the size of a small tent and Bermuda shorts the color of the inside of a conch. A pair of dark sun glasses were perched on his large head. His teeth gleamed as he approached. He hugged Joe, Abby, and I. Cassandra, whom he never met, received an elaborate bow.

"The arrival of summer," I said after the exchange of hugs

and bow.

Calvin laughed, pulled out a chair and sat. "First of all," he announced in formal tone, "I received a large settlement check in this morning's mail, so lunch is on me."

There was polite applause. Abby shouted, "Well done, Calvin!" Joe turned towards a waitress. "Could we have dinner menus, please."

* * *

By one o'clock, the waitress had taken our *lunch* orders, including a second round of drinks, and Joe's briefing had slowed to a stop. While we already knew most of what he said, hearing it in person rather over the phone is always more dramatic or compelling. Calvin took a few notes on what was either a large phone or a small computer. The rest of us listened intently as Joe repeated with remarkable detail his conversations with Dr Kincaid, Special Agent Jake Horan from the FBI and Romano and Cassidy from the Fulton Police. We learned the cadaver dogs had not discovered any remains, but were back this morning for an expanded search. Joe would receive a report on the search and promised to forward it to us.

"I agree with you if one of the bodies is Fox, it's no coincidence the bones were placed on J. Point," Calvin said. "I don't believe in those kinds of things. Cripes, how many people live on the Point, and the bones of one turn up there? No way."

"So, it was a message to Joe?" I said.

"Or Cassandra," Calvin said. "I don't know anyone else who lives on J. Point."

CHAPTER 34

"There's Roosevelt Wilson," Cassandra said. "Remember him? The guy who pointed a shot gun at you."

"Yeah, but he's a fan of mine," Calvin said. "So, it couldn't be my man, Roosevelt."

Joe suddenly stirred and stood. He pulled his phone from his front trouser pocket. "Hey, it's Dr. Kincaid." He took a quick breath. "Hello, this is Joe McDonald." Palpable silence and tension descended on the table. The waitress came by and placed a tray with our orders on a side table steps away. She sensed the changed atmosphere and seemed to freeze.

Joe turned his back to us and took a few steps away. Abby grabbed my hand under the table. Joe was silent and did not move during what seemed to be about two-minute conversation. Our eyes were fixed on him, even as our waitress placed orders before us. I did notice my Reuben sandwich was, as requested, uncut.

"Thank you, Doctor," Joe said. "I appreciate your promptness on this. If you can, I'd be grateful for a copy of the full report once you've sent it to the Fulton Chief." There was a pause. "Why Elaine Blass?" Another pause and then: "Okay, that's fine, no problem. I'll be checking in with her and the Chief later today." Joe terminated the call and put the phone back in his pocket. He turned back to us and stepped forward, but did not sit.

"Kincaid says both dental records and DNA confirm one of the bodies is Samantha Cronin." Joe waited for the instinctive soft groans and sighs you hear when bad news is pronounced. "She also said DNA collected from the bones, and two or three almost microscopic pieces of clothing on the bones tell her the other body is Dr. Fox. She also found Samantha's and Fox's DNA on the blanket. She preparing a full report. It will take a day or two, but she said the bottom line is Fox and Samantha are both dead."

There short gasps around the table.

"No real surprise," I said. "I mean, we've thought both were dead for over a year. Still, it's always sad, or whatever once you hear it."

"But, there's more," Abby said. "Isn't there?"

"Calvin nodded agreement. "You mentioned Elaine Blass."

Joe sat down. "Kincaid says she got a call from Elaine, saying she wanted a copy of the full report. "And not to send it to anyone else."

"Fuck her," Cassandra said. "This is *your* case. The bodies were found on J. Point. You should get the full report."

"Not that simple," Joe said. "Kincaid found DNA on both the blanket and the bones that didn't belong to either Samantha or Fox."

"Yours?" Cassandra asked, incredulity wrapped around the word.

"Worse," Joe said. "Yours."

Chapter 35

"That's crazy," Cassandra said. "That's gotta be a mistake. Can you call Dr. Kincaid back?"

"Cassandra, there are a lot of ways your DNA could have ended up on that blanket," Calvin said. "You shake hands with X. X then opens a door. Your DNA could end up on a door knob you never touched. DNA establishes identity, but it doesn't establish when or how the DNA got to where it was found."

"Dammit, I never shook hands with Fox, or even touched the jerk," Cassandra said. "This is a mistake. That bitch haunted us in life, and now she's doing it in death." She fumed for several seconds and took a deep breath. She turned to Joe. "Is this why Elaine Blass is taking over the case?"

Joe touched her arm. "Elaine is not taking over anything. I'll talk to her tomorrow. Let's try to enjoy our lunch and maybe figure this out."

"I'm all for lunch," I said. "But you must believe, there's a reason Elaine is getting the report. I think Dr. Kincaid was giving you a heads up. You need to be careful when you speak with Elaine."

"And she needs to be careful if and when she speaks with you," Calvin said. "Right now, there's a question to be answered. And until it is, Elaine may not want to meet with you or give you any information."

Joe shifted and pulled out his cell. The buzz of a text message floated over the table. Joe glanced at his phone. "It's Elaine.," he said. "Her text reads: 'WE NEED TO TALK ASAP AND OTR.'" Joe smiled. "All CAPS. Elaine's a friend, I'm not surprised she reached out."

"OTR?" Abby said.

"Off the record," Joe said. "Like I said, she's a friend."

"OTR could be On the Record," Calvin said. "She's a prosecutor."

"So am I," Joe said. He turned to Cassandra. "Everything will be fine. Let's eat."

"You gonna text her back?" I said.

"Already did," Joe said. I used a thumbs up emoji."

"Do me and yourself a favor, Joe," Calvin said. "Don't mention Kincaid's call, or anything she told you. If she asks if you and Kincaid talked, don't lie, but downplay it. Say something like she told me DNA says the bones are Samantha's and Fox, and the full report was being sent to you, meaning Elaine Blass. Do not tell her you know about Cassandra's DNA."

"I can do that," Joe said. "You and Connor can do something for me."

"Name it," Calvin and I said over each other.

"Find out everything you can about Dorothy Kincaid, a forensic scientist at the FBI lab in Bangor, and FBI Agent Jake Horan. He's retired from field work, but still with the Bureau."

CHAPTER 35

* * *

The next morning, a few minutes before ten, Joe waked into the Wicked Brew Café on Park Street in Bangor. Elaine Blass was at a small table sipping from a large mug with the text: World's Biggest Badass. She waved and Joe walked over.

"Elaine, nice mug. I know you're a badass, but it's not very badass to warn everyone else."

Elaine laughed. "I guess you're right, but it's my favorite mug. A gift from an old boyfriend, she said. "Regulars here bring their own mugs. But they'll give you one. Grab a cup of something and we can catch up."

Joe walked to the counter, received some good-natured ribbing about not having a mug, and ordered a large black house blend. He returned to the table and sat down."

"Have you spoken with Dr. Dorothy Kincaid, since the day you found the bones?" Elaine said. She sipped her coffee.

"So, this is catching up?" Joe smiled to soften the rebuke. "She called me yesterday and told me the DNA says the bones belong to Samantha Cronin and Doctor. Fox," Joe said.

"Anything else?"

"I asked her to send me the full report once it was sent to the Fulton Chief. She told me it was going to be sent to you." Joe took the first careful sip of his coffee. "Obviously, that concerned me, but I didn't say that to Kincaid. I told her that was fine. Before I could call you about it, I got your text about an off the record meeting. And voila."

Elaine nodded and smiled. "Good. Sorry about the questions. Let me tell you what's happening, or what I think is going on. And Joe, this meeting never occurred."

"Elaine, we're friends, but don't make a promise you might not be able to keep. One never knows when one might be under oath."

Elaine leaned back in thought. "Yeah, you're right, but fuck 'em. We'll do everything we can to keep this meeting and what was said a secret."

Joe nodded agreement. "It'll be easier if we agree to say, and only if asked, that I found out you were getting the report and I asked for this meet to find out why, and you – Badass that you are- stonewalled me. I left with even getting coffee."

"Will you tell them Kincaid told you I was getting the report?"

"No, I won't tell them. I want to protect Kincaid." He took a careful sip of his coffee and set the mug down. "To quote my favorite badass: 'Fuck 'em,' By the way who's them?"

"Last night, I got a call from John Gibbons, Chief of the criminal division for the Maine AG."

"I know who he is," Joe said. "His friends call him Gibbey. He has the confidence of the devil. An asshole, but a smart one. They're the most dangerous."

Elaine nodded. "Well, he might soon be my Boss," she said. "He called to say the AG was aware of the bones found on J. Point, and he wants his office to take over the investigation. Gibbons asked if I'd like an appointment as a special assistant attorney general to head it up."

"Did your friend Gibbey say why the AG wants the case? You know the FBI has its nose in this."

"He implied *he* played a role in getting the laboratory involved, but aside from scientific analysis, the FBI wouldn't be involved. As for why the AG wants the case, Gibbons said – and this is *really* off the record – that Cassandra's DNA was

CHAPTER 35

found on the bones. He sees a potential conflict of interest and didn't want any of the county prosecutors involved."

"Except you," Joe said. "Any ideas why he came to you? You know I'm not questioning your experience or abilities, but why not someone in the AG's Office?"

"Well, I'd have to resign the county prosecutor's office, so they'd be no conflict. He did mention that Samantha was part of the prosecution's case against Robert Palfrey, and maybe I'd like to seek justice for her since the jury reached no decision on the charges involving her."

"Hmm, sounds like bullshit," Joe said. "Have you responded to Gibbon's offer?"

"I told him I'd think about it, and I was honored to be considered, and blah, blah, blah. He said he needed an answer before the end of the week."

"Look, Elaine, we're getting into a difficult area here," Joe said. "My advice is if you're interested in getting into the AG's Office, tell Gibbons you want a full appointment as an Assistant AG, not this special assistant bullshit. That kind of appointment ends with the investigation, which if they think Cassandra is involved, isn't going to last long. You'll be looking for a job before the end of summer."

"Huh, I like that approach," Elaine said. "I'll do it." She paused and assumed a cautious tone. "So, you don't mind if I take up the investigation, assuming I get full Assistant AG status?"

"No, I don't Joe said. "You're tough but fair. And you know the difference between a case and a bullshit smear to get publicity for a jerk who's planning a future campaign. If there must be an investigation, I'd rather it be done by a person I trust and who knows how to run a real one." He took a swallow of his coffee. "There's a hundred ways Cassandra's DNA could've found its way to the blanket and the bones."

"I know. I asked Gibbons about that," Elaine said. "He told me, and I quote, 'We have a lot more than DNA.'"

"Bullshit," Joe said. "There's no way Cassandra had anything to do with this. Does Gibbey think she killed Samantha, too? He's trying to sell his proposal to you. If this was a slam dunk case, he'd do it himself."

"You want to know the little that he told me?" Elaine emptied her cup with a last gulp of coffee. She wiped the inside with a napkin and put the mug in a large bag at her feet. The meeting was coming to an end.

"Of course, I would, but it would be a mistake for you to do it," Joe said. "Let's wait until you know whether or not you're going to accept his offer. If he won't make you a full assistant AG, and you decline his offer to become a special assistant, then you can tell me whatever he told you. If you end up heading the investigation, I don't want you in a position where you've compromised yourself. If this goes any further, and Cassandra is ever charged, you'll have to disclose it all to me or her attorney."

"That's kind of you, Joe," Elaine said. "God, I hate this is happening."

"I assume Cassandra will be asked to come in for questioning," Joe said.

Elaine stood and picked up her bag. "I would think so. Unless, Gibbons, or whoever he puts in charge, decides to impanel a special grand jury," she said. "If that happens, Cassandra could get a target letter. I'll be in touch, Joe. Thanks for meeting with me."

CHAPTER 35

* * *

On his way home, Joe punched in Sister Alicia's private number, and in a miracle of sorts, she answered. He gave her the news about Samantha and Fox. It was a short call. She thanked him for keeping her in the loop, and said she would pray for their souls.

Joe terminated the call and thought: *Cripes Sister, pray for mine. I'm the one who has to tell Cassandra she might become a target of a murder investigation.*

36

Chapter 36

"You're shitting me," Cassandra said. "A target letter? Because of some DNA on a blanket?"

"She said Gibbons told her there was some other stuff, but she did say it was more likely you'll be asked to come in for questioning," Joe said. "No target letter."

It was now two o'clock, the sun still high in a cloudless, blue,sky. They were sitting on the porch, sipping ice tea. Cassandra's final grades had been submitted weeks ago, and she was in full summer mode, until the bones and her DNA were discovered. Now, she alternated among anger, fear, and depression.

Joe, concerned he was about to lose some accumulated vacation time, had taken off the week of Memorial Day. The discoveries had put him in full battle mode. "We need to get an attorney," he said. "I want Gibbons to know he's about to stick his dick in a hornet's nest."

CHAPTER 36

* * *

The call from Elaine Blass came on Joe's cell at three o'clock. They were still on the porch. The sun a bit lower and whispers of shadows danced on the wood floor.

"Hi Elaine, any news?" Joe gave Cassandra a hush signal.

"Hi Joe, I called Gibbons and told him I would not resign my county prosecutor's position unless I received a full appointment as Assistant AG. And, I told him I wanted to be in the criminal division," Elaine said. "I figured I might as well ask for everything. Besides, I didn't want an assignment to the mail room, or the Eminent Domain section." She paused.

"Good thinking," Joe said. "What'd he say?"

"Basically, a no," Elaine said. "He said that would take time and then he suggested assuming all went well with the investigation getting an appointment shouldn't be a problem."

"Wow, a definite maybe," Joe said

"Yeah," Elaine said. "Solid as a fart in the wind. I told him the condition wasn't negotiable as far as I was concerned. I thanked him for the offer and consideration and hung up."

"I'm sorry it didn't work out for you," Joe said. "But I think you made the right decision. Gibbey's a blowhard. You're better off where you are."

"You should run for AG," Elaine said. "I mean it. The way you handled this morning's coffee was gracious and very kind." She laughed, "I'd work for you in a heartbeat."

"And I for you," Joe said. "But I'm not running,"

"Never say never, Joe," Elaine said.

"Which is why I don't say never," Joe said. "Is this when you tell me what Gibbons said he had other than the DNA?"

"Maybe I should wait another twenty-four hours in case he comes back with a solid offer," Elaine said. "Okay?"

"Absolutely," Joe said. "I should've thought of that. Make it forty-eight. That'd be safer for you." In the corner of his eye, Joe saw Cassandra's shoulders slump. He flashed her a thumbs up and a wink.

"Thanks, Joe, you're the best. I'll call you as soon as I hear, or in a coupla days, whichever comes first."

Joe terminated the call and looked at Cassandra. "We'll hear in a few days," he said. "No way, is Gibbons going to get Elaine an appointment as Assistant AG."

"Why so sure?"

"Because Gibbons is smart enough to know if he goes to the AG for permission to offer Elaine a full appointment, he'll be asked how come the people *you* hired for the criminal division aren't good enough to handle this case?" Joe smiled. "As soon as Elaine told me she was only offered an appointment as a Special Assistant, I figured Gibbons didn't want that question being asked."

Cassandra nodded understanding. "So, knowing that, you suggested Elaine ask for the appointment you knew she wouldn't get."

Joe held up his hands. "Well, I didn't know for sure, and it was also for Elaine's benefit. I wanted to be sure she knew what was being offered and the stakes involved."

"You even told Elaine you'd rather have her head up any investigation because she was fair."

"Of course," I did. "But, c'mon nobody wants the smartest or toughest person heading up an investigation even if she is fair. If there is to be an investigation, I want a dumb klutz heading it."

CHAPTER 36

"And, of course that's also why you played nice and didn't ask her for whatever Gibbons told her he had on me, besides the DNA."

"Yeah, but we'll get that information if there's an investigation. And, it there isn't we don't need it. What we needed was for Elaine to think I was only interested in being fair to a friend."

"Is she a friend?" Cassandra said.

"Yeah, she is, and she still is, but I was also interested in protecting or helping my wife, and I was able to do both." Joe picked up his cell phone from the table. "Let's get back to the business of a lawyer. How you feel about Calvin Washington?"

* * *

Calvin called me on my cell at ten after five. I was at my office on State Street, getting ready to leave. I stuffed the last of Malcolm's report of Dr. Kincaid and FBI agent Jake Horan into my brief case and grabbed the cell. "Calvin, howareya," I said.

"Joe McDonald called me about an hour and half ago. He wants me to represent Cassandra. He thinks the AG is targeting Cassandra because of the DNA on the bones."

"That's crazy," I said. "It's way too early to start focusing on a person. Does he think she killed Samantha too? Is this some kind of grudge against Joe?"

"All good questions, but I called to ask you one, and I'll need an answer pretty quick."

"Shoot," I said.

"I want to hire you, part-time. I'll need you to work on this both as an investigator and paralegal."

"Happy to help," I said. "I don't think it'll be a problem with Malcolm. Put me down for two bucks an hour, or whatever you need to make certain the attorney-client privilege covers me."

"I was hoping you'd take a buck an hour," Calvin said, good-naturedly.

"Well, I have to split it with Abby."

"Seriously, Connor I appreciate this. I have another call scheduled with Cassandra tonight. They're expecting some news on this in the next day or so. I'll get back to you to set up strategy and a work plan. Let me know if this s a problem for Malcolm."

"It won't be, unless he learns I'm doing it for two bucks an hour."

Calvin's laugh came through the line as if he were in the next room.

"Calvin," I said. I have one question. If I had said no, or I couldn't do this, did you have anyone else in mind?"

"Abby," he said. "In fact, she was my first call, but my call went to voice mail."

I heard his laugh a millisecond before he terminated the call.

Chapter 37

A cloudless blue sky and a soft breeze across Queen Lake, gave the morning of the first day of June the feel of summer and the hint of the warm days and bright sun that were to come. At eight-thirty, Joe, showered, dressed and ready for work, was surprised to find Cassandra in her bright, Kelly-green robe sitting at the kitchen table. Both her computers were open, her coffee cup filled, and there was a second full, steaming, cup on the ready for Joe.

"Hi, thought you were sleeping in today." He sat across from her at the table and picked up his coffee cup. This is a pleasant surprise."

"You, or at least your name, is in the *Harley-Fulton Monitor* this morning," she said in a voice laced with fatigue and uncertainty.

Joe picked up on it. "What's wrong? I thought we both agreed last night, we have nothing to worry about."

"Yet, we got a lawyer."

"Yeah," Joe sad. "But that's because we're not going

to let Gibbons, or whomever he puts in charge, poison the atmosphere against us." He took a careful sip. "Is someone taking shots at us in the *Monitor*?"

Cassandra gave a weak smile. "No. It's just about the bones, the FBI and the fact the AG is taking over the investigation." She slid her computer over to Joe.

Human remains found on Jeffords Point

FBI Agent Jake Horan said partial human remains were found on Jefford Point Monday, May 29, about Noon. Caleb County Prosecutor Joseph McDonald discovered the bones near The Road on his way to J. Point's annual census count. According to Horan, the skeletal remains were examined by the FBI Laboratory in Bangor and determined to be of Samantha Cronin, 25, of Bangor, and Alice Ruth Fox, 56, of Langdon, Maine.

Cronin, was last seen on March 25 2022, at a class taught by Fox at the University of Southern Maine in Portland. According to Horan, "Cronin disrupted the class," and seemed to have had issues with Dr. Fox, a tenured faculty member of the Psychology Department.

Fox, was last seen on or about April 8th of last year at J. Point, where she owns a summer home. "Dr. Fox was a friend and a valued member of our faculty. She will be missed," said Harlan Perkins, Chair of the Psychology Department.

State Police returned to J. Point Tuesday morning to resume the search. However, no additional remains or related items were located. Assistant Attorney General John Gibbons said his office would be undertaking an investigation."

"Christ," Joe laughed, "Harlan Perkins told Calvin and me that Fox was like a sharp stone in his shoe. Now that the stone's been removed, she's is a friend and valued member of his department." He took a sip of coffee, and slid the computer back to Cassandra. "Horan didn't waste any time getting the word out, He gave us a break by not mentioning the argument between you and Fox."

"Yeah, remind me again why you told him about that," Cassandra said.

"For the same reason we told the police when she first went missing. Because Horan or the person in charge, was going to find out about it. Then, they'd be asking me how come I never mentioned it. You know this, Cassandra."

I know," she said. She played with her coffee cup.

"You're probably the last person who saw her alive. You're going to get questioned. So, I wasn't going to lie or hide the argument. If it's no big deal, never hide it. That's what *will* make it a big deal. Plus, you were in the right, and Andy will support you on that."

"I know, I know," Cassandra said. "I'm pissed at myself that I let that bitch get under my skin. And, it scares me that Gibbons is already announcing he's taking over the case. By tomorrow, my name will be in the *Portland Press Herald* and the *Bangor Daily News*."

Joe nodded. "Yeah, eventually it will," he said. He reached across the table and touched her arm. "Cassandra, you and I both know you didn't kill Fox. Gibbons, or anyone he hires, will discover that, or at a minimum, will see the state can't meet its burden of proof. We'll both be named and questioned. And we'll both get through this. Together."

He pulled his hand back and glanced at his watch. "I've got to get to the office. Are you okay?"

Cassandra nodded and smiled. "I am. Thanks."

"Good, I need you sharp and ready," Joe said. "We've got some asses to kick."

Cassandra laughed.

Joe approached the door and his peripheral vision caught a bright blue van with yellow Channel 3 lettering across its side, coming onto his property. He stared at the closed door for a second or two. He turned to Cassandra. "The media is here; you might want to change. I'll go outside and delay things. Remember, we do not dodge or lie to them."

Cassandra stood and removed her robe. She was wearing a dark blue business suit, white blouse, and sensible shoes. "Way ahead of you," she said. "Invite them onto the porch. I'll make more coffee. Let's kick some ass."

* * *

Joe stood at the top of his back stairs as a reporter and camera man exited the van. He knew the reporter, Wendy Grisham, a fleshy, dark-haired woman with intelligent eyes and a smoldering resentful aggression that intimidated most. She was the station's top street reporter, and today she was wearing a square-shouldered, khaki-colored business suit that made her look like a tomboy or an archaeologist.

"Take your time, Wendy, I'm not going anywhere.

CHAPTER 37

The cameraman smiled. He was a tall, thin, dry-faced, fortyish guy in faded jeans, plaid shirt with a brush mustache and nicotine-stained fingers.

"You mean, we're not getting a shot of you running away or rushing back into the house?" He said.

"Joe's too smart for that," Wendy said. "Howyadoing?"

"Fine," Joe said. "We were expecting you. If you'd like, you can set up on our porch. Get out of the sun and have some coffee." He gestured to the porch, with its outside entrance a few feet away.

"Works for me," the cameraman said. "I'm Marvin." He looked to Grisham for agreement.

"Porch is fine," she said. "Let's go. I'd like to talk with Cassandra, as well."

"She'll meet us on the porch," Joe said. He glanced at Marvin. "You won't get her hiding or running away, either."

"Going to be a boring piece," he said, with a smile. "Hope the coffee's good."

* * *

Chapter 38

Ten minutes later, they were settled on the porch. Randy White, a twenty-something reporter from the *Portland Press Herald,* who looked like a model for J. Crew, had arrived and was invited to join them. Cassandra brought out a tray with hot coffee, cups and several bottles of ice water.

"I'd have made coffee cake or bought donuts, but that seems too close to sucking up," Cassandra said. She looked to Grisham. "How'd you like to start?"

"Get me a donut from the Holy Donut," Marvin said, "and I'll take the film out of the camera."

Cassandra smiled, but saw a shadow of annoyance cross Grisham's face.

"Joe, suppose you tell us, how you came to find the bones, who was there, what you did, etcetera," Grisham said. "That'll get us started and we can go from there." She looked over the reporter. "Okay?"

"That's fine," Randy said.

CHAPTER 38

* * *

After ten minutes of Joe telling how he found the bones, and everything after, and softball questions, Grisham stood and stepped a little closer to Cassandra. "How do you explain your DNA being on the bones discovered by your husband?"

Joe resisted the impulse to step in. He suspected Grisham wanted him to attempt an answer, so she could shut him down with a practiced authoritative remark, and create footage for tonight's news. All the previous questions had been easy and directed to him. She hoped to catch Cassandra off guard with the sudden turn on her. Joe remained silent and turned towards Cassandra.

"Dr. Fox has been in our home. She was a neighbor. Her DNA could be on articles in this porch, in my house or on my person, just as mine could be in her house. In fact, Ms. Grisham, yours could now be on that chair. It's certainly on the coffee cup."

"Even after the almost two years she's been missing?" Grisham said, refusing to take the bait.

"I don't see why not," Cassandra said. "My house has been cleaned, of course, but her DNA could be someplace. And, her house has been vacant all this time. The point is DNA is transferable, and while it can give the identity of a person, it cannot tell when or how it got to where it was found."

The young reporter cut in, "Ms. Harvey, have you been questioned by the police since the discovery of the bones?"

"No, but I expect to."

"Why's that?" White said.

"I may have been the last person to see her alive. I was questioned when she first disappeared for the same reason."

"Did you tell the police about the argument you had with Dr. Fox, when you were questioned back then?" Grisham said. "The one where you threatened to burn down her house with her inside."

"Of course," Cassandra said. "And I told them what it was about, what I said, and what I thought of Dr. Fox." She smiled. "The fact you know exactly what I said, means you've spoken with the police. So, you knew the answer to your question. Did you ask it hoping to catch me in a lie?"

"What did you think of her?" White asked, filling the pause following Cassandra's question to Grisham.

"She was not a good neighbor. She continually blocked access to our home by parking her car on the right of way, which she considered her driveway. She did it repeatedly." Cassandra pointed to Roosevelt Wilson's house. "Dr. Fox came to our home one night, claiming our neighbor, Roosevelt Wilson, whom she referred to using the N. word, had slashed her tires. When Joe took her out to see the car the next morning, it was partially blocking the driveway, but the tires were fine."

"Why the next morning?" Grisham said.

Cassandra paused and grimaced, as if to show her reluctance to speak ill of the dead. "Because Fox arrived at our home drunk. After making the allegation, she passed out at our kitchen table. Joe carried her into our bedroom and she spent the night there. My memory is she said her home didn't have electricity."

"So, you didn't think much of her," White said.

"I tried not to think of her at all, Cassandra said.

"And when you did?" White pressed.

"Have you ever had a stone in your shoe?" Cassandra said to White. "Not the worst discomfort or pain in the world, but

CHAPTER 38

still a nagging nuisance. Dr. Fox was a small, sharp stone in my shoe."

Marvin, the camera man, covered his mouth with his right arm to muffle a laugh.

* * *

The give and take went on for a few more minutes. Grisham decided to try another subject. "Joe, why'd you suppose the Attorney General has decided to take over the investigation?"

"That's a question you need to ask him," Joe said. "But I'll tell you what I think, for what's it's worth."

"Go ahead," Grisham said.

"Samantha Cronin last known address was Bangor, Dr. Fox's principal home was in Langdon, and the bones were found on J. Point, where she had a second home. That's three different counties, so from that standpoint it makes sense for the AG to either take over the investigation, or designate a lead county prosecutor. Additionally, since I assume he knows Cassandra's DNA was discovered on the bones, and the fact Fox was a neighbor, made it a bit easier to come down in favor of taking over the case."

"So, you don't think it was because your wife is a suspect?" Grisham pushed.

Joe smiled. "There are no suspects this early in an investigation. Any experienced prosecutor or police officer will tell you that. Cassandra is not a suspect, even though, as she's already said, she expects to be questioned, as do I. And we will both cooperate fully in any investigation."

Grisham decided to give up. She had enough for a story, but no headline. "Okay," she said. "Thank you for your time." She looked over to White. "Anything?"

White shook his head and flipped his reporter's notebook closed.

"I have something I'd like to add," Joe said.

"Go ahead," Grisham said, her interest suddenly piqued.

"The bones I discovered belonged to two women, and we've only talked about one. I never met Samantha Cronin, but I have learned a lot about her. She was a twenty-five-year-old woman, who had a difficult life. The last person to see her alive was Dr. Fox. Samantha interrupted a class she was teaching on March 25 of last year. Dr. Fox asked her to leave, which she did. Then Fox left the class, telling her students she wanted to be sure Samantha left the building. To the best of my knowledge, no one ever saw Samantha again, except of course, her killer. She vanished. Her car remained in the college parking lot. Her credit card and phone were never used again. What happened to Samantha?" Joe paused for effect, knowing no one would answer.

"A case could be made, using conjecture and questions similar to what we've heard today, that Dr. Fox killed Samantha." Joe paused again and watched White's hurried scribbling in his notebook.

"We know Samantha didn't drive her car out of the lot, didn't use her credit card or phone after she left the classroom, and we know Fox went after her. Does this prove Fox killed Samantha? Of course not. But if people want to make a big deal about Cassandra being the last person to see Fox alive and having an argument with her, they're free to do so. But what about Fox being the last person to see Samantha alive and

CHAPTER 38

they too had an argument of sorts. Samantha disrupted her class. Fox testified for the defense in a trial of a man alleged to have abused Samantha when he was her coach. It ended as a hung jury, although he was convicted of abusing others. Samantha believed Fox was responsible for the hung jury on her complaint."

"You think Samantha had a motive to murder Fox?" White said.

"I'm saying that's why Samantha disrupted her class. I don't think she killed Fox, but if she did, why'd she leave her car in the college parking lot?" Joe paused again knowing his question would not be answered.

"I'm saying this is a complicated case. The bones of two women, who had some history with each other, show up in a pile on J. Point. How the hell did this happen? Did Fox kill Samantha, and someone killed Fox in revenge? Did one person kill both? If so, why? Is this a serial killer? These are the questions that need to be answered. And, as we've said, Casandra and I plan to cooperate with any investigation established to get the answers to all these questions."

"Do you think Fox killed Samantha Cronin?" Grisham said.

"I don't know who killed Fox, and I don't know, for certain, who killed Samantha," Joe said, certain his qualifier would be picked up by the reporters. "Thanks for coming out here to give us an opportunity to answer your questions and make a statement. I need to get going, unless, of course, you have more questions for Cassandra or me."

The collapsing of Marvin's camera tripod answered Joe's question.

Chapter 39

"So, how'd you think it went?" Casandra said to Joe. They were in the kitchen, cleaning cups and emptying half-filled water bottles.

"About the way I expected," Joe said. "You were brilliant, and I was even better."

Cassandra laughed. "Seriously, what do you think will be on the news tonight?" She sat down. A signal she wanted to talk; not just chat as part of a clean-up routine.

Joe sat. "I was being serious. I think we gave them enough to make this a bigger story than your DNA being on the bones. Wendy Grisham is good. She'll now want to focus on both Fox and Samantha, talk with Roosevelt, maybe Fox's students. You made her a racist; she'll definitely follow up on that. Her students could be fertile ground for throwing mud at the good Doctor."

"That explains your speech at the end, which I thought was brilliant."

"We'll see whether it was brilliant or not. But I thought it was time we bring Samantha into the story and make it bigger than your DNA. The fact is this is a bizarre case, and Wendy will see that. I don't know about the kid from the *Portland Press Herald*, but if he took good notes, his editor will know it's a story and deserves a serious investigation."

"Seems counter intuitive, to want a serious investigation," Cassandra said. "I mean, I'm the one who has DNA on the bones. I'm the one under the microscope."

"Cassandra, this morning, we took you out from under the microscope and put Samantha and Fox in your place. Nobody, except Connor and Abby, Calvin and us, seemed to care when the two of them went missing. Now that they're dead, there has to be an investigation. We want it to include everyone and everything, not just to go after you and me. We wanted a klutz to head the investigation when it was just centered on you. Now that the whole picture is coming into focus, we want a serious investigation," Joe said. "And that will get us the truth. Well, the investigation, plus us, Connor, Calvin, and Abby." Joe waited for a smile, but it never came.

"I hope you're right," Cassandra said. She stood and went back to cleaning coffee cups.

* * *

Elaine Blass's call came at three o'clock. Joe was in his office reviewing police reports. Increasing citations for minor offenses - public drinking, fishing without a license, and loud parties - arrived as they always did on the weekend of Memorial Day. The black flies would soon settle in for two or three weeks, chasing everyone, including the fishermen, indoors. There would be an uptick in loud parties and an occasional disturbance at one of the local pubs.

"Hey Elaine, what's up?"

"Well, I'm still working for the county prosecutor, not the Attorney General," Elaine said. "Gibbons didn't even counter-offer."

"Sorry it didn't work out for you, but you won't regret insisting on a full appointment as an assistant AG, before leaving the county prosecutor's office."

"You're right about that, Joe. Anyway, I called to tell you two things. First, about what Gibbons said he had beyond DNA. The second is something I heard from a source who should know."

"Gimme a second," Joe said. He grabbed a pen and some loose papers from the top drawer of the rolltop. "Shoot."

"Gibbons said Fox had a diary in which she said she felt threatened by Cassandra, and he said they had some nasty emails supposedly sent by Cassandra to Fox. Pretty vague, but that's all he told me."

No surprise about the diary, Joe thought. *Glad Calvin took pictures of it.* "Did he say these emails came from Cassandra's computer?'

"No," Elaine said. "I thought about asking him that, but decided it would be inappropriate unless and until I was assigned to the investigation."

"That was the right decision," Joe said. "Well, last time I looked, Cassandra still had her computers. If Gibbons had these emails, he'd have gotten a warrant to seize them. If they do exist, they must have come from another source."

"I think it's bullshit," Elaine said. "He was trying to build up his case to get me interested in jumping aboard."

"I suspect you're right. What was the other thing you called about?" Joe said.

"Right. You'll never guess who Gibbons recruited to head up the investigation."

Joe laughed. "You're right, I won't guess. You'll just tell me."

"Trevor Chandler," Elaine said. "He represented Palfrey in the case involving Samantha and several others."

"I know who he is," Joe said. "He used Dr. Fox in that case."

"Curious choice."

"He had a reason for picking Chandler," Joe said. "I don't believe in coincidences."

* * *

Joe called me at a quarter after three. I was in Malcolm's office enjoying the view, which had a sliver of Faneuil Hall, and part of a cobblestone walkway with the shadows of a large unseen elm, its branches dancing with the breeze. "Hey Joe," I said. "Howareya?"

"Two bucks an hour?" He said. "What kind of attention will Cassandra get at that rate?"

"The same Abby got from you when I was in the shits, back in the day," I said.

"I did that for zero," Joe said.

"Well, I had to account for inflation and travel to Maine," I said. "I emailed you Malcolm's report on Doctor Kincaid and Jake Horan. You've time to read it?"

"Part of my agenda for tonight. Any surprises?"

"Kincaid's single, lives alone in Bangor, has good credit, lives within her means. No complaints or malpractice suits. Graduated from Johns Hopkins Medical School, and the University of Vermont. Malcolm thinks she worked briefly with the CIA, before going to Quantico and the FBI."

"Thinks?' Joe said.

"Sometimes, when Malcolm hits certain security blocks or can't account for a person's whereabouts or activities for a period of time, he thinks prison, deep cover, or CIA. Prison is easy to crack, so he thinks CIA."

"A guess?"

"Educated guess," I said. "In any case, she left Quantico, and took over the FBI lab in Bangor six years ago. No complaints, controversies, scandals."

"What about Horan? Any issues there?"

"He spent most of his undistinguished career pushing papers in the Atlantic office. Malcolm found internal complaints. Five or six, I think, nothing serious, mostly taking shortcuts, not following procedures and protocols. His finances are in order. Surprising, since he's been married and divorced twice. He requested and received a transfer to the Portland office. He's been there four years. The rest is in the reports I sent. My mind starts to empty after three o'clock." I was more interested in hearing anything new on his end.

So, I asked

40

Chapter 40

It took only a few minutes for Joe to tell me about he and Cassandra meeting the press at their door, and the statements and answers each gave. At first, I wasn't sure if Joe had done the right thing by expanding the story this early. But then I remembered his brilliant work with the media eight or nine years ago, when I ran off on a Halloween night. I wanted to avoid the shame of an indictment, I was certain was coming, for misusing campaign funds for personal expenses like mortgage payments, and my son's college tuition. For almost two weeks I crisscrossed the country trying to find the courage to kill myself. My family and friends searched for me by tracking credit card purchases for gas, and Joe handled press relations. He did a masterful job. The district attorney agreed to hold off on any indictments until I returned. Instead of becoming the subject of an arrest warrant, a police search and coming home in handcuffs, I got the time to come to my senses, and come home with Abby and two friends. We arranged a small press conference outside my house, where I admitted all wrongdoing, and announced I would resign from the House of Representatives. The indictments did come, as well as a year in jail, and disbarment from the practice of law, but I never got the pillaring in the local or state media markets I thought I deserved. And now, I'm back in Melrose. Like the hat says: Life is good.

Joe's news that Trevor Chandler would handle the investigation did prompt a response.

"Chandler doesn't know how to handle a grand jury or a criminal investigation," I said. "Gibbons must have wanted someone he could control, without them knowing he was doing it."

"Exactly," Joe said. "But it took me about twenty minutes to reach the same conclusion."

"Why doesn't Gibbons just handle it himself?" I said.

"Because he doesn't know how to try a case, cross-examine witnesses, make friends with the jury. Chandler's may be an asshole, but he knows his way around a court room."

I laughed and said, "I don't know the guy, but I trust your judgment."

"I think," Joe said, "when Elaine pushed back on Gibbons; said she wanted a full appointment as an assistant attorney general, he realized he wouldn't be able to control her. So, he moved to Chandler."

"Makes sense," I said. "Gibbons will control the grand jury investigation, and Chandler will handle the trial of any indictments. Gibbons will hold the press conferences to take credit for any indictments, or successful prosecutions. Then, he'll leave Chandler out to dry if any prosecution ends without a guilty verdict."

"And, I'm sure he used that argument when his Boss, the

CHAPTER 40

AG asked him what the hell he was doing," Joe said.

"Except during that conversation, Gibbons told the AG he'd be getting the credit and giving the press conferences," I said. We laughed and I said, "You ever have issues with Gibbons or Trevor?"

I don't think so," Joe said. "There's a bureaucratic rivalry between county prosecutors and the AG, and Gibbons has that attitude and smugness that I hate. But, aside from some bar association meetings or events, I don't think we've ever been in the same room together."

"And Cassandra?" I said.

"I'll ask her. But right now, I need to make a quick call. And get home. Channel 3 comes on at five."

* * *

A dot appeared in the middle of a pale blue background on the television screen. It suddenly burst and became a spinning yellow number three, as dramatic music signaled the beginning of the five o'clock news. The three dissolved to an acrylic desk with a man and a woman, both impeccably dressed, with serious faces, and impossible hair. Behind them, a photo of the Maine Coast provided a new back drop for the spinning three to reappear, slow down and stop, as if a signal for the two news anchors to move and speak. It also signaled Joe's arrival through the back door and onto the couch with Cassandra.

"Perfect timing," he said.

"Shh," Cassandra said.

"Good evening, I'm Amanda Brine and this is Channel Three News at Five."

"And I'm Brad Stevens. Tonight, we start with a story of human bones found on Jefford Point, in Fulton, Maine. We have a team of reporters on this. We start with Wendy Grisham on Jefford Point. Wendy, what do we know?"

Wendy appeared on The Road, close to where Joe found the bones. "Brad, Amanda, I'm standing close to where the partial remains of two Maine women, identified by an FBI spokesperson as Samantha Cronin, a twenty-five-year-old from Bangor and Professor Alice Ruth Fox of Langdon. Fox was fifty-six and a faculty member at the University of Southern Maine."

"It's Doctor Fox," Joe barked at the TV.

"Shh," Cassandra said, adding an elbow to his side for emphasis.

"The bones were discovered around noon by Caleb County Prosecutor Joseph McDonald, a neighbor to Fox, who had a summer home on J. Point. I spoke with McDonald this morning."

The screen filled with footage of Joe explaining when and where he found the bones, which added nothing new to the story. The camera cut to the anchor desk and Brad Stevens.

"Incredible, the bones were found by her neighbor, who happens to be a county prosecutor," he said with practiced skepticism. Wendy Grisham returned to the screen.

"This case is filled with twists and turns," she said. "The DNA of Cassandra Harvey, a law professor at the University of Maine Law School and the wife of Joe McDonald, was found on the bones. I also spoke with her this morning."

Cassandra appeared on the screen.

CHAPTER 40

"Ugh," she said to Joe. "Doesn't even look like me."

"Shh," Joe said and gently poked her shoulder.

"Doctor Fox has been in our home. She was a neighbor. Her DNA could be on articles in this porch, in my house or my person, just as mine could be in her house. The point is DNA is transferable, and while it can give the identity of a person, it cannot tell when or how it got to where it was found."

Wendy Grisham reappeared. "Ms. Harvey also confirmed she and Fox had argued the last time Fox appeared on J. Point. In another twist, Samantha Cronin was last seen in a class taught by Fox, and the two of them also had some kind of dispute. Fox chased Samantha out of her class. That was the last time anyone has seen Samantha." Wendy flashed a suspicious and troubled look. "This is Wendy Grisham, Channel Three News."

"Thank you for that, Wendy," Amanda said. "Let's bring in Nikki Tamara, who spoke with two of Professor's Fox's students, who were there the day Samantha Cronin was last seen."

The camera pulled back to show a third person, a thin African-American women in a yellow blazer with a pleasant smile and round eyeglasses perched on a nose so small you had to look for it.

"What can you tell us, Nikki," Brad said.

"I spoke with Eugene Phillips, and Emily Harkins. two of Dr. Fox's students. Both described Fox as a demanding and controversial teacher. She had strong opinions on psychiatry and on controversial issues such as sexual genders for the non-binary and the LBGTQ community. Fox made no secret of her belief government was adopting policies to accommodate people, claiming entitlements based on gender differences that had no basis in science. It caused a lot of tension in her classes."

"What about the incident involving Samantha?' Amanda said.

"Phillips and Harkins told me Samantha interrupted Fox's class and shouted Fox should tell them about Robert Palfrey. Fox asked Samantha to leave, which she did, and Fox went after her. She told the class she wanted to make sure Samantha left the building."

"What do we know about this Robert Palfrey person?" Brad said.

"Well, here is where the story takes two more twists," Nikki said. In January of last year, Palfrey was tried on thirteen charges of sexual assault of minors and one charge of statutory rape. The allegations all stemmed from his former high school volleyball players and a gymnast, who was Samantha Cronin."

"Really," said Amanda with a shocked shake of her head.

The rehearsed interruption did not surprise Nikki, who went on as if it never happened.

"Samantha and the other victims were allowed to testify after psychologists said the memories of the victims had been repressed. They had come to light at varying times as each victim graduated from different colleges and had begun began careers in business, teaching, and, in one case, as a Catholic nun working in an orphanage in New York."

"Incredible," Brad said, his limited vocabulary now stretched to its limit.

"Dr. Fox testified for Palfrey and refuted the reliability and science of repressed memory. Basically, Fox said the testimony of the victims was manufactured by their psychologists. At one point during her testimony, Samantha jumped up and called her an "effing bitch.'"

In another rehearsed interruption, Brad said. "How'd the jury decide?"

Nikki nodded a silent "good question; glad you asked" and said. "Palfrey was convicted on all charges except those related to Samantha. Sources, told me some jurors took exception to her outburst, and so they remained undecided on those charges. Palfrey's in prison on the other charges."

"I understand, there's another twist to this story, which we have exclusively on Channel 3," Amanda added with enthusiasm.

"There is, Amanda," Nikki said. "A source disclosed to me that Trevor Chandler, the attorney who defended Robert Palfrey on those sexual charges, is expected to be asked by the Attorney General to head up the investigation of this case."

Brad stared at the camera. "Thank you, Nikki. Channel Three has reached out to both the Attorney General, and Attorney Trevor Chandler, for comment, but neither has responded. More on this story at the six o'clock edition of Channel Three News."

Suddenly, the smiling face of a man wearing a plaid shirt, jeans and suspenders selling gutter replacements filled the screen.

* * *

Cassandra and Joe sat quietly on the couch each staring at the television and waiting for the other to speak. After a minute or so, Joe took the lead.

"I think it was a good piece," he said. "They explained away the DNA with your remarks, with no follow up or contradiction to anything you said."

"Everything I said was true."

"Exactly, and that's why it needed to be said," Joe said. "And we got even more than we could hope for with the two students."

"I was surprised they knew about Trevor Chandler," Cassandra said. "Did you ask Elaine to leak that to Channel Three?'

"No," Joe said, adding several syllables for emphasis. "I'd never ask her to do that." He stood and stretched. "I called Nikki myself. I think maybe we've boxed Gibbons into not appointing him. Not sure we want that guy running anything."

"Gibbons and the AG will think Elaine leaked it," Cassandra said.

"No, because they don't know Elaine knows. Elaine told me said she got it from a source, who I suspect is someone close to Chandler. In any case, the AG will think Trevor leaked it himself. That's the beauty of it all." Joe smiled. "This has been a good day. Can I take you out for dinner?"

* * *

While Joe and Cassandra watched the Channel Three News, another pair of eyes watched from the Office of the Maine Attorney General in Augusta, about seventy miles away.

Harold Q. Robinson, the Attorney General turned to John Gibbons, his Chief of the Criminal Division. "You still think Trevor Chandler is a good idea? That sonofabitch shot his mouth off and somebody leaked it to Channel Three. He can't be trusted."

"We haven't announced anything," Gibbons said. "I only discussed the possibility with Chandler, to see if he would accept it, if asked. We can embarrass him and Channel 3 by picking someone else."

Robinson smiled. "Yeah, that has a nice feel to it. Kill two assholes with one stone. So, who you thinking about?"

"You're looking at him," Gibbons said. "Let's keep this in house."

"Then, let's have a press conference," Robinson said. "Tomorrow. Embarrass those pricks at Channel Three."

* * *

Chapter 41

At ten o'clock, the morning of the second day in June, I pulled into the wide driveway of Calvin's white two-family Victorian home on Marine Street in South Boston. He bought the place with his signing bonus with the New England Patriots. He lived on the second floor and had his law office on the first. It was a nice set up, and off-street parking in Southie made it Nirvana.

I got out of my car with one of those coffee-take-out-trays they give you at Dunkin' and walked up the front stairs to a large porch with thick, immaculate, white colonial pillars running up to an oak stained ceiling. A small white sign with black lettering next to the door to my right read: Calvin Washington, Attorney at Law & Discreet Investigations. I pulled the door open and walked into a reception area with vintage oak courthouse chairs with red leather inserts on oriental rugs and walls dotted with award plaques and game pictures of Calvin playing for the PATS. Hanging over a fireplace, was a framed picture of Calvin and Tom Brady, in their Patriot uniforms, holding a Super Bowl Trophy.

CHAPTER 41

"In here," Calvin yelled from a room in the back. "Hope you brought coffee."

"I have coffee," I yelled back. "Do you have a law degree hidden in here with all the football stuff?"

"It's upstairs, under my bed. Hard enough being a black man in Southie, without admitting you're a lawyer, too."

Calvin appeared in the door frame to his office. He was dressed casual, jeans, red sneakers, and a black Providence College Sweatshirt. I was in tan slacks, loafers, and a dark green golf shirt.

"Let's use the conference room," he said.

* * *

Minutes later, we were enjoying our coffees, on maroon leather chairs at a mahogany conference table with a glass protective top. I noticed a law degree from Suffolk University. I knew Calvin had studied law at night, while playing for the Patriots.

"Okay, Connor, tell me what you think.

"Calvin, last year, on a Saturday morning in April, you had breakfast in my house with Abby and me. Within seconds of my telling, you about Samantha Cronin, who was missing, you concluded Fox killed her."

"I did," Calvin said. "And you agreed with me."

"I did, and I still believe that."

"So, how'd the bones end up together and on J. Point?" Calvin sipped his coffee. He looked as if he already knew my answer."

"There are three possible explanations," I said. "First, Fox was killed by a person she thought could help her dispose of Samantha's body. Somebody she trusted. But it went south, and that person killed Fox and disposed of both bodies. And before you say it, I know that doesn't explain why some of the bones were moved to J. Point."

"We can deal with that little item later. What's your second explanation?"

"The person who killed Fox, didn't know about Samantha. After that person killed Fox, he or she finds Samantha's body, maybe in Fox's car, house or wherever. So, he or she disposes of both bodies. Again, this doesn't explain why some of the bones were moved to J. point." I stopped to sip my coffee. Calvin stared ahead; a lap top opened in front of him. For all his face showed, I could have been explaining baseball's infield fly rule.

"Third," I said, explains everything, but we don't have proof."

Calvin shrugged. "We don't have proof on anything. Go ahead, there's no jury here."

"I think Fox may be alive," I said. "I think she killed Samantha, and brought the body to the basement of her J. Point home. She cut it into pieces and used acid or some other chemicals to reduce it to bones. Then she puts the bones, or at least some of them, on J. Point. Maybe she wanted people to think she was dead. That would explain leaving them where they could be seen by the people going to the beach for Census Day."

"The first explanation also works better if the person helping Doctor Fox, was with her in the basement. That puts the bones on J. Point. Of course, that also means both she and Samantha are dead."

CHAPTER 41

"You're still calling her doctor?" I said.

Calvin laughed. "Let's assume it's door number three. What's next?"

"We need experts to determine, if they can, which bones belonged to which victim. If there're two pelvic bones, or something vital to life, then we've got two dead women, and we go back to theory one or two. "But if all the bones belonged to Samantha, or all except a finger or whatever, then it's reasonable to believe, even probable, that Fox is alive."

"You discuss this with anyone else?' Calvin said.

"Abby. We sort of worked it out last night," I said. "I wanted to be ready for today's meeting."

Calvin smiled. "I figured as much. Good of you to give her some credit."

"Well, you said you called her first for the job you offered."

"I was kidding," Calvin said. "I knew if I got you, Abby would be part of the package. That was good work."

We toasted our coffee cups

"Maybe, we can get to that Doctor Kincaid," Calvin said. "She was good enough to call Joe and give him the head up on the investigation being taken away from him. We ask her to make a list of all the bones, and who, in her medical judgment, each belonged to. Hell, that should be part of any routine investigation."

"How about Joe making the call?"

Calvin shook his head. "I'll call Joe this morning to give him an update, but I'm not sure I want him communicating directly with her. I'll discuss it with him. Maybe, I'll call her and ask if such a list has been developed. Hopefully, she's a PATS fan."

"Isn't everyone in New England?" I said.

"I suppose, but the real question is whether she knows who

the fuck Calvin Washington is?"

"Wouldn't be a problem if she ever saw your reception area," I said.

42

Chapter 42

Attorney General Harold Robinson and John Gibbons strode into the media room at the Augusta Office and stepped onto the elevated platform. The room was filled with print and TV reporters, along with a few stringers, trolling for news stories for the smaller community news and cable outlets. Robinson stepped behind the podium. Gibson slightly behind him, but in full camera view.

"Good morning, thank you for being here," Robinson began. "As most of you know, I do not normally comment on investigations being conducted by my office. However, a newscast last night, and a story in this morning *Portland Press-Herald* stated there was an ongoing investigation by my office into the discovery of human bones on Jefford Point this past Monday, Memorial Day. Additionally, it was revealed that the DNA of Cassandra Harvey, a professor of law at the University of Southern Maine Law School, and the wife of Caleb County Prosecutor, Joseph McDonald, was discovered on those bones. And last night, one television station reported I intended to appoint Trevor Chandler, a criminal defense attorney, to head up the investigation." Robinson paused for effect. "Let me be clear and unambiguous. Investigations by my office are headed up by my staff and not by criminal defense attorneys. Second, while the finding of these bones on J. Point has been on the news since Monday evening, the fact Ms. Harvey's DNA was found on the bones is part of the investigation, and if I find out the person responsible for this leak, he or she will be prosecuted." He paused again to replace the sternness on his face with his amicable, I'm-your-friend-and can-be-trusted smile. "With me today is the person who will be heading up the investigation, and he'll answer any questions he can about it." With a wave, he summoned Gibbons, to the microphone and stepped away without an introduction or handshake.

* * *

Joe got off the call with Calvin, and shot his fist into the air, hitting the roof of his car. He knew Cassandra was out and about, and decided to call Sister Alicia at the New York Orphanage. He was grateful she had a cell phone, and he could avoid a receptionist and escape the elevator music used for messages on hold. *Maybe they use hymns*, he thought, as he listened to the ring tones."

"Hi Joe, this is Sister Alicia, howareya?"

"Fine, Sister. I'm calling because I may have jumped the gun the other day when I told you about the bones, we discovered on J. Point."

"You mean there're not Samantha's?"

Joe grimaced. "No, I'm afraid they do belong to Samantha and Doctor Fox. But they are partial remains, and until they are more fully examined, we can't say, for certain that both Samantha and Fox are dead."

"I see," Sister Alicia said. "But when Calvin and Connor McNeill were here last year, I got the distinct impression they both thought Doctor Fox had killed Samantha."

I know," Joe said. "And frankly, we still do. What we can't be certain of is whether the pile of bones I discovered last Monday proves both of them are dead. We need to wait for further analysis. I'm sorry I acted too quickly."

"Don't be sorry, Joe. I wanted you to keep me informed. I, too, have concluded Samantha is dead. She would have contacted me, or used her credit card if she were alive. And, she'd never have left her car in the school parking lot."

"I agree," Joe said.

"It was kind of you to call. I'll keep you, and them, in my prayers. Dead or alive."

"Thank you, Sister. And you in mine," Joe said.

"Oh, and Joe, one more thing. Do you think Calvin might be able to get a few sisters and I tickets to a Patriots game, once the season starts?"

* * *

John Gibbons read an opening statement, which sang the praises of the Attorney General, who had left the room, and profusely thanked him for his confidence and support. Next, he meticulously outlined the organization of the office, his own biography and experience, and the necessity of a thorough and competent investigation. The four-minute spiel produced little more than the shuffling of feet, papers, and two audible yawns and a groan. Finally, Gibbons removed his eyeglasses and smiled.

"Any questions?"

"Has a special grand jury been impaneled?" A woman in the first row said.

"No, but one will be in the next five to ten days."

"Why not rely on the police to investigate? The same woman asked.

Gibbons smiled. *Thank you, Alice.* "We will be working with all the local police, and we anticipate their full cooperation. This appears to be a complicated case, and we think a grand jury, with subpoena powers, is a better, more unified, investigative tool. Witnesses can refuse to speak to the police. We want them in a position where they must either testify or plead the fifth."

Wendy Grisham stood. "Have the bones been analyzed? If so, by whom?"

"Yes, by the FBI Laboratory in Bangor. This is getting close to the investigation, so I won't comment any further on details of the investigation."

Wendy pressed. "An FBI spokesperson identified the bones as being those of Samantha Cronin and Doctor Fox. Anything in the investigation, so far, to the contrary?"

"No"

"Are both women dead?"

"I would think that's clear, enough," Gibbons said.

Randy White from *The Portland Press Herald* stood. "Any thoughts on why the bones were found on Jefford Point?"

CHAPTER 42

Gibbons paused as if in thought. "Well, I don't want to speculate, but Doctor Fox did have a summer home there." He gave a who-knows shrug and said, "maybe somebody thought if the bones were found there, everything would fall under the jurisdiction of the county prosecutor."

Several print reporters jumped up. The loudest shouted, "You're accusing Joseph McDonald, or his wife, Cassandra Harvey?"

Gibbons held up hands, palms out. "I didn't say that. Too early to accuse anyone."

"Are they suspects? Will they be subpoenaed?"

Gibbons shrugged. "I don't think subpoenas will be necessary. I expect their full cooperation."

"Are either or both of them targets or persons of interest?" Wendy Grisham said.

"I can't comment on who are or are not targets of an investigation," Gibbons said. He glanced at his watch. "I need to get back to work. That's all for today." Gibbons stepped off the platform and headed towards the door. He passed Nikki Tamara from Channel Three.

"Maybe next time, Nikki, you'll check with me before believing anything Trevor Chandler tells you. That is, if you still have a job at Channel Three."

Chapter 43

Joe was at his roll top desk thinking about possible approaches to Doctor Kincaid. He agreed with Calvin's suggestion that he not call her, but because Calvin represented Cassandra, Joe wasn't sure he was the right approach. Calvin did agree to send Joe five tickets to a late September or early October Patriots game for Sister Alicia. "Want to keep her and other gals warm," Calvin had said.

Jackie's voice cut into Joe's thoughts. "Wendy Grisham from Channel Three is on the line for you."

"Hmm," Joe said. "I may have found the answer." He punched the button on the old black phone. "Hey Wendy, what can I do for you?"

"Please tell me, you didn't give Nikki Tamara the false tip about the AG asking Trevor Chandler to head up the bones investigation."

"Bones investigation," Joe said. "I like that. I was afraid you'd be calling it Bones-Gate. And, I did call Nikki, because I got it from a good source, and I wanted to get it out there."

CHAPTER 43

"Well, your good source was wrong," Grisham said.

"You and I both know Nikki should have called Trevor, or the AG after she spoke with me."

"She did. Neither responded to her call."

"So, then your producer had a choice to make, go with it or wait. Maybe, Channel Three should have waited. Maybe they were too anxious to air *their exclusive*," Joe said. "No reason to be pissed at me."

"You're right, and I'm not." Grisham said. "We fucked up."

"Which, of course, is why I called Nikki and not you," Joe said. "And, by the way, I'm certain the information was correct. I think AG and Gibbons pulled the plug once it was announced by Channel Three and not them."

"You're probably right, Grisham said, "Still, it was sloppy reporting, on our part."

"So, why'd you call?"

* * *

For the next several minutes Grisham told Joe what had occurred at the morning press conference, including the inference voiced by Gibbons that Cassandra might have placed the bones on J. Point to give Joe jurisdiction over any investigation.

"Any comment?" Grisham said.

"Neither Cassandra nor I placed the bones on J. Point. But Gibbons is correct when he says Cassandra and I will fully cooperate with any serious investigation."

"You said 'serious,'" Grisham said. "Are you questioning anyone's motives?"

"Not all, I'm sure everyone wants a serious investigation."

"Anything else?" Grisham said. "I'm sensing you have something to say."

"I do," Joe said. Can we go off the record?"

* * *

Joe told Wendy, off the record, his suspicions that Fox killed Samantha and that she might still be alive. He used the reasoning developed by Calvin, Connor, and Abby, without mentioning their names. He knew Wendy would not tape the conversation, without asking, but he heard the scribbling of notes. As he approached the end, he said "All I'm asking is for these bones to get a serious and professional look, and that a list be made indicating which bones are Samantha's and which belong to Fox. Then it can be determined if the bones indicate Fox is dead or alive."

"What about Samantha? Grisham said.

"Yes, Samantha, too. It's just I've been certain she's dead since the day she disappeared. But, yes, Samantha too."

"The bones are part of a criminal investigation, so an FOI won't work"

"Yeah, and I don't want to wait until an indictment, to get a look at them and have them tested," Joe said. "Look, I don't think Doctor Kincaid will speak to you. She'll tell you the full report, blah, blah, blah, has been or will be sent to Gibbons, and you'll have to speak with him."

"I could go directly to Harold Robinson. The public already knows who the bones belong to, they have a right to know

CHAPTER 43

whether the bones indicate either or both are dead or alive."

"He'll tell you to go to Gibbons," Joe said.

"I know, but if I go to Gibby, he'll tell me to get lost. Then, Robinson will tell me he has to support his Chief. Better if I tell the AG I went directly to him because this is a policy decision for the highest level. You know, play to his ego," Grisham said. "I'll tell him all I'm asking is that he release a public statement affirming that once the examination of the bones is completed, his office will announce whether or not the bones indicate to a medical certainty if Samantha and Fox are dead or alive, and it couldn't be determined, he'd say that."

"That sound like a plan," Joe said. "Make sure the timeline for the statement is after the examination of the bones; not after the investigation.

"Don't wordsmith me," Grisham said around a laugh and hung up.

* * *

The "Bones Investigation" continued to garner print and media attention. Portions of the Attorney General's press conference were covered across Maine. The fact the bones of two missing women, connected by Palfrey's criminal trial and a disruption initiated by one during a class lectured by the other, were found on a small strip of land by the County Prosecutor, whose wife was allegedly the last person to see one of the women alive and was arguing with her was more than any news outlet could ignore. The attention broadened, when Fox's controversial views on both her profession and the various topics she raised at the classes at Southern Maine University.

Suddenly, it was more than a murder case. It became a reason to discuss, mostly by talk radio, the wisdom of policy changes made to accommodate people who identified as transitioning, transgender or as neither male nor female or both. All of this temporarily shifted attention away from Cassandra, her DNA, and her arguments with Fox. That changed when more details about the investigation and emails allegedly sent to Fox by her were leaked and surfaced in local and state wide print and TV news outlets across Maine.

44

Chapter 44

I came into the press room of the Attorney General's Office a few minutes before ten o'clock, the morning of June 12th, a sunny and humid Monday. Abby and I had driven up to Augusta Sunday morning. We had lunch at The Hott Dogg House on Mt. Vernon Street, and then a nice dinner at Otto's On the River. It was a compromise. I love hot dogs and can't resist an opportunity to try them at a new location. Abby loves eating with a water view. If I could find hot dogs with a water view, I could halve our eating out budget. We stayed at a Hudson Hotel, a popular, inexpensive New England chain with an asshole for a CEO. This was not the result of a compromise, but because I had agreed to a two dollar an hour rate, and mentioned it to Abby.

I was here to ask the questions Joe mentioned to Wendy Grisham. He had no reason to suspect she wouldn't ask them, but you never know what will happen once a press conference begins. I called in a favor from years back, and got a twenty-four-hour press credential from the Melrose Free

Press. I bought a reporter's notebook at a Dollar Store. Abby suggested I wear a brown fedora with a white card reading: PRESS sticking up from the band, but we decided that might be pushing it. Besides, where can you find a fedora in Augusta on a Sunday?

I grabbed a seat in the second to last row, behind a Channel 3 camera and a woman I knew from pictures on their website was Wendy Grisham. I glanced at my watch: ten o'clock.

I heard the rustling of something, seconds before John Gibbons strutted into the room and onto the platform. He stood behind the podium and gave the confident smile of a person with all the answers.

"Good morning," Gibbons said. "I have a brief statement, and I'll take some questions upon its conclusion."

The camera man in front of me gave out a muffled groan. That earned him an icy stare from Grisham.

"This morning I received a report from Doctor Dorothy Kincaid from the FBI Laboratory in Bangor. As you know, she and her team collected the bones discovered on J. Point - Jefford Point - to be more accurate this past Memorial Day. She has been examining them ever since."

Never slept, ate, or pissed, I thought. I've always hated expressions like "worked tirelessly, or endlessly, or diligently." Another one is "worked hard." Politicians always say that. Does anyone ever work soft? Or sporadically?

"Dr. Kincaid's report confirms the bones are those of Samantha Cronin and Doctor Alice Ruth Fox, and that given the compilation of bones, both women are dead. A summary of her report will be made available to each of you at the end of this press conference."

"Why a summary?" Grisham shouted from her chair.

CHAPTER 44

"Because the report contains details relative to a murder investigation, which we will not disclose until it has been completed."

"Does her report conclude both women were murdered?" I shouted, drawing the attention of Grisham., who, I think, nodded approval.

"I'm not going into what's in the report, other than what I've already said.

"Where are the bones, now?" I said. "Will they be preserved?"

"They are at the FBI Laboratory and will be handled in accordance with the procedures and protocols of a joint investigation."

"When did this become a joint investigation?" Grisham said.

"I only meant joint in terms of the bones."

"Who has custody of the bones? I said. A woman in the front row shouted over me.

"Has a special grand jury been impaneled?"

Gibbons pointed at her, and smiled. "As we speak. It should be completed by Wednesday. That's all for today. Thank you."

* * *

Cassandra was at the kitchen table re-reading the press clipping on several emails, allegedly sent by her to Doctor For.

"Jesus," she muttered. "I'd have to be a fucking jerk to use language like this in an email. How'd they trace this shit to me? This is bullshit."

Her cell buzzed. She picked it up from the table and saw it

was from Office of Dean Margaret Summers. *Shit, here it comes*, she thought. "Good morning, this is Cassandra Harvey."

"Hi Cassandra," a chirpy voice raced into her ear. "Can you hold for Dean Summers?

And what if I said no, Cassandra thought. "Certainly," she said.

A second or two passed. "Hello Cassandra," Dean Summers said. "How you holding up?"

"I've had better weeks, but I'll get through this. I keep telling the media I've never sent Doctor Fox any emails, let alone the garbage that's been all over the news the past week."

"Well, you know we're all behind you Cassandra, and let's hope this all goes away soon," Summers said.

Yeah, sure you are, and this is not going to disappear overnight. "That's nice to hear, Margaret, I appreciate your calling." *What now Kemosabe? You gonna hang up or tell me the real reason you called?*

"Well, I'm calling for two other reasons. First, the State Police have seized your university computer. The officers who came had a warrant. Our general counsel, Tom Bennett... you know him. Right? In any case, Tom reviewed it, and we assented to their taking it out of the university.

"When was this?"

"Less than an hour ago. "I hope you didn't have any personal matters on it."

"I have my own computers," Cassandra said. "I understand what's mine and what belongs to the law school. What's the second reason you called?"

I received a call from the Chair of our Board of Trustees. Obviously, the Board is concerned about all the attention this is getting and how it reflects on the law school."

CHAPTER 44

Summers paused. Cassandra decided not to make her wait.

"You know I can't do anything about the publicity, and I've denied ever sending Fox any emails. I've admitted the two of us did not get along, and that we have argued. But all our arguments were face to face." Cassandra paused and added: "You know me well enough to know I would never put language like that in an email to anyone."

"Of course, I do, Cassandra," Summers said. "But the Board is putting me in a difficult position. Having the police come here this morning hasn't help. I was thinking how would you like a paid sabbatical for a full academic year? Next September through June. This should all be over by then, and you can return refreshed and with all this behind you."

"Dean, all sabbaticals are paid, and the policy is not more than one in any ten-year period. You know I had one four years ago. This would be viewed by all, including the press, as a paid suspension. I will not do that."

"You want me to tell the Board you are refusing this offer, which you must admit is generous, considering the circumstances."

"The circumstances are that I have not done anything wrong, I have not been charged with anything, and I have tenure."

"But after you're indicted, I'm not sure the Board would agree to a paid sabbatical," Summers said. "Perhaps it would be better to have it all approved before any indictment comes. Can you at least think about it? I'm trying to do the best for you that I can. Given the pressure I'm under."

The pressure you're under? "Tell the Board Chair, I'm aware of his concerns, and would be pleased to meet with him and the entire board at their convenience, or, as you graciously stated, 'after I'm indicted.'"

Chapter 45

As Cassandra was speaking with Dean Summers, Joe was in his office conference room with Jacob Daniels and Joan Foote, two of the five Commissioners for Caleb County. They had come to his office unexpectedly, and Joe immediately knew the visit was connected to the Bones Investigation. He wasn't worried. These two carried no weight. They declined his offers of coffee or ice water, and settled in across from him at the oval, oak conference table.

"So, how can I help you?" Joe said.

Joan spoke first. She was a thin redhead, in her fifties, with a big nose and wide smile.

"Jacob and I are here to express our concern that the current investigation into your wife's possible involvement in the murders of Doctor Fox and the other woman, are going to hamper your ability to do your job."

"Samantha Cronin."

"Excuse me," Joan said.

"Samantha Cronin," Joe repeated. "She is the other woman.

CHAPTER 45

She was twenty-five, and a victim of a criminal assault when she was a teenager. She had indifferent, if not abusive, parents, and she was probably homeless when she was murdered."

"I see," Joan said.

"You should try to remember her name, particularly before you go around saying the investigation into her death might hinder my ability to do my job. And you should also remember my wife is not being investigated."

"No need to get angry here," Jacob cut in. He was a soft-faced blond with gold-rimmed glasses in his forties who looked like a British movie star. "We're all friends."

"You show up here, unexpected, say my wife is being investigated in a murder case, and wonder if I can do my job. And you're my friends?" Joe shook his head. "The short answer is to your question is yes, I can do my job. The longer version is my job does not depend upon your approval or your determination as to whether I can do it."

"The Charter gives us the authority to remove any employee," Joan said, a sharpened edge to her tone.

"That provision applies to employees, not elected officials," Joe said, returning the edge. "The legislature or the Judiciary can remove me *for cause*. Good luck with that. Anything else on your mind?"

"We have some control over your budget," Joan said. A privileged smugness now stitched on her face.

"Go ahead," Joe said. "Try to screw around with my budget. We'll see how that works out for you, and all the family and friends you have working for the county."

"Let's start over," Jacob – the good cop – said. "Perhaps we came on a bit strong. Let's relax and discuss this as friends. Perhaps we can reach an accommodation."

"What'd you have in mind Jacob? "I step aside so you can lobby the governor for an appointment?"

"Maybe just a temporary stepping aside, and I'd only be interim or acting, whichever term you decide," Jacob said.

"No such thing," Joe said. "It's like being a little bit pregnant. I step aside, the governor appoints someone and he or she has the job until the next election. Forget it. Anything else?"

"Be reasonable, Joe," Jacob said. "We're friends, we should be able to resolve this."

"We're friends, are we, Jacob? You're still pushing friendship? The two of you walked in here trying to get me to resign because of a bullshit allegation against my wife. You call us friends? Friends come in and ask how I'm doing, what can we do to help? You two come in looking for my job. Well, if either of you want my job, run against me. In the meantime, get the fuck out of my office."

* * *

I called Malcolm after the press conference. He had agreed to investigate the leaked emails Cassandra allegedly sent to Doctor Fox.

"Anything on the emails?" I said.

"And good morning to you, Connor," Malcolm said. "How's everything in Maine. Mud season in full bloom? Have the black flies arrived?"

"Is this you or a new voice you're practicing," I said. "Good morning to you, Malcolm, hope all is well. So nice to speak with you. Anything on the emails?"

"They're on the lap top Cassandra uses at the law school, it's a Dell. She occasionally brings it home. The other two are Hewlett Packers, both clean."

"Shit. You're sure?"

Three seconds of silence from Malcolm answered the question. "The were scrubbed, but by an amateur. I found them and anyone with any experience will find them. Of course, I could permanently scrub them before the subpoena arrives." One of Malcolm's voices added, "but that would be wrong."

"It hasn't been subpoenaed," I said. "No crime, I think. It not her computer, but she has custody of it with the permission of the law school. Maybe they could be scrubbed."

"Well, you're the disbarred lawyer," Malcolm said. "I yield to your expertise. However, from what I could determine the portions leaked to the media are word-for-word the same as I found on her computer. Assuming Cassandra didn't leak them, I suspect Gibbons already has them."

"Not without a warrant," I said.

"A person with certain skills and no scruples, could use Fox's computer to trace them back to Cassandra's university computer,

"But why not get a warrant to seize the computer? The university will cooperate. And why not subpoena her computers at home before she destroys them?" I said.

"Maybe she's under surveillance, hoping she'll try to do that," Malcolm said. "Or maybe they're just stupid."

"Or maybe, they have their own Malcolm Butts, and they know what on all of her computers," I said. "Could someone have planted them on her university computer?

"Of course," Malcolm said. "Fox could have typed them

herself if she could get into Cassandra's office at night, or when she was in class."

"But could she have planted them without actually being in Cassandra's office?

"Yes, or someone working on her behalf," Malcolm said. One of his other voices said, "but not everybody has my talents."

* * *

About three hundred and forty miles from where Connor was speaking with Malcolm, Sister Alicia was in the Office of the Superintendent of the New Beginnings Orphanage in Troy New York. The orphanage was in a large, granite building, formerly used for manufacture of stoves. Troy is home to Rensselaer Polytechnic Institute (RPI), America's oldest technical research university. But the building housing the New Beginnings Orphanage was closer to Hudson Valley Community College and Sacred Heart Church, where Sister Alicia had a room in the rectory.

Monsignor Mark McGrath, a youthful-appearing, athletic, man in his late seventies, with hair the color of old baseballs, had just returned from a two-day pilgrimage to Lourdes, France, which preceded four days of skiing in the Dolomites in Northern Italy, sat behind a large desk. It was dotted with small pictures of nieces, nephews, and a few professional sport stars he had met on his quarterly pilgrimages. McGrath's left-wing politics put him at odds with the local bishop, Angelo Rossi, who had removed him from several parishes for organizing activities, which conflicted with church policies. When the

CHAPTER 45

Monsignor's brother, Ned McGrath, who owned and operated The Thirsty Shamrock, an Irish Pub a short walk away, told him about a vacancy at the orphanage, Mark immediately requested a position at New Beginnings. Bishop Rossi quickly appointed him Spiritual Advisor and Superintendent. This left McGrath with time for travel, golf, photography, hiking, and pastoral duties such raising funds for New Beginnings, and performing Saturday and Sunday evening masses at any Irish pub in Troy that requested it. "God, Guinness and Catholics; meet them where they're at," McGrath explained to Bishop Rossi after he first initiated the practice.

"How can I help you, Sister Alicia?"

"I need to take some time off, Monsignor. I want to organize a memorial service for a dear friend of mine, whose bones were discovered a few weeks ago on a small peninsular of land in Maine. She was murdered, and only a few friends seem to care."

"That's terrible," McGrath said. "Ah Maine! A wonderful place. Great golf courses, skiing, hiking trails and one of the most spectacular coast line in the world."

"Well, I'm afraid I'll be too busy finding a church for the service," Sister Alicia said.

"Of course. Well, I'm sure there are nice churches in Maine. Names escape me now, but if there is any way I can help, please do not hesitate to call me."

"So, I can take some time off Monsignor? "I was thinking next week."

"Take as much as you need, my Dear. I'm so sorry to learn of your loss. And take time to enjoy Maine, after your done with the memorial service. It will help you through the grieving process. Waterville Valley is nice, unless the black flies have taken over. In that case, try York or Wells Beach."

Chapter 46

The press conference announcing the bones belonged to Doctor Fox and Samantha Cronin, and that both women were dead, received prominent coverage across Maine. In most newscasts, snippets from the conference were followed by reports of the seizure of Cassandra's computer from the University of Maine Law School. This, in turn, fed back to earlier stories about the emails allegedly sent to Fox by Cassandra. One newscast replayed Gibbons' speculation on the bones being left on Jefford Point so the investigation would be led by County Prosecutor Joe McDonald, Cassandra's husband.

"Tomorrow, there'll be reports of growing pressure on the two of us to resign," Joe said, placing air quotes around growing pressure.

"I suppose, I should have expected it," Cassandra said. "Still, for it to come before I'm even charged with something, surprises me. And they call themselves a law school."

"You won't be charged with anything," Joe said. "Tomorrow, the whole team is coming up here to explain how we're going to kick ass on this."

"Why here? We can go to Boston or someplace halfway."

"I asked Calvin that. He told me it had something to do with Holy Donuts."

* * *

Connor, Abby, and Calvin stepped onto the porch the next morning twenty minutes before eleven with notebooks, laptops, iPads, a large dry erase board and easel, and two one dozen boxes from Holy Donuts. They arrived in separate cars, which immediately signaled to Joe, one of them had other business in Maine and would not be going back to Massachusetts. Ten minutes earlier, Joe had arrived home from Dunkin' with a Box of Joe. After everyone got settled, Calvin cleared his voice and started.

"First, some good news to be followed by great news. Joe, do you know who Damien Woody is?"

"Yeah. He played football for Boston College, and several NFL teams, including the PATS. Now he does football commentary on one of the TV sports shows."

"Very good," Calvin said. "Now I'll tell you something else about Damien Woody. He's a friend of mine, and his brother-in-law, Joseph Bettencourt, is the Chief of Staff to Harold Robinson, the Maine Attorney General."

"Hmm, I like where this is going," Joe said.

"Yesterday, Damien called me to say this Bettencourt guy called him to ask if he knew me. Damien told me the AG wanted to know all about me because of the bones investigation."

CHAPTER 46

"He say how they found out you were representing Cassandra?" Joe said.

"He didn't, and I didn't ask. But what I did ask is for a meeting with Robinson, so he could learn all he wanted about me." Calvin smiled. "This morning, I got a call from Mr. Bettencourt telling me I was meeting with the Attorney General tomorrow morning at nine o'clock."

"That's great!" Joe shouted. He stood and extended a fist bump to Calvin.

Calvin returned the bump. "It gets even better," he said. "I'm about to explain how, over a box of Holy Donuts, I'll convince Robinson there isn't a case against Cassandra, and he'll look foolish if he indicts her after the remarks Gibbons made. I'll even try to convince him to appoint Elaine Blass to head up the investigation."

"A box of Holy Donuts got you a meeting with the Attorney General?" Cassandra said.

"That and a signed Tom Brady Patriots Helmet. Damien mentioned to me Bettencourt's been looking to add one to his collection of NFL helmets.

"Couldn't Damien have gotten him one?" Joe said.

Of course," Calvin said. "But Damien told me while his wife is great, and he loves her, her brother is an asshole."

* * *

"This won't take too long," Calvin began, a few minutes later. He took off his blue blazer, revealing a bright orange button-down short-sleeved shirt. "I need to get to Augusta this afternoon. Here s what we know the prosecution has and could present to a grand jury. First, Cassandra's DNA was on some of the bones, and the blanket found with them." He wrote DNA on the board.

"We know DNA can be transferred, and we know Fox spent the night here. That was when she claimed her tires were slashed and got drunk. I will ask the AG where he thinks the blanket came from? I will also ask if he knew Fox wore Cassandra's coat the next morning to get back to her car. And of course, the tires were not slashed. We can explain the DNA and expose Fox as a liar and a boozer. A win win." He wrote the words liar and drunk beside DNA.

As if on cue, Roosevelt Wilson's jeep pulled up the road and stopped. From the passenger's seat, Sister Alicia climbed out and waved. Roosevelt got out and came around the front of his jeep and offered her his arm. The two walked toward the porch.

"What the fuck?" Joe muttered. He stood and opened the door. "Sister Alicia! This is a pleasant surprise. Hello, Roosevelt."

"I found this young lady walking along The Road. When she told me she was looking for you, I told her we were neighbors and offered a ride." *Didn't know she was a religious,* he thought.

"Come in, come in," Joe said.

"I'm sorry to intrude," Sister Alicia said. "I didn't know you had company."

"Well, how could you have known, Joe said. "Please sit down. He pointed to the chair he'd left."

Maybe if you'd called? Cassandra thought.

Hey, Holy Donuts," Roosevelt said. He walked to the box and took one.

CHAPTER 46

* * *

Joe made the introductions, brought out a few chairs and the group resettled. Joe told Calvin the unexpected guests could stay, and urged him to continue.

Calvin wrote fingerprints under DNA, and said, "we expect the AG will say they found Cassandra's fingerprints in Fox's house here on J. Point."

"I've never been in her house," Cassandra said.

Calvin smiled. He loved these moments. "Yes, but a vodka bottle from your home was brought into hers. And, the day the two of you argued, she offered you another vodka bottle to replace the one she took. You grabbed it, and then Fox took it back."

"She can't transfer those prints to another surface in her home," Joe said. "Can she?"

"According to accepted science, she can't," Calvin said. "But remember, she was briefly in intelligence, so who know what she can or can't do. But we know how your prints could have gotten into her house." He wrote emails on the board, and turned to Cassandra.

"As for the emails, common sense and computer science are more persuasive that you didn't send them, than you did. The language is so strong, threatening, and incriminatory, it's crazy to think you'd send them from your university computer. Moreover, Malcolm Butts has assured us your computer could have been hacked and made to appear the emails came from it. Also, he says it's more likely, Fox got access and sent them to herself, as part of a plan to get you fired from the university."

"Any evidence of such a plan?" Joe said.

"Working on it," Calvin said. He wrote Diary. "It's like her diary. Fox writes she's afraid of you, feels threatened by you, but she never complained to anyone about you. We've – that is Connor, and Murph from my office - have spoken with her colleagues, and none ever heard Fox mention your name. By the way, now that Fox has gone from missing to dead, everyone we spoke with said she was an exceedingly difficult person to work with."

"Amen to that," Roosevelt said. "A world class pain in the ass."

Calvin smiled and wrote the words difficult, not liked. "As for your argument with Fox, Andy from the towing company will testify as to the circumstances of her car blocking the road, and the fact she did not move it, after you asked. He'll say he was there only to move it to her parking area on her property. Andy will also testify as to how she tried to avoid her portion of the snow plowing costs." He jotted snow removal on the board, and the words mortgage sale.

"The attorney from the bank, Karen Ferrick, will testify she explained to Doctor Fox, at the time of her purchase of the property, all of her responsibilities under the right of way agreement." Calvin paused a moment to take a sip of water. He looked at Cassandra. "Ms. Ferrick also told me you called several times to see if the property was being sold or foreclosed. She said you were interested in purchasing it."

"I did," Cassandra said. "I think I called her three times. I did not want another asshole to come in and be my neighbor. Can you blame me?"

"I made the same call, for the same reason," Roosevelt said. "But only once."

There was brief, uncomfortable laughter.

CHAPTER 46

I only have one other thing to say, but I will not go into details here. It's no secret that a number of us think, reasonably I believe, that Fox killed Samantha. In fact, our theory makes more sense than the one being pushed by Gibbons that Cassandra killed Fox. I am going to impress upon Harold Robinson that Gibbons has tainted the investigation by suggesting Cassandra left the bones on J. Point because she believed that would place the investigation in Joe's hands. Never mind the fact until the bones appeared there was no investigation or any idea as to what happened to Samantha and Doctor Fox. Also, Gibbons leaked the emails, further compromising the independence and objectivity of the investigation."

"Any proof he leaked it?" Joe said.

"No, and who cares?" Calvin said. "As soon as he denies it, we've accomplished our goal." He took another sip of water. "I'll tell Robinson all I'm asking is for a clean and objective investigation. Let the police and the special grand jury do their job. And move Gibbons to the side. He's an embarrassment, and I'll suggest he appoint Elaine Blass."

There was brief silence followed by polite applause. The kind you'd get from people not certain, whether it was appropriate or not.

"I was hoping for more enthusiasm, maybe a standing ovation," Calvin said with a wide smile."

Joe and Cassandra immediately jumped up and began clapping. They were followed by Sister Alicia, Roosevelt, Connor, and Abby.

A shrill whistle from Abby pierced the applause.

Chapter 47

Calvin and Connor packed the materials into Calvin's car, and he left for Augusta. Connor and Abby stayed for another two hours enjoying relaxed conversations, cold drinks and snacks with Joe, Cassandra, Roosevelt, and Sister Alicia. Connor offered Sister Alicia a ride to wherever. Roosevelt responded, "I got that covered." So, after twenty minutes of the long Irish goodbye, including multiple hugs, expressions of thanks and promises to do this again, soon, Connor and Abby got into their car and left.

Joe had followed them out to their car. When he got back to the porch, he positioned his chair to face Sister Alicia. "Okay, Sister, what's up?" He smiled to soften the moment. "Why are you really here?"

"I received permission to take a few days off so I could arrange a memorial service for Samantha. I had no interest in involving her family. I thought of you and Cassandra and wanted to ask your opinion and for your help. Something simple, small, and outdoors."

CHAPTER 47

"That sounds wonderful," Cassandra said. "You can have it here. Unless you have a location in mind."

"There's no body to bury," Joe said. "Hard to say how long the bones will be tied up with the investigation, and they'll probably be released to her family. How about you plant a tree in her memory, along with a small commemorative stone?"

Sister Alicia's eyes welled with tears. "Those are wonderful ideas. And, I'd love to use this place. God, I'm so unprepared for all of this. I do have some money."

Joe waved the offer aside. "This will not be expensive. When were you thinking of doing it?"

"Perhaps this Friday? At noon? Is that too soon? I'd like to get back to the orphanage by Sunday."

"How'd you get here?" Casandra said.

"I took a bus from Troy, New York to Portland. I used the Orphanage's UBER Account to get to the beginning of J. Point. I didn't know your address, but I thought if I walked the roadway, I'd run into somebody I could ask. Mr. Wilson was kind enough to pick me up."

"Lucky for you," Roosevelt said. "I only came up to retrieve some tools. Usually only here on weekends, after Memorial Day and full-time from July first to the end of September."

"Well, we can drive you to the bus station in Portland when it's time to leave," Joe said. "And, Friday for the memorial service is fine."

"And you can stay at my place," Roosevelt said. "It's clean, has indoor plumbing, and I won't be there. If you need anything or some food to eat, Joe and Cassandra are only forty or fifty feet away. That's where I get most of my food and drink. When I'm tired of eating out of a can.'" He laughed. "Please Sister, I'd be honored."

"You're all so kind," Sister Alicia said. "I wish Samantha had known you."

"I wish that as well," Roosevelt said. "Instead, we had to put up with that bitch, Fox. Forgive me, Sister, but I'm glad she's dead. She was a horrible person."

* * *

The next morning, while Cassandra took Sister Alicia shopping for some food and cooking utensils, and while Calvin was meeting with Attorney General Harold Robinson,

Joe was driving to Bangor and the FBI Laboratory to pick up a small package. He had called Doctor Dorothy Kincaid yesterday, after Roosevelt and Sister Alicia left. She took the call only after Joe assured her it was not about the investigation.

"What I need, if it's possible, is some bone dust that I can say may be from Samantha," Joe told Kincaid. "I'm having a memorial service in my yard this Friday, and I'd like to have something in a bottle or container to bury."

"You need a permit for that?" Kincaid said, interspersed with a brief laugh.

"Probably," Joe said. "I'm not sure, but it's always easier to beg forgiveness than to ask permission."

"Boy, isn't that true, Kincaid said. "I can give you a very small amount of bone dust. Not enough to analyze, and I can't say it's Samantha's, but it probably will have particles from her bones. That's the best I can do. And this stays between us."

Joe quickly agreed, thanked her, and asked when and where.

CHAPTER 47

"It'll be in a package addressed to you, and at the front desk. Come after ten o'clock tomorrow."

And so, at eleven-thirty on Wednesday morning, Joe drove out of Bangor with a small brown paper wrapped package on the front passenger seat of his Subaru. His next stop would be Broadway Gardens in South Portland for a small tree, and perhaps a commemorative stone.

Just in case, Cassandra forgot her promise to create one.

* * *

Cassandra didn't forget, and late that afternoon, Joe, Cassandra, and Sister Alicia picked out a spot, visible from Joe's fire pit, to plant the small fir tree Joe purchased, along with the glass cork-topped vial of white bone powder, and a white stone on which Cassandra had stenciled the words:

Planted to Celebrate
A Life well lived and too brief
Samantha Cronin
1997 – 2022

"You did a beautiful job, Cassandra," Sister Alicia said, her eyes tearing. "We're not even sure what year she died."

"I'm think Cassandra has it right," Joe said. He threw the stone purchased that morning into Queen Lake.

"If it's okay, I'd like to plant the tree and stone tomorrow, and at the memorial service we can say a few words and distribute the bone dust," Sister Alicia said. "Let God's wind take Samantha, where He wishes her to be."

"Whatever, you want is fine with us," Cassandra said.

Joe's cell buzzed. HE retrieved it and read the text from Calvin:

WATCH CHANNEL THREE NEWS TONIGHT @ FIVE.

"This has to be good," Joe said. "Let's get inside before God's wind puts us in the lake."

* * *

The three of them watched the dot turn into the revolving number three, and all the drama that preceded the nightly news. Finally, the familiar anchors appeared behind a desk.

"Good evening, I'm Amanda Brine, and this is Channel Three News at Five."

"And I'm Brad Stevens.

The screen filled with a three second flashing blue and yellow Breaking News logo, and returned to Amanda Brine.

"Tonight, we start with breaking news on the bones investigation. The words, "Bones Investigation" flashed in bright yellow at the bottom of the screen.

"We have Wendy Grisham, live from outside the Office of Attorney General Harold Robinson. Wendy, what can you tell us?"

The face of Wendy Grisham appeared outside a closed oak door with the Seal of the State of Maine. "Good evening, Amanda, and Brad. About an hour ago, I learned from a reliable source that Attorney General Harold Robinson has appointed Elaine Blass, an experienced and well-respected

CHAPTER 47

Bangor County Prosecutor, to head up the bones investigation. She replaces John Gibbons, Chief of the Criminal Division, who made news last week by implying Cassandra Harvey, wife of Caleb County Prosecutor Joseph McDonald, was a person of interest in the deaths of Samantha Cronin and Doctor Alice Ruth Fox. Based on this information, I confronted the Attorney General."

A close-up of Attorney General Robinson, a microphone under his nose, appeared. "This is a complicated investigation. We do not have any suspects or persons of interest. We don't even have a cause of death. The seizure of a computer at the University of Maine Law School was part of the earliest phases of the investigation and was done with the full cooperation of the Law School and Ms. Harvey."

"Are you displeased with the handling of the investigation by Mr. Gibbons?" The person holding the microphone asked."

"John Gibbons is a fine man and a good public servant. As chief of my criminal division, he has responsibility over several attorneys and their cases. I decided it wasn't fair to ask him to take charge of this very complicated case. I have asked Elaine Blass, an equally competent prosecutor, to take over and she has agreed. That is all I have to say."

Wendy Grisham appeared. "My sources tell me that Elaine Blass will be methodical, thorough, and fair. And, do not be surprised if we learn at some point that these women were not *both* innocent victims."

"Thanks, Wendy," Brad Stevens said. "Stayed tuned to Channel Three for extended coverage of the Bones Investigation and Wendy's developing and exclusive stories."

"Calvin's a genius," Joe said. He turned to Cassandra. "Elaine will get to the truth. We're going to be fine. Let's have some drinks? Alicia?"

"A small glass of white wine seems appropriate to celebrate good news, and to toast Samantha."

"For me as well," Cassandra said. "Were you and Calvin her sources?"

"Of course," Joe said. "Calvin was her source today, and I told her our suspicions about Fox killing Samantha." Joe stood. "Two white wines and a Harpoon for me, coming right up. God bless you, Calvin Washington."

"And Connor and Abby and some guy called "Murph." Cassandra said. "I think it was Connor and Abby who first suggested Fox killed Samantha and might not even be dead."

"Victory has a thousand fathers, defeat is an orphan," Joe called from the kitchen. "I don't know if Fox is dead or alive, I just want Cassandra off the hook."

"Calvin's hourly rate is so low, we should ask him to paint the kitchen," Cassandra said.

"Speaking of Calvin, Joe," Sister Alicia said. "Have you had a chance to ask him about those Patriots tickets I mentioned a week or so ago?"

"He said he'll get you five tickets to a game in September or October," Joe said.

"Well then, I like to take you and Cassandra, Connor, and Abby.

* * *

Also watching the Channel Three News, from a motel room, in Calais, Maine, nestled on the Canadian border and the St. Croix

CHAPTER 47

River, was Felix Ketch, the robotic voice from Joe's days with the CIA. Felix had followed closely the Bones Investigation, and was disappointed in the news of Elaine's appointment.

A minor setback, Felix concluded. But only a temporary one. Maybe it's time for Plan B.

***

At nine o'clock, Joe and Cassandra were in their comfortable chairs discussing the day and the plans for the memorial service. Joe's cell sounded the opening bars to John Lennon's *Imagine*. He looked and did not recognize the number. He violated his rule of no unrecognized calls after eight in the evening.

"Hello, this is Joe McDonald."

"Hello, Joseph," the robotic voice said. "Remember me?"

"Hello Felix, Been a long time. What's up?"

Cassandra sprang to life and hurried over to Joe's chair and sat on the rug. She gave him her best what-the-fuck-expression.

"I'll tell you what's up," Felix said. "You ruined my life, and I'm about to ruin yours."

"Not sure what you mean by that, Felix. I never thought you had a life. Why not explain why you called, and what I can do to make certain you never call again. It's a pain in the ass to have to change my number."

"Still the smug, self-important wiseass, Joseph," Felix said. "I won't be calling again, but let me tell you what I am going to do. Tomorrow, all your friends at Channel Three are going to learn about the time you and Cassandra spent with the Company. How you took our money, got free law degrees, fancy housing, and phony stipends every month, and a job with the US Congress and the Intelligence Committee. Then, when it was time for you to do your duty, you left."

"That's not exactly how I remember it, Felix," Joe said. "I think what happened is that your bosses decided your decision to send me to Bahrain for nine weeks of training before another assignment to the United Arab Emirates, without allowing Cassandra to come, was crazy. Your whole project, whatever it was, got dumped. And probably you, too. None of it my fault. And Felix, the stipends were not phony. I paid taxes on them."

"I lost my job, you pompous asshole. I lost everything. When the public hears about your secret lives, money payments, you and Cassandra will know what it's like to become pariahs in your fancy world of privilege."

"Felix, you shoot your mouth off about anything involving the CIA, you'll be in shit ten feet deeper than anything you think you can put us in. And if you even try, I'll bury you upside down in a barrel of loose shit you'll never get out of."

"Just wait and see..."

"Fuck you, Felix." Joe terminated the call.

"Why piss him off, like that?' Cassandra said. "Maybe you could have worked things out with him. Remember, your diplomatic skills?"

"Not after all this time," Joe said. The fact he waited this long to try anything tells me he knows he has no leverage. If he could do what he said, he'd just do it and then call me. The only way to deal with scum like Felix is to threatened him, show him you're not afraid. I may have to get a new number, but I'll wait a few weeks to see if he calls. Pretty sure he won't."

CHAPTER 47

"You're not worried?" Cassandra said, with a skeptical eyebrow.

"Not at all," Joe said. "Tomorrow, you Alicia and I are going to have a discussion, go over a few things and prepare for Friday's service.

"You do have a plan?" Cassandra said.

"I always do," Joe said.

***

Thursday morning's discussion did not take longer than thirty minutes, and the rest of the morning was spent raking, and cleaning the property. Calls were made, and a few purchases collected and carefully placed around the property. All was completed before two o'clock and they spent the rest of the afternoon relaxing and with some anticipation and concern about tomorrow's memorial service.

48

Chapter 48

Friday, June 16, was bright with blue skies, a shimmering sun, and the promise of a summer full of warm days, cool nights, and the songs of distant cicadas. Joe and Cassandra placed a small but sturdy table, covered with a white Irish linen cloth, near the fir tree and commemorative stone. Cassandra placed a white candle, and a laminated card with an Irish blessing, on either side of the vial of bone dust. Joe glanced at his watch: eleven-thirty.

"Wonder what's keeping Alicia," he said. Over the past days, they had, at her insistence, taken to simply calling her Alicia.

"This is a difficult day for her," Cassandra said. "I felt myself tearing up just looking at this table. And I never even met Samantha. This is all so horribly sad."

"You think we made a mistake having it here?"

"No," Cassandra said. "This was the right thing to do. Whenever, we sit around the fire, we can toast her memory and keep her alive."

"The life of the dead is placed in the memory of the living,"

CHAPTER 48

Joe said. He placed his arm around Cassandra's shoulder.

"Cicero," Cassandra said. A sob caught in her throat. "Let's wait inside for Alicia."

* * *

Alicia arrived at eleven-forty in full religious dress.

"I haven't worn this since the trial," she said. "I hope Samantha won't mind."

"You look beautiful," Cassandra said. "Samantha would be proud of you and thankful for all you have done for her."

"Foe what *we* have done."

"Does this mean we go back to calling you Sister Alicia?' Joe said.

* * *

At noon, the three of them walked out to the small table. Sister Alicia picked up the vial, and said a brief prayer. She turned to Joe and Cassandra. "Words are inadequate to express my appreciation for what you have done for Samantha and for me. Whenever I pray for her, which is daily, I will pray for you, as well. God bless you both. Would like to say a prayer for Samantha? It's okay to say a silent one, if you prefer. God will hear it."

Cassandra stepped forward and bowed her head. After less than a minute, she stepped back, and Joe moved to the spot she'd vacated. He picked up the card and said, "Samantha, may the road rise up to meet you. May the wind be always at your back. May the sun shine warm upon your face; the rains fall soft upon your fields and until we meet again, may God hold you in the palm of His hand." Joe blessed himself, and stood back.

"Well, wasn't that special," the familiar voice of Doctor Fox cut through the still air like a straight edge razor.

The three turned toward her house. Fox stood with an AR Rifle with a silencer, pointed at them. She was wearing a floppy canvass hat, a rain jacket, and boots.

* * *

"Well, hello Felix," Joe said. "Nice to see the face behind the voice. You're like the arsonist who stays to watch the fire. Here you are, at the service for the girl you murdered."

"Figured everything out did, you?" Fox said. "Enjoy your smugness, Joseph. You won't have it much longer."

"It all came together for me, when you and that robotic voice called Wednesday night. You gave me all the motives for what was happening. And the call told me what bothered me about the first time you and I spoke on the telephone. It was about snow removal and your telling Andy it would not be necessary. You remember that call?

Fox didn't answer, but took two steps forward. The rifle was steady in her hands and pointed directly at Joe. Experienced.

"I remember it because you called me Joseph, even after I introduced myself as Joe. Only Felix and Cassandra's mother ever called me Joseph." Joe shook his head. "I should have figured this out a long time ago, but it took Wednesday's call to put it together."

"Sister Alicia," Fox said. "Nice of you to join us. Got all dressed up, I see. Like you did at the trial."

"Where you gave all of us the finger, as you walked out," Alicia said. "You are an evil person."

Fox smiled. "I was not expecting you, Sister Alicia. Good thing I have extra bullets."

"We know you killed Samantha," Alicia said. "It's the only scenario that explains her disappearance and her car being in the University's parking lot. But why? She never did anything to harm you."

"Not to be crude, but for the same reason a dog licks his balls." Fox said.

"Samantha was investigating Doctor Fox," Joe said. "She was following her and making a dossier on her. Fox knew she was being followed, and probably discovered it was Samantha. What Fox didn't know was Samantha was only trying to the get her fired from the University, and she was nowhere near discovering her second identity. But our Doctor Fox couldn't take the chance, and when the opportunity presented itself, she killed Samantha."

"How'd you come to know about the memorial service?" Cassandra said.

Fox shook her head and stepped a bit closer.

"Dr. Kincaid told her," Joe said. "When Connor and Calvin started discussing the possibility Fox might be alive, I kept that thought. When the announcement was made that Fox was dead, I knew either she *was* dead, or Dr. Kincaid was lying and was part of the scheme. That's why Connor, Calvin and I kept pushing about the bones, and making them available for inspection. We knew both Kincaid and Fox had some connection with Intelligence. So I told Kincaid about the memorial service. I wanted the bone dust, but it was really a test. And lo and behold, look who showed up." Joe looked at Fox. "You knew the news last night about Elaine Blass heading the investigation ended everything. Investigating the bones would be her first step, and the world would know you were not dead."

Fox remained silent and took a breath.

Joe took the vial from Alicia and help it up. The signal

"You killed an innocent girl for no reason." He stared at the space above Fox's head and the corner of her house. A glint of metal blinded him for a millisecond. He blinked again and saw the flash before he heard the shot.

Fox's hat flew off her head. She took a half step forward, and Joe saw it was not just the hat that had come off. The top of Fox's head was inside it. The hat, aided by a small wind, drifted over to the fir tree, and landed on the commemorative stone.

The rest of Fox stood briefly. The world stopped. No more classes, grading tests, obnoxious students. No memories, no regrets. Nothing. She simply dropped, her mouth open and full of blood, rolling onto the yellow rain jacket, shiny in the high noon sun.

Chapter 49

The following Sunday afternoon, at three o'clock, Sister Alicia waked into the office of Monsignor Mark McGrath at the New Beginnings Orphanage.

"Good afternoon, Monsignor, do you a few minutes?"

McGrath stood. "Sister Alicia, you're back already? Was there a problem?"

"No Monsignor, we had a nice memorial service. Everything went even better than expected. And I wanted to get back."

McGrath smiled and sat. He gestured Sister Alicia to the chair in front of his desk. "Well, we're certainly happy to have you back. But you really should leave some time for yourself. Nobody on their death bed ever regretted not spending more time at the office."

Sister Alicia smiled and sat. "I understand, and I will take some vacation this year. I've found some wonderful people, who've invited me back later this summer."

"That's great," McGrath said. "Get the times you want to me as soon as possible. Do not let the summer slip by." He smiled again. "That's an order, Sister."

"I will Monsignor," Alicia said. She remained seated.

"Is there anything else?"

"Yes, Monsignor. I'd like you to hear my confession."

"Of course." He pulled open the top drawer of his desk and removed a purple stole. "If you lock the door, we can do it here. Saves us having to run across to the chapel."

"Of course, Monsignor. I don't mind." Alicia stood and walked over to the door. She locked it, and walked back to the char and knelt.

"No need to knell, Sister. Please use the chair and we can have a conversation-like confession."

"Thank you, Monsignor." She stood and seated herself at the chair. She blessed herself and started. "Bless me Monsignor for I have sinned. My last confession was one week ago."

"Please confess your sins, Sister Alicia."

"While in the State of Maine, I planned with three other people to do certain things that resulted in the death of Doctor Alice Ruth Fox."

"What the ...., Monsignor regained his composure. "Who is this, Doctor Fox? How do you know her?"

"We, that is the other three people and I, believe she killed my friend Samantha Cronin. The memorial service was in her honor."

"So, this was a revenge killing?"

"No, Monsignor, Fox was about to kill my friends, Joe McDonald and his wife, Cassandra, and myself. My third friend, Roosevelt Wilson was a sniper with the Marines. He was hiding maybe a hundred feet away and he shot her."

Monsignor McGrath smiled. "So, Roosevelt Wilson shot

CHAPTER 49

Doctor Fox in order to stop her from killing you, Cassandra and Joe?"

"Yes, Monsignor, but that was part of the plan, and that's why it may be a sin. I think."

"The plan was to let Doctor Fox think she had the three of you trapped and then have the fourth person, Roosevelt Wilson kill her? Have I got this right?" Monsignor McGrath said.

"Yes, I think so. See, at first, we thought Doctor Fox was dead, but when this guy Felix called Joe, he realized Felix was Fox or Fox was Felix, and the anger Felix had for Joe, which went back to when they were in the CIA, was the motive for why Fox faked her death and tried to frame Cassandra for that murder."

"Was this Fox person transgender or non-binary?" McGrath said. "Is that the correct word?"

"No, she was a woman. But when she was CIA, she used the name Felix." Sister Alicia shook her head. "I know this all sounds crazy."

"Sister, I'm Irish. "It's the crazy things that make sense to us. And I still think you haven't committed a sin. Were the police called?"

"Yes, Joe called them."

"And they didn't arrest anyone?"

"No. You see, Thursday morning, the day before the memorial service, Joe told all us he'd figured out Fox was alive. That she had killed Samantha, and was trying to frame Cassandra and ruin their lives because Fox, when she was known as Felix, believed Joe had ruined her career with the CIA. When the Attorney General announced a new person was heading up the investigation, Joe told us, Fox would have to abandon her plan because the new prosecutor would examine the bones and discover they did not belong to Fox. Joe also told us, he thought Fox would come to the memorial service, so he purchased and we placed cameras and recorders all around the property. The police saw and heard everything."

"Wait a second, Sister. Is this the so-called Bones Investigation? Is this what you've been involved in?"

"Yes, some media people have used that expression."

"Sister, you don't need absolution. You need an agent." McGrath laughed. "You should write a book. I have a brother-in-law, who could help. I could get his daughter to help. She's a better writer. I could get one of our local printers involved. You need to move quick on this. Before one of your friends does it first. And, if profiting on this makes you concerned, you can donate all the proceeds to the orphanage. We won't say anything about this to Bishop Russo. Whaddya think?"

"Monsignor," Sister Alicia said. "My confession?"

"Of course, Sister. I got it. And I'm still pretty certain you did not commit any sin."

"Monsignor, I was hoping Doctor Fox would show up. I wanted her to get killed. I hate what she did to Samantha. But once she was dead, I began to think I wasn't much better than her."

"No, no, no, Sister, you are light years better than Doctor Fox, and, frankly, if it had been me, I'd have been praying for Fox's to show up." Monsignor McGrath smiled. "But to ease your mind, and in case you're right, I'm granting you absolution, in the name of the Father, the Son, and the Holy Spirit. Amen. Sister, you've had a helluva three days in Maine."

"Monsignor," Sister Alicia said. "My penance?"

Monsignor McGrath glanced at his watch. "In just over three and a half hours, you're coming with me to the Thirsty

CHAPTER 49

Shamrock. I'm doing a seven o'clock mass in the back room."

Chapter 50

Eight months from the day of Samantha Cronin's memorial service, the special grand jury, under the direction of Elaine Blass, issued a report concluding Samantha Cronin had been "murdered by a person or persons unknown, but in all probability by Alice Ruth Fox, Ph.D. a/k/a Felix Ketch." It was highly unusual wording, but no one complained, and it provided the answers the press wanted. There were no indictments or any charges brought against Roosevelt Wilson, or any of the other attendees of the memorial service. The report indicated most of the human bones were those of Samantha Cronin. The other bones had been removed from several corpses under the charge of Doctor Kincaid. They were not identified in the report.

Doctor Dorothy Kincaid was indicted for conspiracy, obstruction of justice, and perjury. The charges are still pending. She was allowed to plead guilty to federal charges of conspiracy to interfere with a federal investigation, and falsifying a federal document. She received a five-year suspended sentence, was discharged from the FBI, and lost her pension. Her attorney, Trevor Chandler, is negotiating a plea agreement on the state charges.

Elaine Blass was appointed Chief of the Criminal Division for the Maine Attorney General. Former Chief, John Gibbons, resigned and is teaching Criminal Law and Procedure at the University of Maine Law School, where he has made peace with Cassandra Harvey.

Connor McNeill accepted a position as para-legal and investigator with Calvin Washington. Malcolm Butts & Associates is a client on retainer with the firm. Malcolm also appears as a ventriloquist and part of a comedy team at Giggles, a comedy club on Route One in Saugus, Massachusetts.

Joe and Cassandra bought the Fox property, and rent their former house to seasonal residents, including Sister Alicia, who comes for one week each summer, with two other nuns from New Beginnings Orphanage. Sister Alicia never wrote a book, or appeared on any television shows.

Wendy Grisham, the Channel 3 reporter, wrote *The Bones Investigation*, which enjoyed modest sales in New England. It has been developed as a limited series and sold to Netflix.

The Governor offered Joe an appointment as County Prosecutor in Bangor. It would have required him to move, and he declined, with thanks, the offer. He, Cassandra, and Roosevelt Wilson remain on J. Point, where Joe pays all the costs of snow removal on Perch Lane.

About the Author

Tim O'Leary is a former Assistant Attorney General for the Commonwealth of Massachusetts, a Massachusetts State Representative, and for twenty-two years the Deputy Executive Director for the Massachusetts Association for Mental Health. He is retired and lives in Wakefield, Massachusetts with his wife, Patricia.

Also by Tim O'Leary

The Day Job
  Robes
  The Friends of Ed McGonagle